The Oxblood Effect

The Oxblood Effect

Annabel Johnson

THORNDIKE
CHIVERS

This Large Print edition is published by Thorndike Press, Waterville, Maine, USA and by BBC Audiobooks Ltd, Bath, England.
Thorndike Press, a part of Gale, Cengage Learning.

This is a work of fiction. Any resemblance of the characters to persons living or dead is purely coincidental.
The text of this Large Print edition is unabridged.
Other aspects of the book may vary from the original edition.
Set in 16 pt. Plantin.
Printed on permanent paper.

LIBRARY OF CONGRESS CATALOGING-IN-PUBLICATION DATA

Johnson, Annabel, 1921–
The oxblood effect / by Annabel Johnson.
p. cm. — (Thorndike Press large print clean reads)
ISBN-13: 978-1-4104-0520-3 (hardcover : alk. paper)
ISBN-10: 1-4104-0520-6 (hardcover : alk. paper)
1. Large type books. I. Title.
PS3560.O37134O93 2008
813'.54—dc22 2007046711

BRITISH LIBRARY CATALOGUING-IN-PUBLICATION DATA AVAILABLE
Published in 2008 in the U.S. by arrangement with Annabel Johnson.
Published in 2008 in the U.K. by arrangement with the author.
U.K. Hardcover: 978 1 405 64466 2 (Chivers Large Print)
U.K. Softcover: 978 1 405 64467 9 (Camden Large Print)

Printed in the United States of America
1 2 3 4 5 6 7 12 11 10 09 08

For GIN

Who was with me
from the beginning

My thanks to

David St. John

For reading the unfinished manuscript and giving me the perspective I needed to complete it.

1

She drove carefully. A lot of power under the pedal of the battered pickup, there was a temptation to floor it. But she kept strictly to the speed limit, letting the eighteen-wheelers breeze past in an eddy of backlash. For so early in the morning there was steady traffic on I-25, its twin corridors cresting and falling with the ripple of the land. To the west the foothills of the Front Range pressed like giant knuckles, wrinkling the edges of the prairie. Familiar scenery, but she could spare no thought on homecoming right now. Her attention was on the rear-view mirror. The white moving van had been behind her ever since Trinidad. And the silver Toyota — or one just like it — had been at the pumps in the gas station in Raton. All small cars look alike these days. Her glance flicked toward a road sign:

POINT OF INTEREST — NEXT RIGHT

She took the off-ramp, crossed the overpass and headed west along a gravel road, up a slight rise, then down into the low land along the old Colorado and Southern tracks. The monument stood as she remembered it, lonely in that vast impassive land, the historic dead forever frozen in stone. Sculpted figures ten feet tall were set on a patch of grass enclosed by an iron fence, which was again surrounded by chain link, as if the guilty living had tried to give extra protection to those helpless victims. A forgotten pocket of the past.

Satisfied that she hadn't been followed, Cass cut the engine and got out, stretching limbs that had grown stiff with tension. It eased as she walked over to the railroad tracks, bringing back a rattle-and-click of memories. This had been one of her father's favorite places on earth. He would get out the picnic basket, hand forth sandwiches, pop a can of beer. Comfortable in his jeans — always glad to get out of the Post Office uniform — he would wander over to sit on the embankment, eyes fixed on the past.

Vibrations of violence still emanated from this weedy patch, the rat-a-tat of guns, screams of the women and children, the crackle of flames. Back in 1914 a few thousand striking miners and their families had faced the thugs of a powerful coal company — and lost. It was called the Ludlow Massacre. Nowadays the tragedy was ancient history, and who studies history any more? An annual service was still held by union die-hards, but otherwise few lingered at this spot, peopled by its ghosts.

Only men with long memories like Tom Butterfield. Eyes fixed on the past he was seeing acres of tents spread along the low ground, hearing the noises of a half-dozen languages, miners' families learning to camp together, to communicate. Actually happy in their union with each other, they had stood against the power of the Wall Street moguls, absentee bosses who sent thugs from the slums of Chicago and Kansas City to put the workers down.

"The guards set up the machine gun across the tracks. There used to be a grove of trees, but I guess they cut 'em down later. And over there, the company's goons dressed in militia uniforms formed their ranks, they called it 'Water Tower Hill,' not much of a hill . . ." Her father relived it step by step, until the two girls strayed off to walk the tracks, teetering and chattering, kid stuff.

Izzie usually came along on those trips, glad to get away from that hell which was her home. Weird little kid, face looked as if it had got caught in a trash compacter, mop of black elf-locks worn long around her cheeks to cover some of the bruises, but there was no self-pity in her exuberant grin. "Me, I'm going to Hollywood if I have to jump a freight." Staring wistfully southward.

"California's west, silly, on the other side of those mountains. Anyhow what would you do out there? You're no glamour puss."

"Maybe I could be the Bride of Frankenstein." She would frazzle her hair wickedly. "Look at Lon Chaney, he made millions of bucks being freaky. Come on, Sandy, beatcha to the gully."

Sandy. She said the name under her breath. The name on her birth certificate was Sandra, incongruous as a cocktail dress on a mountain climber. For sixteen years she had been "Sandy." Now it brought a rush of rebellion: *No! I'm Cassandra. I am Cass Gillett of Minneapolis and Washington, D.C. and Dresden, Germany and I don't feel like Sandy Butterfield.*

Then training kicked in and she instructed herself to quit the kicking and learn to live with it, the same way you live with a bad shoulder. Lifting the hatch on the back of the truck she dug into the box of groceries and found the bottle of Tylenol, took a couple with a few swallows from the thermos of cold water. Time to get going. Dragging her feet wasn't going to make things any easier.

Back in the cab she started the engine and shoved it in gear with the heel of her hand. Hanging a U-turn she headed toward the highway. Enough time had passed to flush any trackers. At the overpass she slowed to a crawl, but there were no disabled vehicles down on the shoulder, no van, no Toyota. No highway crew pretending to mend the road. No team of surveyors or lurking highway patrol car. Just a thousand people on the move, trying to get north to Denver, or south to Albuquerque. On the far side of the bridge Cass drove straight on eastward, following a secondary across the swelling plains.

The range still bore witness to the fact that this had been a coastal shelf in prehistoric times, the edge of a vast ocean where tides had left long drifts of gravel. Here and there raw sand thrust through the thin top soil, warning of dunes to come, but for the present the ground was still supporting a scatter of buffalo grass, some fields of prickly pear, a few stunted cedar trees. How those had got there, who knows? Must have been carried down off the mountains. The

Sangre de Cristos over west of the foothills, their blue silhouette rose like delicate trim on the horizon, lacy with lavender shadows. On those heights were heavy forests, full of birds — Stellar jay, magpie, crow — feasting off the berries, then heading on out across the plains, dropping their lime, and with it the seeds. Only a few dwarf juniper had survived the harsh dry environment down here.

As the pickup ran out of blacktop and rattled onto old washboard, the wound above her left ear began to ache, not used to all this cool breeze. The brown wig she had worn ever since the surgery was locked in a safe deposit box in Albuquerque, along with the other memorabilia of a vanished existence. New Mexico had been a good place to regroup. To rest up, build some strength, get oriented on the world of western America. By the time she was ready to move on, her hair had grown back, long enough to lose the wig. After years of dark locks, she had walked forth from that bank a crop-top natural blonde even if the wheat stubble was barely long enough to hide the scar.

Her head gave a throb as the truck hit a pothole. At the crest of the next hogback she slowed to a stop and looked back.

Nearby, a lizard took alarm, skittering across the rocky ground into a hole. A bird flew off in a black flap of wings, crow. And still she lingered, surveying the scenery . . . nothing moved back there. She had only passed one vehicle coming from the east, a brown UPS van, making the mail run from LaJunta to Trinidad. Off to the south the great headland over Raton Pass stood etched in sunlight. The sky was clear as spring water, breeze smelling of new growth. A good day to be reborn.

Hi there, Sandy, old girl.

Facing forward, she put the truck down the long incline past a rock outcropping known locally as Coyote Crags. At that moment, to all intents, Cass Gillett had vanished off the face of the earth.

To reach this point she had used all her expertise to transform herself. As she came across country a couple of smooth switches had morphed her into, first, Dominique St. Milo with a Paris address, and then into Anya Rasenko of Odessa with forged documents perfectly executed, birth certificates, European passports, driver's licenses, the works. Dominique had rented a house in St. Louis and Anya had holed up in a condo in Omaha. Never to return, of course. The expensive paperwork was locked in the safe deposit box, along with her Baretta and the wig and two pair of contact lenses in different colors. She was glad to be shut of those — it was hard to disguise her eyes, that unusual shade of teal she had inherited from her mother. For once she could carry an I.D. that was legitimate. Sandra Butterfield of Panhandle, Colorado. No one in the world had ever heard of her — except the people up ahead in that scrabble of a town.

She drove on through a knee-high forest of staghorn cactus, warped shapes writhing like the damned. Something about this land evoked a vocabulary of perdition. The County was named Las Animas after the river that runs through it, originally dubbed by its Spanish discoverers El Rio de las Animas Perdidas en Purgatoire. Her father had loved to roll that off his tongue. He had been born in Trinidad, relished every gravelly inch of this country. Never realized that a kid named Sandy had suffered a very real purgatory of frustration in those days. Another pothole, and her mended brain gave a sharp throb as she crossed the final bench and tilted downward into a shallow valley where a huddle of houses and trees clenched like a fist around a water tower.

Sprung up like a clump of weeds in the middle of nowhere, a hundred years ago

Panhandle had been a cattle town before drought had finished off the meager range land. Slowly, with the loss of commerce, it had turned into a narrow enclave that existed only by its own incestuous needs. A place where life was monitored and debated and judged by one's neighbors, where the main form of communication was gossip, the most serious business of the populace, to render advice. You were graded on how you accepted it. The ultimate betrayal was for someone to escape. She could imagine the whispers that had followed her departure.

". . . that little Butterfield girl, so young, only sixteen, to leave her father alone like that — downright shameful!"

No, Cass wasn't expecting to be given a welcome-home party. She was almost surprised to find the town still alive. It had been bleeding for years, losing its young people to boredom, lack of jobs, lack of future. And yet, strangely enough, at the edge of town the sign marking the city limits was so new it only had two bullet holes in it:

PANHANDLE, COLO.
Elev. 4,230 ft. Pop. 1,694

Seven hundred more people than she'd been expecting. And it puzzled her to find that Lamar Street had recently been paved. The Texaco station had grown a body shop and a pink stucco annex with a neon sign over the door: EATS. In the next block a banner on a boarded-up building announced the coming of a Payless Shoe Store. The Rialto's marquee advertised a Walt Disney movie that was only six months old. Safeway was doing a fair business, its parking lot full of cars.

Rolling slowly down Lamar Street, she was further shocked to see a video rental mart, a pizza parlor, a men's western-wear shop called STUD DUDS, INC. and across from it, like a sassy retort, the former ice cream parlor was candy-striped cherry and white and hung with a scrollwork sign: BOUTIQUE DE PARIS. Wondering at these alien manifestations, Cass automatically turned left at the next corner. Two blocks down, then right onto Evans, and now the memories were as strong as the perfume from the lilac bushes that still grew around a familiar porch.

As if it had been preserved in a time capsule, the dust-colored bungalow with the green roof stood beneath the budding locust trees, its border of daffodils shaking their heads, reproachful among the weeds growing up around them. She could almost see her father down on his knees, getting the flower beds neat. By now Cass was struggling with emotions that bounded around inside her like unstrung beads. She took care to set the wheels of the truck exactly onto the twin concrete tracks that led to the parking spot beside the house. Turning off the motor, she sat as it ticked.

And in the growing silence, a familiar crawling sensation warned her she was being watched, a metaphysical awareness you build up over the years . . . Harmless this time. It was emanating from the back stoop of the house next door, where a woman stood.

Liz? Liz Burke, my God, she used to baby-sit me. At least sixty now, she was still sturdy, the slabs of her arms folded across pendulous breasts, ungirdled body sagging against the tightness of the print apron. Nothing slack about the aging face — her chin was set as hard as frozen biscuit dough.

"Well," she called across, "I see you finally got here."

Mystified, Cass climbed down out of the pickup as Liz came across the yard, moving on stiff knees. Her hair was different now. Instead of a long roan-colored hank twisted in a bun, it was short and gray and permed all over her head like steel wool.

"So — how are you, Liz?"

"Oh, I do okay." Stopping ten feet away she loomed in unspoken disapproval. "Got the rheumatiz, but it don't keep me from going to funerals."

So that was it. "I'm sorry I couldn't have been here for Dad's. But the day he died I was undergoing brain surgery. They didn't even tell me until I got out of intensive care. And for a while I was in no shape to travel."

The ruddy face began to ease as Liz eyed the scar still angry amid the stubble of hair. Pulling a pair of wire-rimmed bifocals from her apron pocket, she clapped them on. "I can see now, you still don't look too good. You're some pale, girl. Good thing you come home where you got folks to take care of you." Awkwardly her arms flapped as if urged to hug.

Cass moved into them, interlocking for a quick squeeze that returned aromas of fresh-baked bread, laundry detergent, bath powder. *She smells a lot better than I do.* Stepping back she said, "I'm afraid I need a shower. I've been driving since six o'clock this morning." And was aware suddenly that long afternoon shadows were stretching away from the sun.

"Good hot bath would do you good, and you can go right in and have one. Water's turned on, so's the lights. We knew you was coming because there's stuff in your name at the Post Office."

"Already? I ordered some ceramic supplies, but I didn't dream they would get here so quickly."

"Joe'll bring 'em over for you tomorrow. My man Joe."

"Liz! You're married!"

Sky-washed blue eyes brightened with the pride of spinsterhood defeated. "Going on seven years now. He's a union rep, or he was before they closed down CF&I. Now he's retired. Least he does odd jobs, anything you need, fix your plumbing, mow your lawn. And he don't charge a whole arm and a leg neither."

"Golly, I forgot there'd be grass to cut." Cass laughed weakly. "Dad always did all that." She still felt a sharp pang at the thought. She had fed Liz a small lie: no one had told her that her father had died. It was only after she had written him a letter, to ask if she could come home, that she heard from a lawyer up in Pueblo who had been trying to contact her with the news that Tom Butterfield was deceased and had left her sole beneficiary of all he owned in the world: a house.

"He never quit hoping you'd come back." There was lingering reproof in the words as Liz led the way up onto the front porch.

My front porch now! After all these years of never owning anything that wouldn't fit in a suitcase, this was going to take some adjustment. The living room was dim and close, redolent of pipe smoke. Liz pulled back the drapes. In the afternoon sunlight everything looked faded, the awful sofa shabby, the antique Persian rug so threadbare it was hard to pick out the pattern. It had been her mother's pride and joy, brought from Minneapolis after the wedding.

On the mantel over the fireplace stood a studio portrait, a young woman, smiling. Her mother had been a beauty, but already the eyes were haunted by doubt. Next to it was a framed snapshot of a coltish little girl in a dotted Swiss dress. Taken on her seventh birthday — eighth?

"You didn't write him real often," Liz observed, more in sorrow than blame now.

"I used to call him once in a while. When you're off in Germany every time you think of phoning it's three a.m. in Colorado."

"What was so grand about Germany?"

"Well, for one thing, a free education. I had a scholarship to a professional crafts school; I studied ceramics." A good cover story should stick as close to the truth as possible.

"Them boxes, they mean you aim to stay a while? We all figured you'd sell out fast, wouldn't want to hang around a little cow-patty crossroads like Panhandle."

"Hey, don't knock my home town." Cass mustered a bright tone of enthusiasm, but it took full effort.

"In the old days you couldn't wait to git out. Didn't even tell folks goodbye."

"Liz, I couldn't. The word made me want to bawl. In fact, I even have trouble with 'hello'." As she glanced at the easy chair with the dent sculptured into its leathery contours, she felt a stirring in her tear ducts, weird sensation she hadn't known in years.

"Oh, shoot, you're tired, girl. Take that bath and lie down. Don't worry about dinner, you're coming to our house. You got to meet my Joe."

With the sound of retreating footsteps, an emptiness closed in. Cass walked over and collapsed into the contoured depths of the old chair. She wondered what it would feel like to have a good cry? For what, though? The past? The present? Panic over the future? If you're going to make a fool out of yourself you ought to know the reason.

2

Out of a montage of memories a new reality exploded: groceries. Eggs, sitting in the heat of the camper, milk souring, lettuce wilting — Cass was in motion, heading for the back door. *The kitchen's still that awful yellow.* She rushed out onto the porch and down into the side yard. The truck seemed to be making itself at home under the burgeoning lilac bushes. As she opened the tailgate she was reminded by a sharp twinge in the barely-mended rotator cuff: no heavy lifting. Wedging her hip under the sack she had got it balanced, then almost dropped it when she turned to see a black-and-white police unit nosing into the trim tracks of the driveway. At sight of the overhead flashbar she felt a swarm of moths deploying in her belly, all of them armed to the teeth.

They settled as she recognized the man getting out, though the gray uniform was confusing. The last time she'd seen Pike

Webster he had handed over her final exam paper in Trig, gave her a C-minus, the old fuddy. Of course to a 12th grader twenty-four is ancient. Now he seemed younger, the Smoky Bear look was an improvement over that brown suit he used to wear. A square-built man in a red bow tie, as he had stood before the class he looked like a stack of UPS boxes topped by a delivery tag. Now the gray chambray softened his contours and clung to hard muscle as he lifted a large cardboard carton out of the back seat.

"Been watching for you, Sandy." The top of the box flapped up and hit him in the chin. The jaw line was still the leading feature of his face, which hadn't changed much. No sign of gray in the dark hair. A few more squint wrinkles around eyes that glinted in the sun like smoky quartz crystals. The air of authority was still there. It rallied all her native contrariness. Damned if she was going to call him *Mister.* Neutrally, she said, "Hello."

"Soon as I heard you arrived I thought I'd bring these over. They were your dad's. I've just been taking care of them." He led the way onto the back porch and into the house.

Cass followed, mystified. While she set the groceries on the table Webster was continuing down the hall as if he owned the place. *I haven't even gone back there myself yet!* He had turned in at the small bedroom that had once been a teenage girl's sanctum. As she joined him she saw that the maple furniture was gone, the Luke Skywalker poster vanished. Now it was a workroom with benches around the walls, shelves everywhere. She made a fast adjustment: This was going to make a great ceramics studio.

"They could be valuable," Webster was saying as he set the box down. "I didn't want to leave them sitting around for somebody to swipe. Your dad trusted everybody, half the people in town probably know where he hid his door key." When he opened the carton Cass recognized her father's albums. Stamp collecting had been the delight of his life. And now she noticed the shelf of reference books, neat little tools, tweezers and sponges and a study lamp. Her father had turned the place into a hobby room, and apparently found a kindred spirit in Webster. There was reverence in the touch with which he lifted out the top volume.

"He kept these in that drawer on the bottom . . ."

"Uh — wait a minute." Her mind was doing a zero-to-sixty. "They're yours now. He left a letter — with his lawyer in Pueblo, one of those Disposition of Property memos. I'm his executor, you know. He" — she was inventing hand-over-fist — "he bequeathed his stamp collection to you."

For a few seconds Webster stood blinking stubby dark lashes. "Well, I'll be darned. He never let on. We used to work on these together, long winter evenings. Listen, are you sure you don't want them?"

"What I know about stamps wouldn't mail a postcard to City Hall. They're yours, Pike." The name came naturally now. She even considered offering the man a cup of coffee.

Again, he was one-up, leading the way back to the kitchen, running water into the blue enamel pot as if it were old habit. The ancient gas stove brought back more memories. She had cooked her first meal on that stove. It was the day after her mother had walked out on them. Some minor catastrophe had sent the poor woman running, a final straw in a mountain of straws. Which is how a thirteen-year-old had quickly learned to make meat loaf that night and lumpy gravy, undercooked boiled potatoes. Her father had eaten it as if it were a feast, though his heart was obviously shattering. She got down a couple of mugs.

"I never knew you and Dad were close."

"Back in your day we weren't," he said. "But after my wife died we were a couple of lonely bachelors. Didn't matter that I was so much younger, we got on okay." Then, deliberately, he added, "I was his first pall bearer."

Gritting her teeth, Cass mustered her excuses again. "I'm sorry I couldn't be here . . ." etc., and saw acceptance in his nod. "I'm only just out of rehab. How did you find out so fast that I was home?"

"Moccasin telegraph. Ran into Izzie Knudsen in the post office. She saw your truck go by a while ago. You remember Iz? Well, she runs The Boutique there on Lamar. I guess she's been on the lookout for you." He straddled a chair and sipped his coffee, eying her. "You do seem a little skinny, now that I think on it. That scar looks almost like a bullet wound."

"Accident, over in the Alps. I got caught in a bad rock slide. It killed several of my friends. I guess I still haven't got over it totally." She knew she was babbling, some side effect of the badge on his shirt, an outdated tin star.

"That explains it." He nodded. "I can see you've had some kind of grief, and not entirely about your father. I know you loved him, and he loved you a heap."

"He understood why I had to leave, after I graduated from high. I needed my mother, and by then she had married Tom Gillett. He was a very nice man, made me feel at home. And I liked Minneapolis. Then later, after I went off to school there never was a chance to get back to Colorado. When you're young you think life goes on forever, never figure on things changing. So do you enjoy being a sheriff?" *And if you think that's a hint to mind your own business, live with it, buddy.*

Webster grinned wryly as he looked down at the old Wyatt Earp star. "Actually I'm Chief of Police. Ought to wear a shield, but the City Council figured this antique would tickle the tourists."

"Tourists? In Panhandle?"

"Oh yes, we're now even listed by the Triple A. Got us a big dude ranch out south of town, you know that spread that used to be the Pettigrew place? Now they called it the Rocking R, owned by a fellow named Boyd Ruger from Texas. Bunch of tenderfeet, but they help our economy. We got us a motel out in back of Gollagher's steak house. And of course there's The Academy, our school for fine arteests, run by an old friend of yours." His squint deepened with amusement. “Guy is going to be glad to see you.”

“Guy Magee! You mean he’s still here? I thought he’d be off in Paris or somewhere by now.” She saw him again as he had looked twenty years ago, a dapper boy with a cool grin and a million ideas stacked between his neat little ears. Not to mention talent, waiting to be explored.

“Oh, he went over there once I think, but now he’s brought the art world here. Married a Russian lady and they fixed up the old Hacienda, put some cabins on the back pasture and people pay to come live there and paint pictures. Lord knows why, they don’t do the scenery, they turn out some pretty weird stuff, but what do I know? I’m just a dumb cop.” Webster stood up and spun the chair back in place. “Fact right now I better go out and stop some crime.”

“Don’t tell me Panhandle’s got an underworld.”

“Mostly it’s over-the-top stuff. Especially on Saturday nights out at the roadhouse. You remember Mae Ryan?”

Who could forget the fount of all sex information for the sixth grade?

“Well, she married Rafe Gollagher. They took over the old skating rink and turned it into a tavern. Offer a pretty good steak dinner, you ought to try it. But not Saturday nights, not until you're in better shape. Take care of yourself, Bunny."

He picked up the box of stamp albums, unaware of a darkening of the atmosphere. *Where does he get off using my father's pet name for me? Does he think he's going to be some sort of surrogate parent? If so, he can forget it.*

She said as much that evening as she sat over in the kitchen next door. "Pike Webster better not imagine I'm still his high-school student." Eating dinner, while Liz fussed over the stove and her-man-Joe dug into the spaghetti casserole.

"Anh-h-h, don't mind Web," he said. "Like all hick cops, he's showing off that trooper hat and the pistol he don't never use." Joe Spinney was a burlap sack stuffed with Number Nine coal, gritty and hard and ageless. Life's big wheels had left heavy tracks across that face, scars and seams and leathery folds so deep his eyes were only sharp pin-points back in the shadows. Miner, steel worker, jack of the building trades, he watched Cass covertly, he thought, angling with off-hand questions that were subtle as a left jab.

"So you been to Germany, huh? That's a

long ride on the school bus. You speak kraut?"

"Enough to get along." Speak it, read and write it like a native of Dresden, which was why she had drawn the assignment. "In our school it didn't matter much. We were dealing with formulas. Chemistry has its own language."

"Whatcha need chemistry for?" Liz marveled, shoving across the table a plate of her own home-made bread.

"I was studying ceramic technology." Cass searched for a way to put it without seeming to condescend. "I wanted to learn it as a profession. That takes a knowledge of raw materials and their chemical properties."

"You mean you make pots?" Her big innocent face warmed into a smile. "Oh, that's nice. I got one of them myself, wedding present, came from that big factory up in the Springs." She got up and went off into the living room to come back with a huge buff-colored earthenware jar decorated with broad swirls of red and black iron oxide.

"That's — a very striking piece," Cass could say honestly. "I'll bet the raw materials came from out on the plains. I'm hoping to find some sedimentary deposits around here; I'd like to experiment on native clays.

On my way north I picked up some interesting samples just south of Raton. I'll run some tests on them as soon as I can set up my kiln, which is probably in one of those boxes at the post office."

"You do tests on plain old dirt?" Joe sniggered.

"Well, it's this way," Cass told him evenly. "A piece of ceramics is made of clay mixed with flint and feldspar. To get it to mature you have to get the right proportions, which takes experimentation to test it for shrinkage and sag and color. Then you decorate it, usually with a glaze that contains a lot of coloring oxides. It has to fit the body or you get crawling or bubbling, or crazing. You try out combinations of cobalt and manganese, say, or copper and tin. Each reacts differently to the others and to the conditions in the kiln. For instance, if you introduce smoke you will change copper oxide from apple-green to blood-red."

By then Joe's face had shut like a door. Liz stood up. "I got pie for dessert."

Cass sneered at herself for putting on a smart-ass chalk-talk. But it seemed like a good idea to establish her credentials once and for all, so that the town would accept her at face value. Accept and forget and maybe leave her alone.

Her mother would have understood. Martina Butterfield had always hated that glass cage where people were skeptical of everything she did. They never let her forget she was an outsider, from Minnesota, lot of Swedes and such up there. They were critical if she didn't hang out her wash properly, socks with socks, shirts with shirts, shaking heads if she didn't keep the porch clean. "People!" she would mutter as she swept the back stoop, bashing it with her broom. "People!" as she slammed down the bread dough onto the board.

"Wonderful supper. Can I help with the dishes?" Cass recalled the formula from another life.

"Not this time," Liz beamed kindly. "You look tired, girl. Better git you some sleep. It's late." All of nine o'clock.

Back across the dark yards she went, shivering. Used to love the night, used to draw it around her like a sheltering cloak. Now, she found herself listening for footsteps. Yellow windows patched the shadows, and why wasn't there a light in that house across the street? Must be empty, there was a **For Sale** sign in the yard. And yet she could make out a car parked back there at the far end of the driveway, almost hidden in the honeysuckle, some pale color, catching the glint of starlight. Why . . . ?

Cass, shut up! Sandy doesn't worry about such things. She went on inside and locked the doors. Sleep . . . yes, a good night's sleep will mend almost anything. So long as you don't dream.

The Nightmare

She is there again. It is deeply dark, redolent with odors of the Marseilles waterfront, dead fish, oil spillage. A cold sweat breaks out, the fever of despair, as lying helpless she tries to move — even a fraction. The drug they pumped into her is a paralyzant, must be something new, no relation to pentathol. As a trainee she'd been taught to recognize that. This is no anesthetic, just the opposite, everything is intensified. The shadows are thick as black felt, folding around the light of the kerosene lantern. Sounds are sharp-edged, the scuttlings and squeakings and the light fall of rain on the tin roof of the shed . . . warehouse. . . the stacks of burlap bags are marked "Pommes de Terre" with a brand name: "Avignon." The Midi, she took a three-day leave there once, walked through Van Gogh countryside. The memory is vivid, the colors too bright.

Pain unnaturally acute, too. Deep in her left shoulder she can feel the rotator cuff that blew in the struggle. Two men had come at her out of the darkness, wrestlers against a hundred-and-ten-pound woman. Even a black belt doesn't render you invulnerable.

It had been a trap, of course, but she still couldn't see how they had managed it. Used her own secret code to say she was wanted aboard the executive yacht. How did they know about that? How did they find out the leadership was in town for a strategy meeting? Probably going on right now at the boat, tied up at a pier only yards away . . .

She tries again to break the grip of the chemicals. No luck. Control of her body is shut down, except for the brain which is recording every detail with terrible receptivity. Smell of the harbor, din of rain, the clammy wetness of the skirt around her knees. So use that acuity to prepare. You know the questions they will ask. Be ready with vague answers, then false answers, then more false answers as a fall-back.

There are three of them now, one voice doing most of the muttering. In the cone of light from the lantern on the floor, she can see his feet, wing-tipped shoes, creased trousers, not one of the pair that jumped her. Probably their boss. One shoe nudges her inert form as if she were a piece of debris. We're getting to the point of all this. Brace up, keep shut, don't forget your training. At camp she had tested at the top of her group in resistance to interrogation.

From above in the shadows a voice speaks. "Put your thumb in your mouth."

With a sense of shock she feels her hand move, can't stop it. The thing in her mouth tastes dirty, tastes like it's been lying on the warehouse floor — her thumb.

"She's ready." He sounds almost bored.

A heavier voice says, "Tell her to suck it like a baby." Gnf, gnf, gnf, a thick porcine snigger.

"Not now, no amusements. You can have her after I get what I need. All right, woman, who do you work for?"

Never. I will never tell them that. In a flush of panic she hears herself say very distinctly, "I work for the Libra League."

"Who is your control?" The questions come steadily.

So do the answers.

Drenched with sweat, nightshirt clinging, a long T-shirt with a Denver Broncos logo, Cass stripped and staggered to the bathroom. Turning on the shower dead-cold, hanging onto the wall, she stood under it until she felt numb. Then twisted the knob to hot, until the shivering stopped. Back in the bedroom she pulled on a set of warm-ups, heavy socks, desert boots. Going to the closet she took out the suitcases, methodically packed them. Everything she owned. Snap, snap, closed. She yanked them off the bed so roughly her shoulder gave a small scream.

Out in the kitchen she set them by the back door. Dark outside still. When she switched on the overhead light the room came alive in a blaze of assorted yellows. *God, I will be glad to leave this room.* Over the sink hung a china clock made in the shape of a yellow chicken. A Mother's Day present from a time long past, the hands stood at 4:17. She dug in her pocket for the truck keys, and stopped short.

From old practice her training kicked in. Always resist emotional impulses. Unless there's an emergency, take your time. Have a cup of coffee. She moved over to the stove, mechanically, turning on the burner under the pot. As if obeying orders she waited for it to bubble and poured a cupful, taking it back to the table.

Next, ask the hard questions: What good will it do to run? It won't bring them back, will it?

In a rush of grief, she laid her head on her

arms. Eyes closed, she called the roll one more time, saw their faces, felt the love they had all shared. Her team.

Ian, with his loose blond mop of hair, crooked teeth that he rarely revealed, but a man of great humor. And bravery. He was like strong fiber, mending her when things threatened to come loose at the seams. Especially, he was a big brother to Biscuit. Shy little brown imp from Jamaica, looked like a choir boy, but there was no building, no room, no window, no safe he couldn't get into. Poor kid was madly in love with Koontz. She never knew it, dark, sexy, black-eyed little twit. She had learned her street smarts in the alleys of Marrakesh. She was their honey pot, collecting a wealth of pillow-talk information and enjoying every minute of it. Then there was Yuri, a woodchopper out of the forests of Rumania, broad shoulders, wild black hair, you expected folk songs. But it was Bach that he whistled whenever he dismantled a bomb. And finally Renée, horse-faced, Gallic, brilliant at chess, a wicked computer hacker. She was the silent member of the team. *My team!*

No use telling herself it wasn't her fault. She knew that. Once they'd stuck the needle in her she would have walked in front of a speeding train if they'd commanded it. *I wish they had.* To be left alive, knowing you were responsible for the deaths of others — that was the true essence of Hell. Fault or not, nothing would ever strip her of this deadly guilt.

But you can atone. This she had worked out from the beginning, from the day when she had walked away from the rehab hospital. She could become a non-person, a life sentence of trying to redeem herself by not living, by accepting a state of limbo. This was her punishment, Panhandle was her Alcatraz and she would stay.

Grimly Cass . . . Sandy . . . picked up the suitcases and took them back to the bedroom.

3

In training you were taught to go into new venues, assess the temper of a neighborhood or village, sense its collective soul and especially the subtle forces that channel the currents of its daily life. Then adapt to them, create for yourself whatever image would work in that setting. It was a strange assignment to take with you out onto the streets of your own home town.

After her bad night, her renewed avowal to stick with this mission, Cass felt the same jitters as if she were venturing into unknown territory. In fact she thought it might be even tougher to conform to a manufactured identity among old friends. Izzie especially had always been quick to scorn all phonies. It would be a test of her tradecraft, Cass thought, if she could establish a revamped Sandy that Iz would accept.

With sunshine pouring out of the east across the plains behind the little house, she went about the business of getting dressed. Grudgingly she put on the truss, a device her therapist had fashioned to fit over the joint of humerus and scapula, a sort of harness made of strong elastic. Wincing, she squirmed into the straps that went across upper chest and lower rib cage. At least it wouldn't show under the large saggy sweat shirt. She had found the thing at a roadside curio shop coming across New Mexico, some sort of tribute to the Day of the Dead, black skull and crossbones on it. *If Iz doesn't scathe me unmercifully, we are finished forever.*

Belly grumbling, Cass ate a nutritional bar, all chocolate and chemicals, and stepped forth onto her front porch into a brilliant Colorado morning. Around the steps the orphaned daffodils waved hopefully.

"Okay, okay," she muttered. "I'll weed you this afternoon." She was in no mood for optimism. What she needed was a really stunning opening line to wipe away all her old friend's resentment. You have to assume resentment, the woman's been stuck here all these years, no Hollywood, no adventures.

And yet as she crossed the street to The Boutique she had to admit that it didn't look like a consolation prize. Those brash vertical candy-stripes across the front were cocky, and the window display was stunning. Stick-figures made of black papier-mâché were draped with swim suits and beach towels in jewel tones. A large and terrible china frog sat in a pile of sand wearing Ray-ban sunglasses. The backdrop was gold fishnet. Not the work of a soured middle-aging smalltime shopkeeper.

The door chimed *La Vie en Rose* and Cass was back in the old ice cream store, but with a difference. The fixtures were still in place, the soda fountain stacked with tulip-shaped glasses behind the scuffed marble countertop. On the high stools sat several handsome mannequins posed in outfits that looked a lot too expensive for Panhandle. Opposite was a wall hung with a whole gallery of paintings, clever knock-offs of Lautrec and Brach and Klee, oils on canvas, unframed. Up on a tall ladder a workman was installing a sensuous Gaugin.

Searching for other life forms, she became aware that she was being scrutinized from a near corner of the shop, where a woman sat at a delicate Provençal writing desk. A softly rounded little person, she wore a length of lilac chiffon draped around her, held by a gold chain at the waist. Light hair and a small pearly chin, she sat so still she could have been a mannequin herself, except that she was glaring at Cass with open antagonism. Then reluctantly she glanced back toward a bead curtain at the rear of the store. It seemed to conceal some sort of office where a light cast a silhouette that looked familiar.

Cass headed for it. Amid a clutter of papers Izzie was hunched over a ledger, one ankle doubled under her. She always did sit crooked, seeking new contortions to ease the kink in her spinal column, a souvenir of her childhood. Before his suicidal death her father had been a brutal drunkard. Iz had survived by learning to move fast and adopt a variety of camouflage, anything to confuse the eye. It had developed into a way of life.

Today the wiry figure looked like a pop-art invention: lemon silk blouse, a vivid pink neck scarf and fuchsia skirt. On anyone else the clothes would have been ridiculous. Iz gave them a mysterious panache, like the black hair moussed into wild spikes all over her head. A long leg in a white lace stocking was twined around the chair rungs, and on the floor two yellow spike-heeled pumps lay like dead canaries.

Glancing up, she tilted her “do” and smiled, the same grin she used to wear in movies where people were ripped apart by chainsaws. Her dark eyes, behind the huge designer glasses, had a sadistic gleam. "So, the native returns. Rather bald, but wearing a stylish shroud. And how was the House of Usher? Crypt comfortable?"

Cass suppressed a rush of relief. "Not really. Getting out was tough on the fingernails." Edger Allen Poe had been their running gag. "I see you've been to Paris. How did you find The Rue Morgue?"

"Turned left and looked for a giant ape eating a human liver. Got blood all over my shoes, of course."

"It's what happens when you monkey around." The giggle came naturally enough, but it startled them both. "Can a conversation ever be called 'déjà vu'?"

"We do seem to be reprising another life." Iz surveyed her thoughtfully. "You aren't really a ghost, are you? I mean you look pretty pale. Come back to haunt our dreary sidewalks?"

"Actually I thought I'd try out for a position as the town eccentric." Cass looked down at the sweat shirt.

"You'll have to stand in line. Our librarian is psychic, the Mayor is into U.F.O.'s, he thinks they're rustling our cattle. And Guy Magee's students are as flighty as a flock of cuckoos. You'll feel right at home. Maybe not as much fun as the Left Bank, though. Don't you miss all those student princes and starving artists?"

"You've got me wrong. I was in Dresden, studying ceramics. But I did get to Paris once in a while, often enough to say this shop would fit right in. Iz, the look is fantastic."

That pleased her. "If you're going to be nice I will forgive you for deserting me all those years ago."

"I know I was wrong to run off without a few last words, but if I had to say 'goodbye' I thought I might as well go on and commit suicide."

"Oh, I understood that. Forgiven, forgotten."

"All the same, I thought about you a lot. Figured you were out carving some new exciting future — and you were. Wouldn't it have been a blast if we had bumped into each other on the Champs Elysées?"

Izzie discovered her shoes and put them on. "What the hey, I guess I might as well level with you. The Boutique de Paris should be titled La Dress Shop de Lower Manhattan. I work with importers."

"They must be dynamite. Of course, originality is something you can't buy. This décor is pure class," Cass said as they gravitated out into the store.

"That's Ilsa's touch." For the first time Izzie's face took on genuine warmth, her smile was soft and vulnerable. "Come on, you must meet her." Leading the way over to the seraph at the desk she said, "Pickle, darling, this is the once and famous Sandy Butterfield. San, meet my alter ego, Ilsa Calhern." With a playful gesture she tugged at the golden chain and suddenly everything came clear — the soft little woman's fear, the instant hatred.

"Hello, Ilsa. Izzie always did need an alter ego." Cass tried to put a message of reassurance into her smile: *Hey, I'm straight, but I'm cool. Glad for you both.* It didn't work. The creature's hazel eyes sent her an uppercut of jealousy so fierce it was staggering.

Iz seemed unaware. Or else she mistook the tension for something else, because she frowned at Cass and observed, "You know, you seem older. Of course, who isn't? But honestly, I've seen Annabel Lee look sharper in her seashore days."

"Yeah, I'm fine. The pallor is a parting gift from the hospital. Surgeon gave me a hole in the head. Remember how we always said that's what I needed?"

"Gawd, you aren't kidding. That scar . . . Pickle, would you go brew us some tea please? I left the kettle on."

The child/woman fluttered off like a feather on a passing breeze. Iz had gone to drag a chair over to one of the ice cream tables that wasn't patronized by dummies. And the workman was descending his ladder, sticking a hammer in the pocket of stained denims, grinning over his shoulder. The face was familiar, even though partly hidden by tufty gray eyebrows and a small goat's beard.

"Guy?"

"The one-and-only." He thrust out a grimy hand. "Gad, I can't call you Butterball any more. You're so skinny it would take three of you to make a good Modigliani." In a graceful gesture he brushed her fingers with a chin-fuzzy kiss. " 'Home is the hunter, home from the hills,' and all that. Welcome prodigal."

Cass found herself smiling. "I see you're into your Michelangelo phase, perching on ladders and so forth. When do you start on the ceiling?"

"Actually we thought the old stamped tin gives the place authenticity. Of course if you have any advice — I understand you've just come from the hallowed halls of the old country. I knew you'd turn out to be an artist."

"Not me, I never thought that," Izzie contradicted. "I figured she'd go underground in service of her country, sneaking about the world on fake passports, breaking up spy rings."

Cass forced a laugh. "You've found me out! Just call me Hairy Matty. My most dangerous assignment" — lowering her voice — "infiltrate a ceramics school. There's a lot of skullduggery in chinaware."

"I've heard they sneak cyanide into the glazes, get rid of people right and left." Guy regarded her with delight in his eyes. "Cook up any plots around the old kiln?"

Ilsa was back with a tray of cups delicately steaming of oolong, Cass hoped there wasn't any cyanide in hers. "Actually," she said, "you've got to watch out for the kiln itself. You know the story of the Chinese royal ceramist who accidentally produced the first oxblood vase?"

"Tell, tell!" he demanded.

"It just turned up in his batch one day, this piece that was uniquely red — red is a difficult color to achieve at high temperatures. Well, the Emperor really liked it and demanded another to match. So the poor potter tried and tried, but his copper glazes remained green because he didn't know the principles of reduction. Finally, having lost all face, he stacked his shelves one last time, then jumped into the firebox. Ashed himself out. Of course, when they opened the kiln the ware was magnificent oxblood red. He had pulled off the miracle when he went up in smoke."

Guy let out a hoot and Izzie chortled happily. Raising her teacup she said, "Our telltale heart is back and telling tales. Here's to Sandy."

So . . . she had survived the first test. Her blood pressure subsided slowly as she walked home, a little tired, but she'd got her welcome mat. The forsythia waved yellow accolades at her from the front yards as she passed. Finally when a clump of salmon colored tulips burst into floral cheers, she muttered, "Okay, okay, I get the message."

4

"Unless you're a leopard, protective coloring doesn't come easily. You've got to work at it." The gospel according to Kuzu. Their drill instructor at training camp, he was a walking example of camouflage, in aviator sunglasses, Army fatigues, a stubble of beard that almost hid the scar on his jaw. "You have to assess the background patterns around you and reshape yourself to match them."

Sunday morning, the ambiance of Panhandle Colorado was one of reverence, as people gravitated toward their various churches. Bells chimed distantly while Cass stood at the kitchen window and watched Liz and Joe settle themselves in their old black Chevy sedan. She had been invited.

"At First Baptist we open our arms to ever'body. I could lend you a hat." Liz was togged out now in a pink pillbox set squarely on her grizzled frizz, hugging to her a dated fur-trimmed coat, one wrist dangling a scuffed leather handbag. Beside her, Joe looked grimly dogged in stiff collar and tie. Cass gave him E for effort. He must care for Liz a good deal to get himself up in a wool suit and shined shoes.

And maybe religion was a solution of sorts, she thought, a different perspective on survival. But she couldn't bring herself to it yet. The prospect of all the tomorrows was too bleak. It had to be grappled with face to face, not through the soothing words of a preacher's dispensation.

She had thought about God, they all had. Most in her profession simply dismissed the idea of a deity. Cass didn't. She had felt too vividly the powers of good and evil, opposing force fields struggling toward Armageddon. Her problem was that the bad guys seemed to be winning. She couldn't frame the proper prayers to the leader of a lost cause. Of course she would go some Sunday as a matter of practicality — what better way to help establish her legitimacy. But today, she thought there must be some other way to authenticate Sandy Butterfield, one that she might possibly enjoy a little.

So who is this character? A ceramist. What would she be likely to do, just for fun? How about rock hunting, go search for clay deposits out on the prairies. Get out of this yellow kitchen. Setting her cup in the sink Cass went to the fridge and got out the makings of a sandwich. Bread, bologna, mustard, a six-pack of cream soda, and where's a paper sack to carry them? Add an apple — she reached for it and her shoulder pinged.

For the love of pete, girl, go put on the truss.

In the bedroom she tossed aside the blue cotton bathrobe, a keepsake from the day she had walked away from the hospital. Some instinct had told her not to wait for an official discharge. The League had paid her medical bills in Marseilles, sent her up to Paris for rehab, but they were suspicious of her story. The blood tests had shown no drugs in her system, so the new chemical must be a wonder, to be so powerful and leave no traces. Of course it was hard to argue with a bullet in the head, so they had left her alone temporarily. Sensing that she'd never be able to gain their trust again, Cass had left under her own steam on a snowy afternoon last December, stole a coat from the locker room, put it on over the bathrobe and walked out, to mingle with the Christmas crowds and disappear off their radar.

By then the rehab people had fitted her

shoulder with a support system. As she squirmed into the elastic contraption she caught sight of herself in the long mirror on the vanity. A reminder of her mother. *She wouldn't recognize me now.* The wiry body was skin and bones, looked downright anorexic. Quickly she pulled on jeans and a denim shirt.

Hesitating a moment over the open drawer of the dresser, Cass fingered the stiletto. From Spain, the best tempered steel, carved ebony haft, in a tooled leather sheaf, it brought back all the dark corners, dangerous streets, hand paused for the quick draw — *no more of that!* Shivering slightly, she shoved it back under a pile of cotton briefs.

Pulling on a parka, an old quilted blue thing she'd bought at a Salvation Army thrift store, she went out onto the back porch, pausing a minute in the chilly spring breeze to consider her options. Behind the house the prairies stretched off to the north in prickly undulations, native grasses still winter-brown, bushes barren of leaf. Yet somewhere out there a meadowlark flung its improvisations onto the crisp air. Where, in those fields of cactus and cocklebur, would it find a place to nest? She finally spotted it perched on the topmost sprig of a scrubby juniper a few hundred feet away.

Go for it, bird, the place is all yours, I'm outa here.

As she backed the truck down the drive Cass noticed again the house across the street, weedy yard forsaken, and yet there was that car still parked behind the honeysuckle bush. A silver Toyota, it didn't look like a junker. An anomaly. She'd been taught to watch out for them. The late model car was inconsistent with the FOR SALE sign. Some buyer looking at the house, going to fix it up? Or using it for surveillance? Foolish suspicion — old habits die hard.

Scorning herself for a paranoiac she pulled off slowly down the back street, fighting an impulse simply to floor the pedal and head for parts unknown. She was all gassed up, had stopped at the Texaco station yesterday. It hadn't been a great encounter, meeting Freddie Foreman, another incarnation from high school.

"Yo, Sandy. Heard you was home." In greasy overalls he was as scrawny as ever, his Adam's apple big as a wing-nut in his throat, looking her over with curious green eyes, prowling the truck.

"Sounds like she could use a tune-up." He fingered the padlock on the hood.

"Whatcha got under there? The crown jools?"

"The rig came like that, I bought it second-hand," she said, handing him a twenty for the gas.

When she'd answered the ad in a New Jersey paper the blue '69 Ford pickup had been exactly what she needed — a solid basic engine, a granny gear and a power train that was easy to work on. Price was right, the widow had been glad to be rid of it. She hadn't even removed her husband's fishing tackle. The engine had delighted the young mechanic in Omaha who had rebuilt it, souped it up, installed new brakes and overloads. She had field-tested it driving across Nebraska at ninety miles an hour, the old crate vibrating and rattling, but full of pep. *No, Freddie, you aren't going to get your mitts on that engine.*

He hadn't even checked the tires, but they were new. Cass wasn't worried about driving them off-road, and she was pretty sure she'd have to if she were to discover any sedimentary deposits. They would only occur in a dry lake or an arroyo where centuries of rains had drained down off the mountains and settled into flat ponds. You'd have to be lucky. Today she'd settle for a few agates; she had slung her rock hammer from her belt.

East of town where Lamar Street turned into a two-lane black-top a neon sign rose garishly: GOLLAGHER'S. The old roller rink seemed to have been reborn, to judge by the bawdy billboard on the roof, a reclining bikini-clad woman holding a bottle of beer. *I'll bet the town had a hemorrhage when that went up.* On a blackboard out-front were the scrawled words:

BREAKFAST
ALL YOU CAN EAT
$3.99

To the rear of the old barn of a building stood a row of cabins, imitation logs, shiny with yellow varnish. From a pedestal of red wagon-wheels rose a sign that glowed faintly in the bright daylight.

VACANCY

A mile farther she passed another indicator of Panhandle's new age. A tall wrought-iron gate arched over a graveled road that led to a distant huddle of outbuildings, corrals, a haystack. In the grillwork above was a large "R" equipped with rockers. She felt a small stir of amusement. If all the guest ranches in the western United States that were named the "Rocking R" should be gathered in one place they'd make a carousel.

And then she was free of distractions. Driving on across the plains she began to enjoy the sense of anonymity that came with those vast stretches, wide open and surging as the prehistoric sea. They reminded her always of the timelessness of the land which looked as though no one had trespassed on it for centuries. And yet a hundred and fifty years ago this corner of the West had produced heroes. Her father loved to tell their stories.

"Not far from here old Joe Meek got jumped by the Comanche. With no place to go for cover, he and a friend had to shoot their own pack mules and fort up behind the carcasses to hold off the Indians' attacks until nightfall. One thing about the native Americans, they were sensible about getting a good night's sleep." Her father would chuckle. Joe and his buddy slipped away before the moon got up, shanked it at a trapper's trot to the nearest post, which was Taos, seventy miles to the south. "Man, those guys were tough," he marveled.

She could almost picture them, a couple of ragged men in beaver caps and slung carbines, loping on foot across this endless prairie. Cass slowed the truck to a crawl. Over on the left there seemed to be an arroyo, worth a look. She turned off, carving a crooked track around stands of stag-horn until she could see that it was only a minor dry wash, four feet deep and fifty yards wide, drifted with gravel banks. No clay here, but it might yield a few agates. Cutting the engine, she got out. In deference to the faint throb of her scar she clapped on the old fishing hat she had found in the back of the truck and left the Ford ticking and settling like an elderly dame in the sunshine.

When she walked over to the edge a pair of doves burst out of the underbrush on the far side, whimpering *trespass!* Closer at hand a jackrabbit leaped up and went jinking away down-country. For the first time in a long while Cass began to relax. Jumping down into warm sand she headed across the dry stream bed searching for any rounded stone with a cratered surface that would indicate chalcedony.

A hundred yards up, she headed for a low island of rocks left by the runoff, good spot for geodes. Spotting a possible, she bent to pick it up just as an insect buzzed past her head and hit the opposite bank with a soft *thwick.* Before the sound of the shot reached her Cass was in motion, flinging herself behind the gravel bar, scrambling for shelter beneath a meager clump of rabbit bush. As she tried to work her way deeper she drew another shot. If there'd been any doubt that this was some guy out popping at ground squirrels it was gone.

In an odd way she almost felt relieved. She realized that for months she had been expecting something like this. Especially since arriving in Panhandle her sixth sense had been warning her, as it did when she walked down a street that was too quiet, or entered a locked building too easily.

She took off the fishing hat and raised her head a few inches, hoping her light hair was a blend with the sparse dry vegetation atop the bar. The distant figure stood gripping a rifle, just a guy in hunting clothes, too far to make out his face. Behind him, a silver Toyota. Must have followed her out here. *But how did I miss that?* Don't try to figure it out, just be thankful he's a lousy shot.

And impatient. He blasted one at a ground squirrel that jumped up ten yards away. Missed. Cass plucked a branch of rabbit bush and used it to ease the fishing hat upward into sight — oldest trick in the world, but it worked, drew another shot. He banged off a couple more, wildly. And . . .

yes, he had to reload.

She was up and running hard, back toward the shooter's side of the wash, scuttling to shelter under the overhang. It took her out of his view, but it was no permanent solution. Just upstream the arroyo curved back into his sights, broad and shallow, no hiding places. No escape route. She crawled over to investigate a narrow gully that might have provided a way out, but it was choked with tumbleweed that had piled up around a stunted juniper.

Mind on fast-forward, she considered the little tree, gnarled, thick with twisted branches. Searching quickly, she found what she was looking for — a sturdy fork. Hacked off the limb with her hunting knife, keeping an ear out for any sound from the sniper. Taking his time now. *He doesn't have to hurry, he knows I'm not going anywhere. And I might have a gun, so he'll be careful.* She risked a quick glance — the man still stood hesitant on the brink of the arroyo. One minute he'd had a pat hand and now he was drawing to an inside straight.

Laying the stripped branch aside, Cass shucked off her clothes and squirmed out of the truss. Slicing a length of elastic, she used her bootlaces to tie it to the arms of the fork. When she looked again he was beginning to move her way. Hastily she laid out shirt and jeans, set her boots below the pants' legs, a small boulder for a head, covered by the tatty fishing hat. It didn't have to stand close inspection. Just needed to be lifelike enough to make him stop and look closer.

As she heard gravel crunch she snatched up a pebble, discarded it, found a better one and nocked it into the elastic. The heft felt pretty good. Using a slingshot was a skill best learned young. By the third grade she had made life unpleasant for every tin can up and down the back alleys of town. The secret was not to aim with the eye, but with the hand, the way you throw a stone. Draw back the rubber in your right, then lunge with your left as you let go. A shiver ran over her, sweat trickling down her bare ribs, *where is he?*

He was there not thirty feet away, hesitating. *Over here, stupid.* She rose and ducked fast as he squeezed off a shot. With an agonized cry she back-tracked into the cascade of tumbleweed, skeletons of dry white twigs like the ghosts of party balloons, thorny, but perfect to blend with a naked body. Lumbering footsteps now, and a lizard lunged over the brow of the bank and down its hole, pretty thing with a turquoise collar.

Then he was above her on the bank, sunglasses, baseball cap, flannel shirt, just a guy out hunting varmints, but the rifle could have brought down a moose. Another step, to peer down at the dummy. Adrenaline surged, with its terrible high. Cass rose from her crouch, drew and zinged the stone at his head. Ducking she had picked up a second rock before he hit the ground. Doing a loose jackknife off the bank, he lay flattened out face down in the bottom of the wash.

Weapon ready, she moved toward him. Piece of luck to have knocked him out cold. Circling watchfully she picked up the rifle, a Winchester .270 with a scope. When she nudged his shoulder with it he lay still — the total inertia that only comes with complete systems failure. Cass gave his ribs a good kick with her bare foot, but there was no sound of expelled air. His face was half buried in the sand. Bending over him, she felt for the carotid, no pulse. Only a slight red mark where the stone had struck, that terribly vulnerable spot in the temporal above the jugal point. She touched it and felt a sickening softness, the bone beneath had fractured inward. But his skin was warm as if he were still alive.

5

Never killed before. Shouldn't there be some kind of revulsion? For the moment all Cass felt was an awful elation, to be alive, to have won. To survive, that was the bottom line. Kuzu had reminded them over and again in training: when it's you or the other guy, go for it, no regrets. Backing away from the body she went to get her clothes, hauled them on. Beginning to feel queasy . . . *I killed . . .*

It lay so still, with such finality. Who? Who was he, and who sent him, who wanted her dead? Especially, how did they know where to look? In fact he must have been here ahead of her. The silver Toyota had been parked across the street when she arrived that day, so long ago — what? Friday? Day before yesterday. Confusion stirred her mind like a slotted spoon. *I should take a closer look, maybe it's somebody I know.* She hadn't even tried to see his face. Reluctantly she moved back to the side of the inert figure and, with ginger fingers, took hold of the heavy jacket by the sleeve, grabbed a pants leg and heaved the body over with an effort.

Reaction struck fast and hard, a fluxing sweat started out all over her body, knees jellied, she stumbled aside and vomited convulsively. Ended up on all fours, retching into the sand, dry painful spasms. When she tried to stand up, she had to use the rifle as a prop for a minute, but when she'd got her balance she was drawn back to the dead man by the irresistible force of recognition. She knew him of course, that was the face which had hung over her in the warehouse, hideous in the glow of the lantern. Even in bright daylight it was ugly as sin, pocked skin, bulbous nose with broken veins. All that thickened flesh was probably why he made that guttural *gnf gnf, gnf* snigger. She could hear it, hear the rats scuttling in the shadows of the warehouse, smell the stink of the harbor, feel the slap of waves against the piers of the dock. Marseilles had come to Panhandle.

Her stomach twitched weakly. There was still no answer to the question of *why.* Why go to all this trouble to take out a failed spook who's retired from the game? God knows they got everything they wanted out of her that night. *Except my life, they didn't get that.* But what difference? Why should they care?

Unless it was something personal with the sniper, bungled the job and wanted to make it right? Maybe he had to make it right, under penalty of sanction. They'd told him: you messed up, so finish the job. But that didn't make sense. The pros of her world didn't bother with the nuances of the game, they had to get on to other innings. Who ever heard of embarrassment or delicate feelings in the contention of life against death?

The killers do worry, though, about reputation. If he was a hired gun this could have been his personal challenge: to remedy the little oversight of having let her slip from his grasp. His own vendetta — An inkling of hope trickled through her arid dread. Maybe the Flea Circus wasn't behind this after all.

If the man was acting solo, maybe they never even knew that he had caught up with her. Especially if it were written off as a hunting accident?

FREAK MISHAP FELLS TOURIST

Cass crouched beside him, searched his pockets until she found a wallet with a Wyoming driver's license. Robert Willows, the picture didn't even come close. So the car was stolen — poor Bob, rest in peace. She put the wallet back, let it confuse the local law. The State Highway Patrol wasn't trained in forensics, maybe if she set a convincing scene they wouldn't dig into the thing. Just a car thief who stopped to take potshots at the jackrabbits and fell off the bank, hit his head.

She turned the body face-down again, positioning the brow against a fair-sized rock. The gun — she went back to her pickup and searched for a rag, found one that smelled of oil and wiped the stock of her fingerprints. If nobody had noticed two vehicles parked here, it might work. It was all she could come up with, given her limited props. Cass took the rifle back and pressed his fingers onto the stock, the barrel. Finally roughing the sand, she left it too choppy to read foot prints. Covered her vomit and then went in search of the rock hammer.

Found it over near the island of gravel where she had slammed to the ground the first time. The hasp was bent, but she could get it fixed. A good tool, it was edged with tungsten carbide, well worth saving. She dropped it down the back of her shirt where it lodged against her belt.

One last look, and then she returned to the truck, took a long pull of coffee from the thermos. It threatened to make a hasty exit. She held it down and got behind the wheel, driving slowly along her own tracks, avoiding his. If somebody did remember that there were two vehicles here, they wouldn't be able to read her tire tread. In a few days the elements would soften the whole scene of detail. If she could make it back onto the road without anyone seeing her . . . at which point her luck ran out.

The car coming from the direction of Panhandle was a familiar black-and-white Crown Vic. Groaning inwardly Cass knew there was no way Pike Webster was going to forget that he had seen her out here, at some later moment when the body was discovered. He might be small-town law, but he was no fool. There was only one way to handle the thing now. She set herself to morph into Sandy mode and pulled up at the road's edge, waving vigorously. The shoulder sobbed. She had wrenched it again when she hit the ground back there, hadn't even noticed the pain. Now all at once her whole body pulsed with assorted aches and smarts, bruised and scratched from crashing around in the nude. It didn't take much acting to look distressed.

The Chief pulled over window-to-window on the deserted road. "What's up? You look kind of pale. Are you hurt?"

"I'm not too great," she admitted thinly. "I just discovered a man over there, about a hundred yards from that Toyota. He's down in the arroyo and I think he's dead."

Pike frowned at the distant vehicle. "What were you doing over there?"

"I went out rock-hunting this morning. When I saw the car I thought maybe it was one of the locals, figured I could get some tips on where to look for agates. When I got there he was stretched out cold."

"Did you check to see if he was alive?"

"Yeah, I couldn't get a pulse. Looked like he fell off the bank and hit his head on a rock. What are you doing way out here?"

"Oh, one of our citizens created a ruckus over in Lamar last night and they called me to come get him out of the hoosegow, give him a ride home. That'll wait." Webster's face had stiffened into its procedural set. "Would you mind coming back with me while I check this out? Might want to ask a few more questions." Without waiting for a reply he pulled around her and set a new course several yards away from the other sets of tracks, studying them as he drove slowly. Where they all came together by the arroyo the ground was a mishmash of dusty ruts. Cass hoped that the Chief was no expert tracker.

Twenty feet short of the Toyota he stopped and got out, stuck a neat gray Stetson on his head, completing the official look. The uniform was immaculate, pants creased to a cutting edge, so professional it gave her a sickly unease. Motioning her to stay back, he moved on up the bank of the arroyo, jumped down lightly and considered the dead man. Crouched over the body he didn't touch it. Glanced at the pitch of the embankment, the position of the rifle. Picking up the latter by the tips of his fingers he sniffed it, then laid it back down.

Cass shivered, though the sun was straight up by now and the breeze had died. The midday stillness was broken only by the stir of insects in the sage, the scuttle of a ground squirrel. Webster spotted her gully and went to stare at the tumbleweed. It was broken of course where she'd hidden in it, *but all those tiny twigs, he won't notice that, will he?*

"So what you think, Pike? Guy hunting rabbits, tripped and fell?"

He gave her a quizzical look. "Would you

hunt rabbits with a high-performance rifle and a scope?"

"Maybe, if they were high-performance rabbits." The humor sounded lame. "Probably the only gun he had. Wyoming plates, up there everybody carries an antelope gun. Don't they?" *You're talking too much, shut up.*

He climbed out of the draw and led the way back to the cop car. Opening the front door on the passenger side he said, "Sit down, Bunny. You look like you're halfway in shock. Have a jolt of coffee."

"Uh — I'd rather have water, if you've got it."

From the back seat he took a thermos and poured some into the top, handing it to her. "Tell me: If a person trips and falls forward, what do they do first?"

"Excuse me?"

"Look." He thrust out his hands. "It's a reflex, to try to catch yourself. Like you must have done — looks like you fell down recently." There were abrasions on her palms. "No cuts on his hands, only that one bruise on his face, which is odd. I don't get it — the gun has been fired but I couldn't smell any powder, there's too much fresh oil on it. Only it isn't gun oil, more like machine oil, motor oil."

Cass laughed feebly. “You part Indian?”

Soberly the Chief said, “My mother is a full-blooded Navajo. Dad was killed in the Korean War. I grew up on the Big Rez. You learn some useful arts and crafts.” Taking a swallow from the thermos he put the top back on. “One thing I know for sure. You were here first. Right over yonder his treads cross yours plain as day. Bunny, you want to tell me what’s going on?”

The scar on her head gave a sudden throb. She waited for a rescuing surge of adrenaline, but she’d used deeply of it earlier. All she had left were the dregs, bitter in her mouth. She was tired, so depleted she had no more cleverness. She had botched the cover-up, underestimated local law enforcement. Kuzu would have kicked her out of camp.

All that seemed like another life. Now she yearned to make it simple, to speak the truth. She wanted to stay alive and for that she needed to tell Pike Webster enough to enlist his help. A brief thought of sworn oaths, secrets to be taken to the grave, flashed across her embattled mind and she almost laughed. Pretty much too late for that. Taking a deep breath she leaned back against the seat.

“Pike, I hate playing games. It’s what I’ve

been doing for years, a matter of survival. Lying becomes a force of habit. The fact is, I hoped the guy's death would be written off as a freak accident. Which it wasn't, of course. He followed me out here and tried to kill me. Missed, fortunately. I hid over there, you saw the tumbleweed. I drew him into an up-close situation where I could bean him with a rock. I was only trying to knock him out so I could get the gun. But the shot was lucky — or unlucky, from his point of view."

Webster listened, frowning, processing. "Why on earth would anyone want to kill you?"

"Because he bungled the job the first time." She tapped the scar over her left ear. "Bullet just grooved my skull, it didn't penetrate. The surgery was to remove a blood clot."

"This same man shot you once before? Why?"

"Nothing personal. He was a hired gun then, following orders. Now, I don't know. Maybe he was acting on his own, trying to make up for botching the job. Otherwise I can't explain why he'd be after me. The men who hired him wrecked my career, I'm no threat to them any more."

"This career that got wrecked — ?"

She hesitated again, the habit of secrecy so deeply imbedded it was hard to convince herself that the situation demand disclosure. With a long sigh she said, "We swore never to talk about our work."

"Girl, there's been a death here. In my back yard. I need facts."

Cass stared up into that broad, honest face, needing desperately to tell the whole story. Slowly she began. "You know — everybody knows — how the world is threatened with terrorism. But ten years ago it was a hidden disease, incubating in the dark, spread by unknown fanatics. Average people wouldn't believe it was a threat, 'Not in my country!' you know how it goes. The big governments wouldn't even cooperate with each other in releasing their intelligence reports, all jealous of their secrets, full of suspicions. There was no way to coordinate an effort against the cells of anarchists, the little bands of neo-Nazis, the Arabs and all the rest. So a group of hard-nosed businessmen formed their own organization, they called it The Libra League — scales of justice. With an international anti-terrorist agenda they began to recruit people like me, young, motivated, ready to learn the tricks of undercover operations, the mission: to infiltrate and bring down the destroyers. My gift was linguistics. I went to an accelerated school in Washington, D.C., expecting to try for the Diplomatic Corps."

"Languages? How many do you speak?"

"Conversational in eight or nine, I can understand a few of the Middle Eastern dialects, speak Russian with a French accent, but I am fluent in German and that's where they needed foot soldiers. So they sent me to Dresden. I really did attend an art academy, learned ceramics as cover for my real work, to infiltrate the student underground which had been perpetrating atrocities all over Europe. There are more terrorist gangs than you've ever read about in the papers, little pockets of angry, hateful people bent on creating chaos in the well-ordered governments of the world. And they're succeeding in a lot of ways — look at our own experience. After the World Trade Center the United States went into a panic, threw out some of the Bill of Rights, began to argue that we need a whole new discipline and to hell with the old protections. We've almost bankrupt ourselves setting up defenses that aren't going to stop anybody. You can't fight fleas with a cannon. That's what we called them, The Devil's Flea Circus, because they're spreading a new Black Plague of fear."

Webster was listening intently, unconvinced. "This bunch you worked for, they're political?"

"Not really. Their goals are a stable economic climate and a balance of power. The League is secretly funded by corporations in a half-dozen countries, including ours. They don't work with any other organizations, they write their own rules, whatever it takes to bring down the mass-murderers and stop the panic. It's a life or death matter to all of us to protect the foundations of law and order."

"So you were a kind of spy?"

"For want of a better word. I've retired now, my cover was blown, I was almost killed. My usefulness is over."

"But in essence you were off fighting outlaws all these years?"

She almost smiled. "Dad would have loved that description."

"He didn't know about this?"

"I told him I was going underground for a good cause. I wanted him to understand why I had to be out of touch. He was great. He wished me luck."

"Yeah, he would. But Bunny, why on earth would you choose such a cra — such a life?"

Cass shrugged. It seemed so naïve now. "I figured maybe I could make a difference in the world. It was exciting. It was a sort of noble profession, I thought. We were highly trained."

"They taught you to kill a man with a rock?"

She shuddered. "I always did know how to use a slingshot."

"You carry around — ?"

"I made it. After he started sniping at me, I didn't have a weapon, I had to do something. Hey, it's the truth. Go look over in the back of my truck."

He caught the keys she tossed at him and went over to the pickup, lifted the rear hatch and took out the whittled tool. Bending down he scooped up a rock and zinged it at a cactus twenty feet away. Dead aim. "Pretty good balance for make-shift. I doubt if I could kill anybody with it, though."

"It was a shot in a million. Pure luck. I hoped it would get written off as an accidental death, because if it makes the news you could have the Flea Circus all over Panhandle like an epidemic. They may not have sent him, but they'd be sure to follow up on it if they thought he was executed. I still think you'd be best off to make it a low profile item in the papers. Just makes sense."

He tossed the slingshot back in the pickup. "Makes sense to me to call the FBI."

"Then I will say my final farewells right now. Because they will probe me, find out my connections, write multitudinous reports which will leak through the cracks in the Bureau and I would be in the cross-hairs of a whole new sniper, or several, maybe some of them even sent by my own people. We didn't part on good terms. The League doesn't like blabbermouths. I shouldn't have told you this much, but I felt you needed to know. I am trusting you, Pike, don't feed me to the wolves."

She had made him uncomfortable. His troubled gaze kept going back to the spot up the draw where the corpse still lay on the sand. Just a local cop, poor man, never figured on having to cope with a mess like this.

Driving home, Cass tried to sort out the tangle of unanswered questions in her head. The biggest one: How did the gunman get here ahead of her? It made her sick, she wanted to wring her brain for answers, but it was dry. She tried to force a picture of what was going to happen next, but the screen was blank. What it came down to was one fact: the future was in the hands of that unworldly man back there on the prairie with his corpse, his confusion and that antique tin star.

6

Who was it that first came up with the idea of a flea circus? Cass couldn't remember — if she had ever known. It had been part of her training, to think of terrorists as filthy insects. The idea apparently had risen from the time in history, the 14th Century, when the Black Plague was spread by fleas, hopping from rat to rat and infecting a whole continent. Europe lost half its population in a couple of years. Nobody knew how to fight it, the little bugs are almost invisible, ferociously prolific. And in those days they were ubiquitous. Now we have insecticides — for each deadly disease humanity has found an antidote. Cass had been proud of that role. Now her usefulness was over, so how did one specific flea track her across the face of the earth, and why should he bother?

The only data about Sandra Butterfield would be deep in the secret files of the

League. For the fleas to access it there had to be a mole, an idea which had been nagging her ever since the night on the docks. Very few people knew about that conference on the yacht, only the top echelon. As a team leader she had been told, of course. Her orders were to wait with her group at a safe house nearby until she received further instructions. They were going to get new assignments, trouble was looming for the United States. They might be sending her home — a prospect that filled her with mixed feelings.

When she'd got the summons to go to the yacht the note was written in her personal code, one that no one knew except her team and her handler, a man called Jacques. Plus the Directors, she supposed. Cass had no idea how many of the top brass were privy to the confidential files. There were no secrets from the founders. Jacques had been one of them, part of the original core of the League, it was unthinkable that he could have somehow relaxed the security rules, unless — was it possible that he was a double agent himself?

He'd been her control since she graduated from the camp. A Frenchman — she never did know his real name, *thank God I couldn't tell them that.* More than a handler, he'd been a good friend. Came to see her in the hospital, warm and reassuring, it will all turn out well, etc. When he left — they both sensed it was a final parting — he had kissed her hand. Frenchmen.

No, it couldn't be Jacques. He had persuaded the League to make her a team leader, give her the first difficult assignment. She had infiltrated a tough student cadre of neo-Facists who played at anarchy as if it were a team sport, which didn't mean they weren't deadly serious.

"The kiln will fire off at one a.m. tomorrow night." Skulduggerous whisper.

"This will be a Cone 7 operation." Sepulchral tones.

Silly dialogue out of a novel. But the target would be a big one, a major bank or an embassy, and the explosives were real. She helped set them herself. While down the street Ian and the team waited her signal to move in and disarm the bombs, call in the cops. Her long-term goal had been to discover the master mind who gave the orders. And she had begun to feel herself closing in, though she hadn't told that to Jacques, wanting to present him with a *fait accompli.*

This had been brought up in her debriefing in the hospital. Still woozy from the sedatives she had wakened in a sterile white room to find a gray homunculus of a man sitting by the bed. Business suit, thinning hair, narrow body, his spidery hands kept fingering his notebook.

"We need some explanations here. You gave us no indication that your mission was about to achieve success. Our theory right now is that you were playing both sides."

Skull pounding like a jackhammer, shoulder aflame with torn nerve ends, Cass tried to grasp what he was saying. "You mean . . . you think I . . . tortured myself, shot myself in the head and threw myself in the bay to drown?" If she laughed even a little she thought she might never stop.

"It wouldn't be the first time the fleas got rid of an informer. Especially if they thought you were a double agent. You take that chance when you consort with vermin."

"Consort . . . ? Mister, I was assigned to consort with them. Somebody drew me into that trap. I was drugged — didn't they run any blood tests?"

"They came back clean. No sign of pharmaceuticals."

"Well, it had to be something new, fast-dissipating. Lab didn't know what to look for. Maybe you ought to investigate that. It's a devastating chemical. Maintains total power over you."

"So you say. If you weren't bent on treachery why did you go to meet these people?"

"I was lured there by a note in my own personal code, instructing me to report aboard the yacht."

"We found no note."

"Of course not. I destroyed it immediately, S.O.P. Looked totally legitimate — exactly as if it was sent by my own superiors."

Cold eyes. "Are you trying to imply that *we* betrayed *you?*"

"Maybe. Maybe you've got a mole in the top ranks. We talked about it before — it would explain some odd things that have been happening."

"Why would we need to interrogate you about your team? Information we already had? Your group was one of our most valuable cells, why would we want to roll it up? Only the Flea Circus benefited. So I ask you once more: why did you sell out?"

"I didn't sell out! I loved my team! I was kidnapped, I was tortured . . ."

About then the nurses monitoring her vital signs had come barreling in and removed the little creature bodily. She never saw him again — or anyone else from the League. They silently paid the bills, sent her to the rehab hospital, and left her in limbo.

As soon as she got her feet under her, Cass had walked away. From her safe deposit box she'd retrieved her fake i.d.'s — all agents kept a couple of identities they had acquired privately. She had bought a wig and gone to ground. If the League searched for her, it wasn't very extensive. She had no trouble arranging passage on a tramp steamer back to the States.

Ever since then she had more or less expected to hear from them. Loose ends are anathema to a spy organization. And yet she had never sensed anyone on her trail. Unless they were the ones who hired old *gnf gnf.* That would mean a double-cross of such proportions it made her sick. She had gone over it all again in the long hours of the night.

Finally rousing from her bed, she saw that it was still dark outside, but the eastern sky was shifting. Anyway, she couldn't lie still any more. A terrible restlessness surged within her, uncertainty about her shifting identities, about her role in this familiar town which was no longer familiar. The house had begun to feel like a trap; she needed to get out of it, be around people, strangers, an indifferent world where she was no one in particular.

Pulling on slacks and a sweater, she went

into the kitchen. The hideous yellow chicken proclaimed the time to be 7:10. The reason it was still so dark was in the clouds, weather on the move. Across the yards the lights were on in Liz's kitchen. *No!* That was the last place she wanted to be. She hurried out to the truck and sent it backward out of the drive as if she were late for an appointment. With what, though? Death? It was pretty obvious that if old *gnf gnf* could ferret her out, others could too. Her whole instinct told her to run, far and fast toward the nearest horizon.

"Which is a good way to get yourself killed." Kuzu had once warned them. Anonymous behind the black goggles, his scarred face twisted in a sneer. "You were born with eyes on the front of your head, so you could see trouble as it comes. Your back makes a great target."

Maybe go at least as far as Trinidad, get something to eat. She felt caved in by now. No appetite, but her stomach needed nourishment. At the far end of town she was caught by the bright neon sign: EATS and remembered seeing it the other day when she stopped for gas. Not that she was anxious for more chitchat with Freddie Foreman, but sometimes truckers know where the food is good. Two big rigs were pulled up idling in front of the diner, its red-striped curtains giving off a cheerful glow. Cass pulled in and parked the pickup.

When she went in the door she was met by the scorched smell of the deep fryer, mingling with the aroma of Pinesol and a subtler *essence de trucker.* The two haulers in their windbreakers and baseball caps were gabbing with a waitress, whose red-and-white checkered apron matched the curtains at the windows. Something familiar about the woman, thin hair in braids across the top of her head, ears like jug handles and those teeth — Cluny Warren. Shades of sixth grade. Cass took a seat at the far end of the red Formica counter.

Picking up the coffee pot Cluny ankled back, gathering a thick mug and saucer along the way. "So, San', heard you was home." Her indifference was positively invigorating.

"H'lo, Cluny. How's everything?" She seized the cup of hot java, warming her hands on it.

"Oh, good. I got my own place." She waved a hand to encompass the diner. Arm slightly lardy, and from the bulge in her apron it seemed likely that in a few years she would be a tub. "Me and Freddie got married, y'know."

Match made in heaven.

"Got hitched right out of high school. We got three kids." Shoving a menu across she added, "Hot cakes is on special."

"Sounds fine to me. A short stack with a couple of eggs over easy and one sausage." Remember your Sandy routine. "So how are your folks?"

"Pa died a couple of years ago, left some insurance. Ma bought that land across the way and set up the trailer park. It ain't exactly a gold mine, but we get a few tourists. Couple of old Social Security feebs live there year-around, covers expenses." She poured three small puddles of batter on the grill and slapped down a paper napkin, plastic knife and fork.

"Hey, Clu, gimme another one of them flapjacks." One of the truckers. She grinned at him and lavished a huge round on the griddle. Road warriors get extra treatment, a jug of dark syrup, whole stack of butter patties. Sandy Butterworth only rated one, and a small sealed plastic envelope of yellow glop. Not that it mattered, it filled her inner cavern with calories. Eggs were overdone, but they represented protein. Cluny had forgotten the sausage in her rush to get back to the boys. When they paid up each of them dropped some folding green into the tip jar. As they headed out the door, a blast of wind swept in. Out in the parking lot, little dust devils swirled in antic glee.

An elderly man gusted in as they left. "Hoo-boy," he wheezed, blowing his nose on a big red miner's kerchief. "This-here weather ain't so good for my az-i-mah, tell you that."

Cluny moved quickly to put away the jug of syrup.

He snickered. "Don't fret, Clu, only want a cup of java. Y'hear the latest? About the dead body? Yessiree, we got us a killin' right out there on the highway east of town. Pike Webster found the corpse."

Cass froze, the food in her belly turned to brick.

"Go on. Where'd you hear a story like that?"

"M'cousin's boy, Dunbar, y'know, the one fills in at the police station when the Chief's out of town? Well, he says Web phoned in a while ago and said he's tied up with the Coroner over in LaJunta, won't get back here 'til later today."

Cass went to the register. Absently Cluny accepted her five-dollar bill. Cass dropped seventy-five cents into the tip jar — she was never going to rate real syrup anyway.

"So how'd the guy get dead?"

"Who knows? Some eastern dude, maybe he got lost out there in the cactus and died of thirst." The old man thought that was marvelously witty.

As she went outside, the wind gripped her in a chilly clasp and let go, as if she wasn't worth bothering with. Across the road it shook the Trailer Park sign vigorously and moved on across the open fields, raising a swirl of debris, paper cups, take-out sacks, napkins like lost souls spinning away into space.

Depressed, Cass turned the truck for home trying to settle the flutters. What else could you expect? Of course it's going to be news around town. The Panhandle Courier would be ecstatic to have a real story to run, and the LaJunta paper would get delusions of Pulitzer. If the Pueblo Chieftain is short of news they might even assign a reporter to come here and poke around, interview Pike. What small-town cop can resist the headlines?

Tired to the core with trying to figure all the angles, she swung into her driveway, parked the car and got inside before Liz could flag her down. The sleepless night still had its claws in her; all she wanted was to curl up under her electric blanket and try to find oblivion. Popping a Tylenol to take the edge off her aching shoulder, Cass crawled into bed, praying she wouldn't dream.

The Nightmare

"Ah tell ya, them rats gimme the grues." That one is hill-country bred, the twang in his voice like a badly tuned banjo. His are the heavy leather boots. The other one's wearing Nikes, top of the line. The third man, the interrogator, has gone, casting instructions back over his shoulder as he went out into the rain. It's still pelting hard on the corrugated iron roof.

She tries with every ounce of will power to move — the most infinitesimal fraction. Can't. Exhausted, she warps inwardly with such intense anguish it's almost unbearable, the very essence of enslavement.

"Hell," the second one has a strong Hoboken accent, "this is a palace. Gnf gnf. You shoulda seen some of the really dirty holes I been staked out in. Greece, that waterfront is a sewer. And Portugal. Talk about rats, they make these look puny."

"Well, me, I wish we wuz back in the U.S. of A."

Which suggests a question: Why did they go all the way to America to import these thugs? Can't find hoodlums in France?

"So why don't we finish up and git out of this-here stink-hole?"

The smells of the waterfront are vivid, the sound of waves lapping against the pilings beneath the warehouse, the splash of water running off the eaves.

"We'll go when the time comes. You heard the boss, gnf gnf, we don't pop her until it's almost daylight. He wants the big boys on the yacht out there to find her floatin', send 'em a message. Meanwhile, we gonna relax and enjoy ourself." As he bends over her she can see his face now, a contour map of venality, shaped by every gross appetite in the subhuman repertoire. "This pore lonely lady come all the way to the docks lookin' for some action, which she didn't get yet. We don't want to disappoint her, do we? Gnf gnf."

Dear . . . God . . . in . . . heaven . . .

7

It was Marlowe, wasn't it, who described hell's fires? "And from those flames no light, but rather darkness visible."

Cass moved stiffly around the house turning on every fixture, clutching the dowdy bathrobe around her naked body. The big picture window in the living room looked out upon the gloomy street beyond. On the coffee table was a Chinese porcelain lamp, she switched it on. House must look like a Christmas tree. A wet splatter at the window signaled that the wind had brought in the storm. More light —

When she reached up to switch on the floor lamp by the big leather chair her shoulder gave a minor screech. Going back to the bedroom she retrieved the butchered truss and a roll of elastic bandage. Her mother had a mending kit stashed somewhere. She found it in a drawer and got out the stoutest white thread, a big needle. Sitting on the bed she sewed with clumsy stitches, unsteady fingers, whipping the seam over and over. When she slipped it on, the pain in the shoulder steadied into an ache that was manageable.

"Give it time," the therapist had told her cheerfully. "Your body wants to heal."

"Yeah, but what about my mind?"

The surgeon, for all his austerity, had been more sympathetic. Of course he didn't know the whole story, thought she was just another rape/shooting victim. But he didn't minimize the trauma. "You will experience debilitating dreams when your brain will relive the assault. It's nature's way of cleansing the nervous system of stress-related sludge. Don't try to ride it out. Be kind to yourself, take these." Block-buster capsules. But he didn't have to think like a rabbit in hawk country. Even if one sniper was dead there was no guarantee there wouldn't be another. At least take a few precautions.

Pike's words came back: "Probably half the people in town know where your dad stashed his house key." So change the locks, dummy.

She glanced at her Timex — still a few minutes short of noon. She hadn't slept more than an hour before the horrors had taken over. Exhaustion was a chronic condition by now, deep in the bone, but she wasn't going to try again, not for a while. She might as well get busy and secure the house. Squirming into the parka. She pulled up the hood and ducked out fast into the pickup.

Anderson's Hardware store looked different from her memories of it. The old man had run a cracker-barrel operation where farmers congregated and traded gossip around a pot-bellied stove, chewing snoose and guffawing among the milk pails and rolls of barbed wire. Now the display in the window was of Toro self-propelled lawnmowers.

On the door she saw in gold lettering the words:

Hollis Anderson, Proprietor.

Hollis, for pete's sake! Cass had pictured him as long gone from this sorry neck of the woods. Once her partner in crime, a dark-haired boy with fierce, mocking black eyes, he had been the instigator of crazy stunts all through high school. No dare was too wild for the kid. She could still see his lanky adolescent silhouette against the moonlit sky, that time he had hauled the lawn furniture up onto the roof of the schoolhouse, a Fourth-of-July impulse. They had sat there in woven-web recliners and watched the town's official fireworks display over on the soccer field. His ambition had always been to become an astronaut.

The store was a far cry from the wild blue yonder. It had become a sterile place of fluorescent tubes ranked above aisles of shelves, racks of prepackaged items, screws, nails, nuts and bolts all sealed in plastic. She wasn't two feet inside before she was confronted by a tall, dour man — he hardly looked familiar in the gaudy red vest with the TORO logo on it.

"Sandy," he spoke the word as grimly as if it were an accusation.

"Hey, Hollis. How's it going?" Something about the dark stare of those eyes made Cass keep moving, on down an aisle where locks hung, each with screws, a pair of keys, all shrink-wrapped. Only one brand offered a deadlock that might possibly stop a specialist for five minutes.

"So you finally got around to looking up your old friends." He spoke from so close behind, she dropped one of the locks on her shin.

Hollis stooped and retrieved it. His long equine features had aged, the spark of deviltry that once livened them was gone, his face set in the concrete of bitterness like a concealing wall.

She stepped back, instinctively preserving her own space. "I've only been home a week. Had to get settled in. So how are things in the hardware business?"

"What you see is what you get." He shrugged.

"Coming in here I was thinking of the old days. High school, we were all kind of crazy. Remember the time you did a one-handed stand on top of the flagpole in front of the post office?"

"Oh I remember everything," he said with hidden significance.

"By now, I figured you'd be on your way out to the space shuttle."

"Stupid kid stuff." There was still that odd overtone of hostility. "My senior year of college Pa had a stroke. I quit school and came to help out here. Then he died and left the whole works in my lap. I never had time to go lollygagging all over the world."

"Ye-ah. Well, all that lolly can gag you, it's not what it's cracked up to be." She couldn't seem to strike the right note of jocularity. "Anyhoo, you've sure fixed the old place up."

"Pa would hate it."

"Uh — right. Well, that was a long time ago."

"You got out, though. Why'd you come home?"

"I heard my father left me the house. The time was right. I thought I'd settle down."

"That's funny, you never came to his funeral. Whole town was there. Talked some about you. But then you aren't much like him — he'd never put deadbolts on his doors."

"I guess I'm spooked from living in the big city," she said vaguely. "Listen, can you recommend somebody to install these?"

"I do it sometimes, but you'd have to say 'pretty please.' " He had her hemmed into a corner between the hunting knives and the fishing tackle. She could tell he hadn't worn a clean shirt this morning. In a swift move she was past him and over at the cash register, getting out her credit card.

"Never was much at pleading," she told him lightly.

He rang up the sale and handed the card back. "You won't find anybody else."

"Well, then, I will install the things myself." She flipped the remark over her shoulder and marched forth into the downpour. Pneumatic mechanism, won't even let you slam the door properly.

Of course, you have to come down off your high horse if it breaks a leg. A half-hour later, as Cass sat on the floor by her back door, ready to install her new security devices, she discovered a problem; a dead-bolt is only a lock. No doorknob is included. You can't just take out the old mechanism and shove in the new. You have to make a second hole in the door exactly two-and-one-eighth inches wide. From somewhere in the Great Beyond she could hear Biscuit giggling.

"Cut it out," she sneered. "I never was a lock specialist."

There used to be tools in the shed out at the rear of the yard. Her father was a jack of all trades, most men of Panhandle in the old days had to be. She got up and trotted out to the small neat building, snug place. The corrugated tin roof, the rain sounded friendly pattering on. He always liked hanging out here, even ran a conduit so he could have lights and a plug for his bench saw. It held place of honor in the middle of the room, while around the edges hung a variety of hand tools, electric drill and sander, level and square, drawers of nuts and bolts neatly sized. She sorted through his drill attachments on the work bench, but nothing looked remotely able to create a large hole for a lock.

On the opposite wall his gardening equipment caught her attention, spade and pitchfork shining clean just as he had put them away last Fall. The long loppers gave her a twinge: she could still see him pruning his lilac bushes. In a corner a bundle of new white pickets waited for a time of fence mending. Her intentions veered in a whole different direction.

Gathering the pickets, she took them over to the bench, and where did he keep that cross-cut saw? Found it. Ducking back over to the house, she measured the windows, then returned to her project. When shortened and nailed inside the sash the pickets would block each window from being raised more than six inches. Ought to let in enough air. Not safe to leave a wider margin — Biscuit could wriggle through an eight-inch opening. They had once laid a bet on it; she lost. The skinny little brown kid stripped down to his jock strap, rubbed lard on his shoulders and chest and inserted himself through the narrow slot without so much as a scraped elbow. *Biscuit . . . I'm sorry!*

Having cut the pickets to length, she went to work grimly, hammering them into place with heavy blows that left unsightly dents around the nail heads, *who cares?* It felt good to slam into something. When all the frames were secured nobody was going to slip in through a window. She tested the last one, opened it a fraction and closed it fast. A gust of wind rattled the locust branches sending a cascade of water down onto the roof, almost covering the sound of a knock at the front door.

Another throw-back to the thirties, the door had been cut with three slits through which she could see out to where Hollis Anderson stood on the porch. Hunched under a plastic slicker, shedding water off a battered wet fedora. He was carrying a carpenter's tool kit. When she opened the door he gave her a thin sheepish grin, and she could glimpse a ghost of the boy she remembered.

"Come on in out of the storm." Not going to fall on his neck in gratitude, but she was glad to notice a large drill in the box.

"I see you didn't have time yet to install those locks."

"Actually I was just about to go to Dad's shed and look for the right tools."

"I doubt if he had one like this." He pulled out a circular attachment obviously intended for the drilling of two-and-one-eighth inch holes. "Nobody ever buys anything you only use once every ten years or so."

"Good point. Thanks for coming," she said stiffly.

"No, thank *you.* For not being sore. I don't know why I came on so heavy this morning. Guess I was ticked off because you didn't drop by. Seemed like everybody in town was talking about you. Then I realized, you might not figure I was still around. If you'd known, of course you would have come sooner." He gave her a strange, meaningful smile as if they shared a secret.

It made Cass uneasy. "How about I make us some coffee?"

"The hotter the better." With cheerful expertise he shucked off the slicker and went about installing his gadget in the drill. He obviously knew his trade — the job was done before she had the cinnamon buns warm. Coming out to the kitchen he went straight to the back door and set about changing that lock too. Big hands, efficient, in an odd way possessive, as if he felt perfectly at home here. When he finished he went over to the sink to wash up.

"I miss your dad. Bet you didn't know we used to play cribbage right here in this kitchen. Friday nights."

She filled his cup with coffee and set the buns out on a plate. "I'm glad. He loved that game. I never had much knack for it, never could count my hand right. Poker's more fun."

"You were always a great one for fun." Munching a bun he eyed her with an oddly slanted amusement. "We had our times, didn't we? You were a tomboy, but I always knew there was a lot of woman underneath. I admit I was sore when you kited out and left us. Felt as if you'd . . . you'd divorced me."

Cass burned her tongue on the coffee. "Hollis, we were just kids!"

He brushed that off. "We were a team. I was the stunt man and you were my catcher. Without you I felt as if I lost my whole personality. But that's water over the dam. You're back now, that's the main thing."

How do you tell someone politely that you don't want to be his "main thing?"

She said, "And I'm sure by now you have a wife and ten kids. I mean, every girl in the school had a case of hero-worship." And it was true, they did go for Hollis, but never for long. She realized now, he never had a gang of buddies.

"Oh there were plenty of chances," he admitted bluffly, "but nothing serious. Flirty little chicks, I can't stand all that cute stuff. Of course I did get high on one gal a few years ago. During that Desert Storm thing, my reserve unit got called up, I was sent over to Israel to help install Scud-busters. Naomi was doing a hitch in the Israeli army — one tough young woman, smart, kind of bold. The way you were — she liked a challenge. But she was a Sabra and her folks didn't want a gentile in the family, so it wouldn't have come to anything, even if she didn't get killed."

"Sorry to hear that."

"Not even in action, either. On a bus from Haifa to Tel Aviv when it was bombed by some terrorists. Well, at least they were caught, their home base was destroyed — you know the Israelis, they don't pussyfoot around. Not like this country, all our stupid civil liberties, be the death of us yet." His tone was bitter again.

Silently she sympathized. Her mind flipped back to the days when she had been recruited — she'd thought it a great adventure to be an anti-terrorist. Didn't have a clue as to the real meaning of the word. Just a romantic picture of a secret band to dispense justice where laws fail to apply. It was only later after she'd seen bombings, mutilations, women and children dying in agony that she began to get mad. And after the big one on 9/11 outrage had hardened into a red-hot core of anger that drove her like a run-away steam engine, her and the whole team . . .

"Hey, what? Did I say something?" Hollis was peering at her uneasily.

"No. No, I'm fine. I just got distracted by a memory — I lost a friend, myself, to terrorists." Five of them.

"Tough. Listen," he set down his cup, "I'm sorry I ragged you about wanting new locks on the door. You need all the security you can get, a woman living alone."

"Hey, I'm just glad you came over and saved my bacon. What do I owe you?"

"I'd settle for a date. That is" — his body language was defensive, expecting a rebuff — "if you aren't sore about me making a fool of myself?"

She hesitated, but Sandy would have accepted. "Sure," she said, "why not?"

"How about Saturday night. I close early. We could go out to Gollager's, they serve a pretty good steak. Live combo. Dancing. Sometimes it gets kind of wild, but you never minded that."

Oh God. Well, I can always sprain my ankle. "Fine, let's try it. Kids today don't even know it was our generation that invented 'wild.' "

"Ain't it the truth." He winked and grinned, as if at some private joke. "Mae's tending bar out there, you remember her?"

The girl who taught me you don't pronounce the "w" in "whore." *Ah yes, Mae.*

"Good, then it's a date." He gathered up his tools.

It was still pouring as they went out onto the front porch. The Panhandle Gazette in its plastic cover lay to one side. As soon as he was on his way she snatched it up and went back inside.

The murder had made the front page big-time. Black letters: DO YOU KNOW THIS MAN? And a ghastly death portrait of old *Gnf-gnf.* According to the story his papers were faked, the car stolen. He'd been in town a month, staying at Gollager's Motel. She seized on that piece of news — so he'd just been using the abandoned house next door as a stake-out, probably under the cover that he was looking to buy it.

Gears beginning to turn again, Cass processed the new information. Beginning to spin a story that would get her inside that cabin.

8

She had never liked guns. For the men in her training group it had been the ultimate goal, to earn their firearm, a phallic symbol. Cass had gone through the motions, finished fourth in her class at the range, been given a Baretta, which she had put away. The weapon of her choice was the knife.

She took out the stiletto, reluctantly. A reminder of a life she'd left behind, she hated to resurrect it. But next time there might not be a handy juniper tree. Slipping the thong around her neck, she slung the tooled leather scabbard around until it lay between her shoulder blades. Tried her draw — none too smooth. "What? I teach you my best move and you no practice?" Koontz was beside her for an instant, rouged cheeks, pouting red lips, *Oh Koontz, you little slut, I miss you . . .*

Pulling on a turtleneck sweater, Cass moved on out to the kitchen. In the small plastic trash bag under the sink she rummaged until she found a sliver of wood swept up after Hollis had departed. As she went out, closing the door behind her, with a furtive gesture she inserted the splinter into the crack. She felt sticky with the sensation of eyes watching her every move. Liz, probably, not to worry.

At a slow roll as she drove through the rainy afternoon, on all sides Panhandle was quiet under the gray sky. Shops all lighted, spilling yellow reflections across the wet pavement, eaves spouting freshets into the gutter. Then she was out in open country where weather was taken for granted, even welcomed by the wet weeds that lifted their heads along the roadside, looking greener than they had yesterday. Above, the broad sweep of clouds showed fissures, the front moving on through, a leakage of yellow sundown up there.

By the time she reached the parking lot at Gollager's the windshield wipers were beginning to squeak on dry glass. Only a few drops falling as she stepped out into the marvelously washed air. Cass paused for a minute to study the motel units. There were ten of them, mostly small, each with a window box full of defunct petunias. Square buildings that looked as if they were made with a child's Lincoln log set, the one nearest the road had an extra room set on at a right angle, a double no doubt. It was the only one connected to the main building by a telephone line. A few scraps of yellow crime-scene tape hung from the doorknob.

Moseying over, she tried to look in the window but thick green curtains blocked it. The trash container behind it was empty except for a beer carton. The killer had drunk MGB while he kept his secret watches. Fresh tire tracks beside the cabin and a large clot of oil shed no particular light on the man. Such as explaining how he knew to come to Panhandle, Colorado and wait for his quarry. Or why.

By the entrance to the roadhouse the blackboard sign conveyed a new message:

TUESDAY SPECIAL
BEEF STEW
$3.99

Cass felt an inward caving. Long time since those flapjacks of Cluny's this morning.

As she went in she was met by rich aromas of onions and coffee and bacon. The big room was dim, the overhead lights hadn't been turned on yet, too early for the evening crowd. In the shadows she saw it as it had been once, memories wheeling past on old-fashioned strap-on roller skates while somewhere a jukebox played . . . *She loves you, yeah, yeah, yeah . . .* The bulky old machine still stood over by the stone fireplace. But the wonderful hardwood floor, marred by all those wheels, was now dotted with pinewood tables and chairs. Booths had been installed along the east wall and the south was lavish with glass, windows down the whole side of the building.

To her left at a long bar a small huddle of men drank beer and made talk. She strolled over and hitched onto a stool apart from their group. The bartender detached himself from his conversation and came to wipe the counter in front of her.

"What'll it be?" Short and stringy, his face networked with fine lines, his skin ruddy, blotched, the way red-headed people get when they overdo the sauce, he was almost a comic caricature of an Irishman, but the squinty green eyes were sharp as broken glass.

"I hope your special is ready?"

"Rarin' to go. Drink?"

"Draft. Whatever you've got."

He turned toward the window into the kitchen and yelled. "Stew and a brew."

Cass asked, "Is Mae around?"

"Around twice my size." He glanced at his pals who dutifully snickered. "She'll be bringing you your order." And he went on back to his buddies, sinking into hushed conversation with them.

Talking about me, obviously. What else do locals do in a small town? Overalls and beat-up Stetsons and scuffed boots, men of the range or the cattle barn, they were curious, but not unduly. Hadn't connected her yet with the news. Cass reached over and helped herself to the paper that someone had left on the bar. *The Pueblo Chieftain.*

Trying not to search too avidly, she turned the pages, read the headlines, glanced at the sports sidebar. Basketball, some kind of elimination series. In the second section she found it:

BODY DISCOVERED
NEAR PANHANDLE

Just a paragraph: Accident victim reported by rock hunter. Authorities are investigating, no names. So far so good.

"Well, hey there, stranger." Mae was juggling a bowl of stew, a plate of cornbread in one hand while she drew a mug of beer. Cass was surprised to see a handsome woman who carried herself with buxom confidence. The little pug-nosed flirt who used to flap her false eyelashes at the boys had grown tall, put on body weight to match her bust and topped it all with a shining glory of neatly piled hair that was pure silver mink. It was especially startling since her face was still young and smooth as cream, stretched now into a broad smile as she set down the order. "Doggone it, San', I thought you was never going to come out here and see me."

"I've been recovering from an operation — seem to move slower these days."

"I can see it. You look like a half-starved pup. Here, wrap yourself around this mulligatawny, I made it up fresh this morning. Turned out I am a pretty fair cook. The secret's in the beef — we buy ours out of Kansas City. Colorado steer is only good for stirrup taps, is what the boys say. You gotta come out and try our steak dinner."

"I'm looking forward to it. Saturday night, in fact. So how long have you had this place?"

"We picked it up for back taxes a couple of years ago when the town began to boom. Hey, old Panhandle came into prosperity these days, new enterprises hitting town. Chamber of Commerce spreads the word:

low rents and plenty of cheap labor and some chain stores start moving in. Plus that dude ranch over-east puts out a heap of advertising and all of a sudden this old burg is on the Triple A maps. Just in time for us to clean up at this business, me and Rafe. That was him took your order. Ain't he cute?"

"Nifty as a red-headed peckerwood." One of her father's favorite phrases.

It made Mae laugh out loud. "You don't know the half. And the little cuss is lucky, too. Always knows how to get his hands on the money. He's the one makes the place run."

"I heard different. Everybody I've talked to mentions the good food." Cass was spooning up stew like one of the homeless. "That wouldn't be the same old jukebox?"

"Sure is. The very one that almost got busted that night when Hollis Anderson was showing off for you, trying to skate backward on one foot like in the ice-capades, remember?"

"I'd forgotten that."

"Now, of course, we don't skate, but the floor is great for dancing. The old bubble-box has some of the original platters: Credence Clearwater Revival, Beach Boys, the Doors, Three Dog Night. Then on

Saturdays we got a live combo from Pueblo, country-western, square dancing and Lord knows what-all. Excuse me a minute . . ."

Down the bar one of the men was waving an empty glass. Mae moved gracefully to fill it. Grace, that was the word Cass had been groping for, that light way the woman carried herself. Probably a trait she'd inherited from her father who was once an acrobat with a carnival. They'd been playing the Pueblo State Fair one year when her mother got a heart attack, which was why they got stuck in Colorado, moseyed down to Panhandle and settled like a stone in a pond. Nobody had ever figured Mae would stick around, she was too sharp, too hyperactive as a kid. Now she looked relaxed and cool as she came back along the bar.

"So how's the chow?"

"Even better than its reputation." Cass scraped her bowl with a last scrap of corn bread. "You've got a gold mine here, even a motel too. By the way, I may have some friends coming through next month. Are any of your units big enough for a family of four?"

"Just that front cabin by the parking lot. Would you like to see it?"

"If you're not too busy."

"Nah. Supper hour's not going to happen

early on a bad day like this." Turning, she hollered full-voice. "Rafe, you got the duty."

"I ain't cookin' no special orders," he roared back to a chorus of masculine snickers.

Opening the leaf in the counter, she led the way toward the front. "He's okay, just likes to throw his weight in front of those studs, but what man doesn't? So tell me, how old are the kids, these ones your friends are bringing?"

"Uh — five and seven, I believe."

"Too young to sleep in a separate unit and too old to share a bed. That's okay, we got folding cots." She found a bunch of keys in the pocket of her jeans and opened the cabin door. "Well, shoot! I just remembered I didn't clean the place yet. The fellow who was staying here's the one they found dead out on the prairie. Web told me to leave everything untouched 'til he looked into it. You remember Pike Webster? He's Chief of Police now. Got hisself a real murder, I bet he's strutting like a old partridge."

"You mean that thing I read about in the paper?"

"Yep. The bozo stayed right in this cabin. Three weeks he's been hanging around, said he was looking for real estate. Seedy character, but he paid cash. Can't argue with that.

What a mess . . ." She began to pull sheets off the unmade bed. "By now Web must have searched the place, can't do no harm for you to look around."

If the Chief had already tossed the cabin there was probably nothing left to find. Cass glanced in the wastebasket — empty. Slight dent in the cushions of the cheap green-plush chair. The maple chest had the drawers half-pulled. Nothing there or in the closet. She wandered into the bathroom, wondering what she was looking for.

"Bring those towels, will you, San'?"

"Sure thing." She returned and dumped the linens onto the pile on the bed. Beside it was a table and a phone. "I see you can call out from the room, that's nice," she remarked carelessly.

"Goes through the switchboard most of the time. Nights, I hook the line up to the system and leave it all tied in to the outside trunk. First thing I checked, see if the jasper ran up any long-distance calls but there weren't none. Guess I got lucky." Heading for the door, her arms full, she went on, "Listen, hon, I'd better get back over there."

"Sure. Nice place. Thanks for the tour." Sandy straightened the phone, casually palming the scrap of paper that had been stuffed underneath it. "If my friends come

I'll bring them over. Of course they may never make it, he's a newsman, gets sent on assignment at the drop of a hat. . . ." And you are talking too much, nervous excitement over that number on the paper.

"Sometime you got to sit down and tell me about yourself. I know you been all over the world and Europe too. Must've seen some pretty places. Anyway, you be sure and come back now, and don't even think about paying for that lunch."

"Thanks. I owe you." Waving goodbye Cass felt a bit smug, to have turned up something old Pike had missed. Piece of luck. Hit-men are dumb. Only an idiot would keep anything around in writing, but this — a number twenty digits long — would have been way over his head. Something about the sequence seemed familiar, it looked like a Paris telephone number. She had a sudden hunch.

Question now was what to do with it?

9

Cass sat on the top step of the stairs that led down into the cellar below the house, just a dugout with walls rough-cut out of the virgin earth, originally a place for the housewife to store the jars of jelly and pickles she put up in canning days. A spot for the furnace from which to blow its up-drafts through the ventilators and later enlarged to make room for a washer-dryer combination. The wiring included a 220-volt line, which was the reason she had tucked the kiln down there in the few feet of space left over.

Joe had brought it from the post office in his old pickup truck and manhandled the heavy thing down the narrow stairs. She had started the first test firing, she could hear the elements humming now. It was time to go check out the pyrometer, hanging from a big hook driven into the rude wall of the cellar. This first test should only run to 500°

so go down there, ditzy!

Foolish to balk at a cellar, equipped with an overhead light fixture and plenty of air space. But the few minutes she'd spent in the hole had made her feel as if the walls were collapsing inward, the sensation of a trap. A lifelong bugaboo — claustrophobia. It had started as a child when a baby-sitter had locked her in a closet for hours. She'd been hysterical by the time her parents came home and rescued her.

Of course that was long years ago, and she'd thought she was over it, after the rigorous demands of the training camp. Kuzu would be sneering at her right now. Cass forced herself to go down the stairs in a rush. The kiln was a neat piece of equipment, 2-1/2' × 2-1/2' × 3', made of heavy fire brick contained by metal sheathing. Set on metal feet, it had a good heavy lid and an inner chamber two feet square, which would do very nicely for the small ware she planned to make. The pyrometer showed 525°. She switched off and scrambled back up into daylight.

Next step was to try out the potter's wheel. She had put it together last night in spite of the instructions: "Place Bolt B within Receptacle C but do not tighten until all receptacles have been engaged." Of course no electrical gadget could ever replace the joy of swinging one's foot and kicking a heavy hardwood wheel balanced on sealed ball bearings. Hers, in Dresden, would spin for sixty seconds on one kick. But this motorized version would do for Sandy Butterfield.

She invested the thought with contempt. Then felt a twinge of guilt. It was poor tradecraft. When you take on a character you must sympathize with her, pull for her to do well. *You'd better hope she can pull it together, this is the first day of the rest of your life.*

Opening the various sacks that stood around the wall she began to measure out raw materials on the scale, a simple basic batch of throwing clay to be tested and tweaked later. So — one pound of nepheline syenite, two pounds of Kentucky Old Mine #2, which she changed to one-and-a half, then a pound of Georgia Kaolin, lacking in plasticity but a beautiful cream-colored clay. Finish off with one-and-a-half pounds of flint, a little whiting and talc and add water. It was somewhere to start. She'd whip up a couple of test pieces and see how they matured at Cone 5. The kiln was certified to Cone 7, but she wouldn't push it. You can make fine stoneware at 2150°. When the mix was complete she covered the bucket to cure for a few days.

Next job: set cones. Mixing a small batch of ball clay and grog she ran enough water to make it sticky and began to knead it on a paper towel for lack of a bat. She needed to cast some plaster bats. Forming it into a pat she set the graceful triangular spires in a row, Cones 4, 5, and 6. Pyrometers are useful indicators, but the only exact way to judge your temperature in the fire was to watch the cones go down one at a time. They were engineered to such a high degree of perfection that, when set at the correct angle, they would bend over and touch the base with perfect accuracy.

She had just put them aside to let the base dry when she heard a knock at the front door. Going to Pike-alert, Liz-alert, Hollis-alert, she was not prepared for the top of a small head to show through the slotted windows. Opening up, she found a girl out there on the porch. How old? Cass was not sure, children were an unknown quantity. She had never had any motherly instincts, and had learned to be wary of waifs. In Europe some of them were skillful con artists, even occasionally carrying bombs under their ragged shirts.

This one had intense dark eyes beneath a

fringe of black lashes, long straight black hair held back by a ribbon. Not in rags, exactly, but the stone-washed jeans were shabby and the shirt so faded you could barely make out the words: HORSES HAPPEN. From behind a large Safeway sack she said, "Hello. I'm the Welcome Wagon lady. Welcome to Panhandle." Walking straight in past Sandy she headed for the kitchen, trailing her prepared speech. "I know you used to live here before, but not lately, so we want to welcome you back. If you need anything we're here to help." Setting down the bag on the table, she took from it a box of Jell-o Pudding Mix, a fat bag of potato chips, a box of Fruit Loops, a small jar of French's mustard and a squeeze bottle of catsup. Lining them up, she turned and held out a thin hand. "I'm Jessie."

"Uh — hi. I'm Sandy. This is very nice. Would you like a cup of coffee?"

The kid's precocious act almost came unstuck as her eyes betrayed the truth: coffee was a forbidden adult fruit. With wriggle of anticipation she plunked her skinny butt onto a chair. "Thank you, that would be nice."

Cass turned up the heat under the pot and got out cups, not the man-sized mugs that her father had used, but some pretty little shells of Limoges china that she had found on a top shelf of the breakfront.

Jessie picked hers up cautiously, examining the hand-painted flowers. "I never saw *these* before." Which confirmed Cass's hunch that she had been a visitor to this house.

"They were on the top shelf of the cabinet in the dining room. They were my mother's," she added. "Sugar? Cream?"

"Thank you." Jessie took a sip. By now the brew in the old blue pot was fairly strong from sitting on the stove for two days. Even with milk and sugar it should have brought a grimace. Her elfin face did twitch minutely, but she was able to say, "That's very nice coffee."

"It was kind of the Welcome Wagon to send you over to greet me. Who sponsors it?"

"The Chamber of Commerce."

"I didn't know we had one. Anyway I am pleased to get to know you, Jessie. Where do you live?"

For the first time the black eyes flickered nervously. "Over there, south of town," she said, waving vaguely toward the window. "I almost forgot — here's your library card. Everybody gets a library card." The yellow square that she dug out of her pants pocket looked as if it had been around since Carnegie first funded Panhandle's literary barn. "I work there," she added. "At least — I don't get paid, that would be child labor and it's illegal, for some unknown reason. But after school I do the shelving and Charmian — Miss Smith, the librarian — gives me books, like when they get too old and all."

"Sounds like a good deal for both of you."

"Oh, it is. I love to read. And everybody comes in the library, you always know what's going on. For instance, I heard you were interested in rock hunting. I know some places where there are agates."

Cass stood speechless. First time she'd ever been kicked in the gut by a kitten. "Who . . . mentioned . . . about me being a rock hunter?"

"Oh, I don't know." Flustered, the girl took her cup over to the sink. "I have to be going now. Would you like to go agate hunting some time?"

"Actually," Cass said, "I'm more interested in finding local deposits of clay. I'm a ceramist."

"Yeah. I heard you make pottery, *I don't know who told me, I'm sorry!* It's just, word gets around, you know?" She was edging toward the door.

"Well, it's true. I just made up a batch of throwing clay, would you like to see it?"

Curiosity won out. The girl followed down the hall to the work room. Uncovering the bucket Cass scooped out a handful of the wet muck and formed it into a ball. "This is how a pot starts out."

Jessie nodded. "We made ashtrays back in second grade, we cooked them in the oven."

"This will be fired a bit higher, over two thousand degrees. When it vitrifies — which means when it changes to stoneware or porcelain — it will hold water without leaking and stand up to wear-and-tear for a thousand years. Here, try it."

Jessie accepted the ball, plucked some ears out of it and indented a couple of eye sockets. "You could make a horse."

"The Chinese did some great ones. Life-size. They're still standing after centuries."

Forming the clay back into a ball Jessie returned it to the bucket. "I know where there's mud like this. It gets all slithery when it rains, you need to keep your horse away from it."

"Sounds promising. What is it, a dry river bed?"

"More like it maybe once was a lake. It's real flat. I could show you," she added, "but you'd have to ride a horse."

"I have ridden some." Cass thought of a donkey she had perched on going across the Bavarian Alps, but that probably didn't count.

"Okay, I'll let you know. I can't do it this weekend, we have a science project for school." Jessie led the way back to the kitchen where she washed her hands at the sink. "I'd better run, now. See you."

As she trotted off across the back yards she looked completely at home in her habitat. Still mystified, Cass put away the cups and turned to the welcoming groceries, inspecting the packages for pinholes, odd odors, broken seals. It wouldn't be out of character for the Flea Circus to send a child to do their dirty work.

At the bottom of the Safeway bag she discovered one more item, a copy of *The Panhandle Gazette.* On the front page was a headline:

CHIEF WEBSTER
SOLVES MYSTERY

Putting an end to speculation on the identity of the body found by a rock hunter last Sunday on the plains east of town, Chief Pike Webster has announced the results of his investigation.

The victim's name was Virgil Hames,

alias Virgil Harramon, alias Vern Hartman, with a record of arrests for drug trafficking, assault and violating probation. There is a warrant out for his arrest in Delaware in connection with the bombing of a bus station outside Dover.

It is thought that he may have been pursued by members of his own gang, who provoked the gun fight in which he was killed. For lack of evidence as to the perpetrators, Chief Webster has closed the books on the case. Further details on the story may never be known.

Cass reread the article with new-found respect for Panhandle's Chief of Police. Positively inspired. To relegate the guy's death to the realm of run-of-the-mill drug-related crime was to consign it to the waste basket of dead stories. *I couldn't have done better myself.*

10

It had begun to burn a hole in her conscience, that long number she had lifted from the cabin. Now, it was time, since she had another reason to go and see Pike Webster. As Cass trudged across town her feet could have been thirteen years old, finding their way down one block and up another, while her mind was elsewhere. Struggling with diplomatic approaches, tough approaches, angry approaches, revealing her own uncertainties and fears. Didn't want to do that.

She checked step at sight of the schoolhouse. She could feel again the weight of the book bag on her shoulder, hear the squeak of new tennis shoes. Almost see the ghost of a tow-headed girl scuffing across the weedy yard in bell-bottom jeans, late for math class. Scene of so many minor failures, the old frame relic was boarded over now, itself a failure. Beyond, a new modern red-brick building flouted multicolored playground equipment, a hockey field. It seemed to scorn the old clapboard structure, and Cass felt a touch of sympathy. It's hell to outlive your purpose.

On a slight elevation next to the school grounds stood a two-story Victorian house, part of Panhandle's historic heritage, if anybody had an inclination to sentimentalize. From its porch Chief Webster was watching her.

"Brings back the old days, doesn't it?" He sighed as he waited for her to climb the stairs. "I wish they'd tear the old eyesore down."

Created a heart-sore too, to think of being that young. "Thanks for letting me disturb your day off," she said, following him into a hallway that led to a long flight of steep stairs which disappeared upward into shadows. To the right, a parlor had been preserved in lavender and old lace, overstuffed furniture covered with antimacassars. The draperies at the tall windows were heavy satin in shades of rose, lending the room a lovely gentility.

"My wife was into antiques," Pike explained. "She was in the process of restoring the house to its original elegance. That love seat is a collector's item, solid rosewood frame, handmade needlepoint upholstery. I didn't have the know-how or the desire to go on with the job after Maria died."

"How long ago?"

"Six years. Auto accident, ten-car pileup on the ice in Raton Pass. Maria Cordez, I don't think you'd have known her. She was from Trinidad, worked for the State Board of Education on a special bilingual program. She loved to get kids chattering in two languages at once." There was fondness in his tone, but time had obviously dulled some of the pain. "She's the one who taught me how to use a computer," he added. "Which brings us back to your problem. When you called you mentioned a number — in code or something? How'd I miss that when I searched the cabin?"

"It was under the base of the telephone, out of sight."

"Well, it's for sure that I'm no high-crime sleuth, don't get enough practice. But maybe I can help on the p.c."

"Good. I'm not all that tech-smart myself." The team had always relied on Renée, her quick long fingers dancing across the keyboard, the monitor flashing new images so fast it was hard to follow them. Shaking off the memory Cass followed him back through the house to a small room that must have been a pantry originally. Pike had made it over into a snug den, with photos on the walls, bookshelf above the desk which was yellow oak, looked like school issue. To one side stood a blackboard which had been erased, but she could still read remnants of abbreviations: *adj gross . . . Deduct . . . int.* Webster had been doing his I.R.S. thing.

"So let's see what you've got."

She took up a piece of chalk and wrote:

3312714444180669981

"Good memory," he murmured as he studied it. "What does it mean, though?"

"Puzzled me too until I began to feel as if I had seen one like it before. Look —" She wrote again:

3312716473120244 7

"I'm impressed," Webster grinned. "You never showed that much aptitude for numbers in my class."

"It all depends on motivation. This —" she tapped the second — "was my lifeline when I was working in the field, my direct contact with my handler. It breaks down into segments." Amending it now, she wrote:

33-1-27

"That's an overseas call to France." And went on to write

16-47-31-20

"That's a Paris phone number and 2447 is probably an internal routing code. Then I would enter 961, my own personal identification."

"And you think the one you found is something similar. So if you're right, why not call it? Why do you need a computer?"

"A telephone call can be traced. I thought maybe we could just fool around on the net and see what happened."

"Makes sense, but what does that have to do with you now? Why not just hand this over to the feds and be done with it?"

"Because I don't know who to trust any more. You did a great job with that news story. If Virgil What's-it was working off a personal grudge, his superiors still probably haven't guessed where he is or what happened to him. But I'm beginning to doubt the grudge angle. This number would indicate to me that he was sent here for the express purpose of taking me out. He was probably supposed to call back when the job was done. The question is, who sent him? If it was the Flea Circus, they must have had help from one of my colleagues at the Libra League."

"Why would one of your own people want to eliminate you?"

"Because I was good," she said, without emotion. "If there was a mole, a double agent, he probably was getting worried. My team was very good at gathering intelligence. We — there were six of us in the cell — we might have been getting closer than we knew to exposing the traitor. He had to take us out in a way that would discredit us." Cass had thought long and hard to come to that conclusion.

Pike mulled it over. "What was it you called them, a flea circus?"

"It was our name for the terrorists. Fleas infest the world, carrying infection wherever they go. Remember the Black Death?"

His whimsical smile faded as he made the connection. "Got it. So maybe your human fleas have found a new form of virus, the well-known 'weapons of mass destruction.' But why would they want to follow you to a dry wash in Colorado?"

"Pike, I don't know. They succeeded in

ruining me, even if the bullet didn't quite kill me. I'm no longer a threat, so why go to all this trouble? I have no idea. But tracing that number may answer a few questions."

He slung himself into the seat at the computer, erased the I.R.S. forms and went to a search engine, while Sandy watched with new respect. Webster knew his way around the keyboard, blunt fingers barging down electronic passageways that led him finally to an international criss-cross directory. It linked to another connection; he punched in the number, waiting while the cursor blinked: *Working.* Abruptly on the monitor the message appeared: ENTER ACCESS CODE.

"Try mine — 961."

The cursor hung there blipping as if someone, somewhere, was doing a double take. Cass felt the hairs on her neck begin to prickle, almost as if another mind had reached out and touched her. Abruptly the monitor went blank.

"I think we rattled a cage," she said.

Webster tried coaxing it. "You'd think they would at least say 'Access Denied.' "

"Only if the code was not legitimate. I'll bet my personal password hasn't been erased yet. I think we just connected with the mole in our organization. Somebody at the far end of the sniper's link who also knows my League i.d. number."

Abruptly the ache in her head surged into a red-hot migraine that made her dizzy. It had happened several times since she left the hospital, seemed to be ignited by anger. She was aware that Webster had led her out into the kitchen and sat her down in a chair at the table. Put a cup of hot tea in her hand.

Cass burned her tongue. "Would you happen to have an aspirin?"

He gave her the bottle and a glass of water and set a plate of oatmeal cookies in front of her. Raisins. Homemade. Pike looked proud of himself as she chomped one thankfully and nodded approval.

"Now then, you care to tell me the whole story?"

"I hate to get you involved in this business."

"Too late for that," he informed her cheerfully. "I am in. This is my territory and any man who would hunt a woman down with a high-powered scope is the enemy. I want to know whether he's got any friends on tap, either here or half a world away."

"I think" — she set down the teacup — "the best thing I could do for Panhandle is to get out of here fast."

"Uh-uh. Running is no good. They'd just

follow you and next time you might not have any backup. You feeling a little better now?" For a minute his hand rested on the nape of her neck, strong fingers massaging. It was an oddly personal gesture, but she was grateful. It came to her fleetingly that she was fairly tired of fighting her battles all alone.

"I guess I'm reluctant," she said, "because my last partners wound up dead." She hadn't intended any melodramatic effect, but she felt him absorb the word soberly. *See what you got yourself into?*

"You're on home ground and you're in my jurisdiction, so let's assume we'll handle your fleas with a good hard swat. But I need all the information you can give me."

Helplessly, Cass looked around the kitchen, such a quaint, naïve old room with the original china countertops, a tin sink, massive cutting block in the middle of the Congoleum floor. In one corner stood a huge black-iron wood stove, brass bound and polished to a high gloss. Next to it a Hi-Point Range was totally modern and, beyond, a matching refrigerator with an ice dispenser in the door. They looked uncomfortably *nouveau* in the blue gingham ambiance.

She stood up slowly and walked to the

window — testing, testing. The pain in her head had subsided. Carefully she said, "I came home as myself, expecting to live quietly. I certainly didn't dream that any of my recent associates would track me here. They didn't. They were already here waiting. I haven't figured that one out yet. Until I know more about what I'm up against, I will be putting innocent people at risk. Already word has got out linking me to the killing out there on the prairie."

That jolted him. "What makes you think —"

"There is a charming child around town somewhere who knows I am a rock-hunter and —"

Webster's broad readable face tightened like a knot. "A child?"

"Female, white, five-one, seventy-five pounds, dark hair, dark eyes, eleven years old going on thirty."

He groaned and muttered a word to himself. "That little punk."

"Oh yes, I believe her name is Jessie. You know her?"

"Not well enough, apparently. I never dreamed she would snoop through my official police reports. I think I will tan her backside — she's not too old for that."

"Yes, she is."

"My daughter," he explained. "The light of my life, the gray in my hair. How did you happen to meet her?"

"She came over to visit. Said she was the Welcome Lady and was very gracious about it, bringing me cereal and potato chips. She even offered to take me riding, to find some clay deposits."

"That's it!" he muttered. "She's off that horse until further notice!" Then rousing from his private anger he added, "You have my solemn assurance that she will never sneak another peek at my records. From now on I'll keep them in my safe. For what it's worth, I doubt that she will spread this around. I have given strict orders against her ever talking about police business. I will reinforce the point tonight when she gets back from the ranch."

"That wouldn't be the Rocking R, by any chance?"

"She keeps her filly out there. It's all she lives for, riding."

"Then don't ground her. I used to have a consuming curiosity when I was her age."

"You still do. And don't tell me how to handle my daughter."

"Okay, bully her all you like. I'm glad you can't brow-beat me." Cass took her cup to the sink and ran water in it. "See you later."

The Chief flushed a dull red and hunched his big shoulders. "I'm sorry. Bunny, please, don't rush off. I just get frustrated when I flub up."

"Me too. I wish I had never come home to pollute this nice little town. And I will definitely butt out of your family affairs. Only I don't want the kid to hate me for finking on her."

"Don't worry, I know how to handle Pony, appearances to the contrary."

"Pony? That's nice, it fits her."

"Her grandmother gave her a private Navajo name that translates into 'Hoof of a Young Horse.' I'll clear the way so you can go riding with her. If you want to, of course."

"Are you out of your mind? Just because one sniper is dead, doesn't mean there aren't more, or will be soon. I intend to get clear out of Panhandle, draw the fire in some other direction."

"Now let's think on it a minute. These people, whoever they are, may decide not to pursue it further. Why don't you sort of lie low and let me do some more checking. I can backtrack that rental car, talk to the cops in New York who had the man in custody. Somebody had to pay his lawyer to get him off the last assault charge. Of course

I may have to give that number to the Fibbies. This is serious business you've got yourself involved with."

"You put it so nicely."

"You know what I mean. You seem to have led a dangerous life. So maybe right now you should keep a low profile. But that doesn't mean you have to go on the run. Alone out there, in the cold, as it were? Let's take it a step at a time. Only don't get any ideas of sleuthing around, I don't want any more dead bodies. And if you're going to wear a knife, you'd better know how to use it."

Without thinking, Cass reached over her shoulder and brought her hand forward in a sweeping split-fingered draw that Koontz had taught her. With a rapid down-thrust she threw it, the slim blade quivered in the cork bulletin board across the room, having neatly split a small note that read: DRAIN ANTI-FREEZE.

Webster stood silent, then very quietly he went over and retrieved the stiletto.

"That was a dumb, show-off thing to do," she said irritably, "but I'm beginning to feel fed up."

"Join the club," he said, with a quirk to his lips, handing her the knife. "I'm sorry I went into my school-teacher mode. It still comes out at times. But I'm stumped about all this. I'm used to solving problems logically, A plus B equals X. Only now I get the feeling this equation is more like A plus B, plus G, R, and W amounts to X squared. It's too big to fit on the blackboard."

Cass stifled a sigh. *Start thinking like that, Pike, you'll make a great agent.*

"Anyway, stick around," he advised. "We'll figure the thing out. If we have to, we'll call in the feds — discreetly, of course."

Cass shook her head. "Like somebody once said, 'Hey, General Custer, let's discreetly take that short-cut down the Little Big Horn.' "

11

"When your mind is being buffeted by emotional winds you need a helm to clutch, a way to maintain control while you find your compass points." The therapist must have been a wannabe poet. "If you feel those waves of panic rising, go to your potter's wheel. It will take you past the bad spots." Reaching into the bucket Cass dug out a handful of wet clay. Its earthen smell took her back to the big drafty studio in Dresden, the ghosts of other students, the lightness of heart, the optimism — memories that almost sank her precarious little boat. So much for figures of speech.

Slamming a wad of sophisticated mud down onto the wedging board she kneaded it, then split it across the taut wire, kneaded it again, slammed it down as hard as she could. The process was supposed to get the bubbles out; she wished it could flatten away the pockets of insecurity in her thoughts.

The whole hard shell of self-confidence that the tough training at the camp had induced was cracked, almost beyond repair. The extent to which she had retreated from the bold risk-taking life became painfully evident now as she tried to rally to the challenge. Make the tough decision: to go out into the world and dare them to come after you, to present yourself as a target and use that to turn the tables on them? Or to crouch at home in fear the rest of your days with your curtains drawn and wedges of wood in the door above the new locks. Slam, split, slam, split, the texture was beginning to even out. *Maybe when I get it on the wheel everything will start to make sense.*

The Japanese may not have known how to phrase their instructions, but they made a neat little workhorse. Sitting on the seat with the tray between her knees and her foot on a lever that controlled the speed by rheostat, she started the wheel spinning. Slow at first . . . adeptly she flipped the ball of clay onto the middle of the bat and captured it with her left hand, straightening it, feeling the pull of the shoulder injury. She was wearing the elastic harness, but the muscles still complained at any stress.

With the mound of clay centered she wet two fingers of her right hand and stuck them into the top, bearing down while still steadying the muddy mass with her left. As she increased the speed the round ball flattened and spread into a bowl, crude, thick, lopsided. Bringing it to a solid round, with four fingers inside and the other hand opposing she began to draw the wall of the bowl upward, thinner, steeper, coaxing it in again at the top, bowl no more, it had become a vase. To make the neck she drew the clay higher, gradually easing down to three fingers, to two, and finally only one, then feathered it out to a delicate edge and let go. The whole operation had taken less than five minutes, a flowing stroke of creation. It was the way she had always worked — the result would be either a botch or an accomplishment, but it had to be done swiftly.

When she sat back to look at the little piece spinning there before her, she felt a pleasant jolt. After months of disuse her potter's touch hadn't failed her. The structure was good, solid strength at the bottom contrasting with the delicacy at the top, the width and height in proportion. Cass took a deep breath, you always hold your breath those few moments when you're making it happen. All systems are suspended, you are in a primitive state of sensation, hands, feet, eyes and mind. You are thinking: *beauty.* Sometimes you almost achieve it. Or not. Either way, the act of creation is like scouring powder on the soul, you come out cleansed and refreshed.

She took a wire and carefully sawed the bottom free, transferring the vase to a clean bat. In the kitchen she set it in the oven with the door open and the heat turned to "low." In some future time — if there ever was a future — she would set up a proper dry room. Right now, this would do. The warmth from the oven felt good.

Her mind had quit darting around like a cornered fish. She could devote it to the contemplation of this pretty little ornament and how it should be embellished: what color, what kind of decoration, underglaze, overglaze, an engobe — clay on clay?

Her reverie was broken by a knock at the back door. She found Liz out there, shivering, with a shawl over her housedress, bearing a covered dish that gave off aromas of cheese-and-something. "I was just cooking lunch for Joe and I thought, 'Why don't I make an extra pot for Sandy?' " Her ruddy face was so infused with pleasure at her own good deed, it demanded equal enthusiasm.

"Whatever it is, it smells wonderful. Here, let me take it . . ."

"Potatoes-o-grotton. Girl, you are some thin. You got to learn: the trick of living alone is to treat yourself like company, especially when it comes to eating. I done it for years." And her portly dimensions gave tribute. Then she saw the vase and stared. "You done that?"

"Yeah, just got it off the wheel."

For a long minute the jowls and brows and strong lips worked in judgment and finally resolved into a look of approval. "It ain't nothing like my jar, but then you wasn't trying for big and handsome. You wanted small and sweet. It's right nice. How long do you have to cook it?"

"I'm just drying it now so I can clean it up. It has to have a foot put on it and some sort of decoration before I fire it in the kiln. Maybe tomorrow, I don't know. I haven't tested the kiln to full heat yet. Here, sit down, I'll make us some tea."

"Oh, I can't stay, hon. Joe's waiting for his lunch. But I did want to mention" — she took on a lofty, cautious look — "I noticed Hollis Anderson was over here putting on new locks for you. So I brought this back." She took a key from her apron pocket and laid it on the table. "Your pa always liked me to keep an extra for him."

A neighborly formality — her father had usually left the back door unlocked, except when he took a trip to Pueblo. The implication was for Liz to "keep an eye on things." Cass understood the gesture perfectly, the dignity with which Liz stood waiting, uncertain.

She's wondering if I trust her the same way. "Well, call me chicken, which Hollis did, but I get a little nervous about living here alone." Against her will she got out the extra copy of the new key. "It now takes two to open my door. That is, if you don't mind keeping it?" She was threading the two onto a paperclip together, handing them back to Liz, who seemed to bloom under the warmth of friendship confirmed.

"Oh shoot no, I don't mind. I got extra keys to every house on this block, I keep 'em in an old cigar box. But if you're some nervous, I'll put this up in the gravy boat that I never use, it's on the top shelf, just to make sure nobody ever tumbles to it. It's true, a woman living alone got fears sometimes, middle of the night. By the way, what'd you think of Hollis?"

"I guess like all of us he's changed a lot. I'll know more tomorrow night. We've got a date to go out and have dinner at the road-house."

"Well, land-sakes." Liz looked troubled. "You watch out for that Gollager's place, it can get real rough on a Saturday night. Tell you what — you just plan to go to church with us Sunday morning and the Lord will bless all that sin away. I mean them tight pants and sexy skirts, all that hip-switchin' around, the evil rubs off on you before you know it."

As she watched Liz walk back across yards, Cass realigned her thoughts in the direction of her wardrobe — not a trace of a date dress in it. She had bought a nerdy collection of pre-owned clothes at a thrift shop in Albuquerque, the kind of thing Sandy Butterfield would wear. Only Panhandle was turning out to be a little more up-to-date than she'd figured.

As she sat over the casserole, noshing potatoes straight from the bake-dish, she took mental inventory of her closet and found it wanting. And all at once she had no patience for Sandy's dull duds. Besides, to go shopping at the Boutique was exactly what she needed, to scare off the demons. Briskly, she put the kitchen in order, ran the utensils under the tap and turned off the oven.

Pulling on the blue parka with the hood she stepped onto the back porch, bracing against the icy cut of the wind. A transient thought: *What if this was the last time I walked out that door. How would it feel, to leave the only place I can call "home?" Forever?* She tried to cast aside the element of necessity, to conjure up a moment of free will. *Where would I go?*

The empty spaces that met that question startled her. Not one of the many venues where she had plied her craft overseas had appealed as a permanent setting. Her focus had been on job, to find out how and why and who and stop them from doing more damage. Within those limitations, the where had always seemed unimportant. Now she had no desires to go back to Minnesota and its graves. Both parents killed in a car bomb. Colorado was home country — it had actually begun to feel comfortable. The elements were here to achieve peace of mind. To let go the tensions that had propelled her and just live normally around people you know, who care for you, at least a little. People who might rally around you in an emergency . . .

And that's a trap, girl, don't you forget it. Never depend on others to pull you out of the mud. She stripped a twig off a lilac bush and inserted it into the door crack. *Nobody — engrave it on your brain — nobody is going to save your skin but you.*

The window display in the *Boutique de Paris* would have fascinated a plumber. There must have been a mile of copper tubing in it. Dominating was a stylized tree and a loopy mannequin with steel-wool bangs; on the circle of piping that was her head an orange straw hat was cocked casually. Draped over the nonchalant copper shoulders a calf-length tent dress in garish blocks of yellow and blue and green separated by thick black lines, shades of Mondrian. Cass rather liked it. Not her style, of course. *What is my style? Maybe Izzie will know.* The thought warmed her, a chance to turn a decision over to someone else, to admit that another might know best?

She walked in slowly under the chime of the doorbell. The place looked empty, until she spotted Izzie perched on a stool at the soda fountain, looking like one of her own mannequins in a severe white linen sheath that would have seemed virginal except for the wicked wide orange patent-leather belt. To her incredibly long nails she was applying orange polish and decorating each with a glittering star.

Glancing up, she waved them gaudily. "Fifty bucks a set. They cured me of biting my nails. Want to try some?"

"No way. When you throw pots on the wheel you have to keep your nails short or you put gouges in your work."

"I can see how that would be. Long talons would skewer a ewer. You do do ewers?" She flapped her eyelashes in silly affectation of the rich and famous.

"You do ewers when you are in a ewer mood." Cass was happy to be able still to match her silly-for-silly.

"Ah, we're moody. Inspirational, I hope?"

"Not really. The old block is having a bit of a bloc. I thought it might help to buy new clothes."

"You have come to Valhalla. Heed the message on our escutcheon." Izzie waved the fingernails toward the shield above the door. The coat-of-arms was a clever send-up of ancestral heraldry: two coat-hangers crossed above the silhouette of a naked woman, with a banner woven around in the form of a tape measure and below it the motto:

NIL DESPERANDUM
USE CREDITORIUM

Cass found herself smiling. "It's great."

"Ilsa's contribution. She has a marvelous sense of humor when you get to know her."

"I'd like to. Where is she today?"

"Stayed home. She hates this wind, it absolutely ruins her sinuses."

"You still live in the house over on Taylor Street?"

"Uh-uh, that got torn down to make room for McDonald's. Perfect site for ground meat and rancid fat. No, we live over south in the old part of town, an adobe with thick walls, makes you feel insulated and removed from the world. It has a huge fireplace in it — Ilsa cooks herself in front of it by the hour. Awfully thin blood." The tone of concern was pervasive and touching.

Cass felt a twang of envy. To be adored . . . Briskly she said, "Speaking of adobe, where did the old-timers get their clay? Do you know?"

"Don't tell me! You're going to dig your own raw materials. How totally classy of you." The homely, mobile face screwed in thought. "I heard there's a deposit out on the Rocking R — that dude ranch east of town, you know? They might rent you a horse. That's what they do, take bunches of city slickers out on the trail, fry porterhouse steaks and hire a Mexican boy to play guitar music in the moonlight. But be sure and wear fringes on your leather jacket or you'll feel totally outré."

"Whangs. The mountain men called them whangs and used them to darn their moccasins. My father was big on western trivia, if you remember."

"I do. I miss him, I really loved that man." For once, Izzie wasn't kidding.

"So did I," Cass came back, a little defensive. "And he knew it. I kept in touch. He understood why I had to leave."

"I'm glad he did. I sure didn't."

"I never was very good at explaining myself. Then or now." *In other words, don't ask me too many questions, okay?*

"We were too close to see each other in perspective," Izzie said. "I took it for granted that I knew you, like you can see to the bottom of a pool. Only it turned out it was deeper than I thought. And now, you're practically a tarn."

"Well, darn that tarn. I hoped nobody would notice. Can you do something about this skin and bones I call a body?" Cass looked down at her scrawny angularity. Hadn't been able to put on more than a pound or two since she left the hospital.

"You want to change your image!" Nothing could have tickled Izzie more. "Sit right down." Slipping off her stool, she went to the nearest ice-cream-parlor table and pulled out a wire-backed chair. "What sort of price range are we talking about? I suppose you'd rather not go into bankruptcy."

"Not to go out to Gollager's," Cass confessed wryly. "From what I've heard its ambiance is rough-and-ready."

"And Hollis Anderson is a bully boy," she added with a smirk. "Don't glare. I haven't been spying on you. But the town has big ears. You're the new kid on the block, people are bound to talk. I saw Mae in the Post Office this morning and she mentioned your boyfriend had made reservations for two."

"He's not my —"

"Oh, I know that. But you made quite a pair in the old days. Not exactly Romeo and Juliet, more like Peter Pan and Tinkerbell. He could fly, but you could glow in the dark. Yeah, yeah, that was a long time ago. Let's see. What do I have at a reasonable price . . . ?"

"Actually, I haven't bought anything new since I had the operation. I sort of owe myself a blowout." All those years in Europe, wearing student rags, Cass had looked longingly at nice clothes, yearning over the occasional hand-woven wool, a silk blouse, real leather shoes, always dreaming of a day when her undercover work would demand a whole new vocabulary of style.

Izzie had disappeared into the room behind the store. When she came back color spilled from her arms like pirate's treasure. With a flourish she held out some slacks of rust-colored silk corduroy, a turtlenecked pullover of peach cashmere. "Evan Picone, for the informal evening." Hanging that outfit on a nearby rack, she brandished another. A jumpsuit in light gray velvetine, with a crimson blazer draped over the shoulders. "The jacket is by Dior, and don't tell me you can't wear red. Finally we have the wonderful world of Liz Claiborne." Lilac wool slacks and a matching scoop-neck challis blouse with a cardigan of pure Merino knit in triangular patterns of sherry and claret. Like a genii who had popped her own cork, Izzie grinned. "You're speechless."

"I want them all!" And how could anyone have picked, so unerringly, the kind of look she yearned for, when she didn't even know herself? "Iz, you are good!"

"As you will notice, they can be mixed to match. It's the equivalent of six different outfits. They will start you on the road to a new you, which I suspect has been lurking there all along. What was it, in the old days . . . ?" Izzie snapped those long ornamental fingers. "Yeah, you always wanted to be called Cassandra. Well, let me be the first: Hello, Cass."

12

Under a huge wagon-wheel, hung from the ceiling and set with bulbs to make a chandelier, Gollager's was simmering with boozy festivity. Home-towners in flannel shirts and Levis nudged elbows with a welter of tourists in pristine white Stetsons, red flannel shirts with enough buttoned-down pockets to keep the factories of Korea busy for a week. Cass was relieved to see a mother lode of turquoise around her, bolos, earrings, belt-buckles. When she wore the stiletto with a low-cut shirt, she pinned a chunk of turquoise to the thong at the base of her throat to disguise it as jewelry. She had debated leaving the weapon home, but it gave her shoulder blades a measure of self-confidence, though it remained to be seen what would happen if Hollis insisted on dancing.

Something about him made her uneasy. When he had picked her up his eyes had seemed to glaze at the sight of the lavender slacks and cherry blazer. Mouth came ajar, then snapped back together in a smile that was both smug and arrogant, like a man who has just found a five-dollar bill on the sidewalk. It permeated his demeanor all through the meal, which was excellent. The steaks were a perfect medium-rare, the salad crisp, the strawberry pie deliciously caloric. Cass began to enjoy herself. "This dessert is terrific."

Hollis smirked as if she had made an improper suggestion.

And now the band was setting up on the stage at the end of the room, wrestling drums into place, connecting a microphone for the singer, a glittering cowgirl with long legs beneath the short sequined white suede skirt, a fringed leatherette jacket over her size 38 bust. At sight of her the crowd gave its inevitable salute: "YEEEE-haw!"

While the musicians jangled their instruments through a quick tune-up, the band leader, a pudgy boy in tight white pants and a huge purple cummerbund to hold in his beer belly, blew into the mike and launched the show. "Hey, thar, all you rustlers and buffalo gals, we gonna play y'all sweet and hot and low to the ground. So take off yore shoes and git yore feet on them bare boards.

Here we go!"

The girl shivered her tambourine and they launched into an old country-western with a driving beat. ". . . silver threads and golden needles will not mend this heart of mine."

Hollis grabbed her elbow and half lifted Cass out of her seat. Biting back a whimper of pain, she clenched her jaw and let him lead her onto the floor. The pump-handle two-step wasn't too nerve-shattering, all it required was energy. Jockeying her around the room, Hollis was flinging his chaps like a Crazy Dog Cheyenne with a death wish. The metaphor came to mind because of the lanky black hair and the Indian duds — he was wearing a beaded deerskin shirt and moccasins that looked hand-made. With more muscle than finesse he yanked her around until finally the cymbals smashed the song dead.

Cass headed for the sidelines.

"Hey, we're just getting started." He seized the elbow again and this time she yelped.

"Take it easy. My shoulder is just held together with safety pins."

Dropping her as if she had the plague, he frowned ferociously. "Sorry, I didn't realize. I thought it was just your head got banged."

"My whole body took a beating." *Which is*

an understatement. "I need to sit the next one out." But they had arrived at their table only to find it appropriated by a new party, four easterners who ignored their irritation and sat there looking rich and immovable.

"Lousy short-horns, I ought to teach 'em some manners," Hollis proclaimed with clenched fists. Cass bit her tongue. *Lovely. Now we're going to have a brawl.* Then a voice cut through the fiddles and banjos.

"Over here." It was Izzie, who got up and wedged in beside Ilsa on one half their booth to make room for Hollis and Cass in the other. "Please join us."

Hollis jutted a jaw, his face turning a sullen red. But Cass had already accepted the invitation. Sliding to the far side of the bench she said, "Thanks, I needed to sit down. We'll buy the next round. I'll have draft beer."

The waitress had been quick to come over. "Make mine VVO," Izzie said with a wicked grin at Hollis.

"Gimme a brew," he muttered grimly, scowl deepening by fractions. A touch of homophobia? Cass wondered.

"I don't care for anything more." Ilsa's piping voice emerged from the depths of a wrap of rose velour, her small face in retirement behind a delicate chiffon scarf. Izzie was making her own statement in a green velvet tuxedo, black hair slicked tight to her head.

"Pickle didn't really want to come tonight, but I thought a little merry brouhaha would be good for us."

"And you do know how to brew the old haha," Cass said, automatically. Word games between the two of them were such old stuff, she could hardly believe that Ilsa would find that an excuse for jealousy. The sequestered face grew a fraction icier. Trying to steer to safer grounds Cass went on, "Is the place always this crowded?"

"Tonight we have a few extras, the ghoul crowd. April 20th? Remember? Our favorite massacre?"

"Ludlow. Of course." There were always a scattering of history buffs who came to lay flowers on the memorial. Cass flashed on a picture of her father giving an impromptu chalk talk to the visitors one year, his broad kindly face infused with respect for the long-gone victims.

"People still flock to the site for tears and ceremonies," Iz was saying, "after which they come here to celebrate their own viability. Speaking of which, you look pretty lifelike in that outfit. I didn't think you were ready for that particular combination."

"She's not." Ilsa spoke up sharply. "Red is all wrong for her. She should wear umbers and charcoals."

"Even in April, Pickle dear?" Izzie was deferential. "I thought I did pretty well. Sandy seems positively chipper, or maybe that's the company." She winked at Hollis, who shuddered visibly.

Squirming out of the booth he said, "That's Red River Valley. Want to try it? I'll be careful of the shoulder, promise."

Cass hesitated, but the moment was saved by the arrival of the Chief of Police. Webster looked all-cop tonight in fresh-pressed uniform and Smoky-bear hat. "Excuse me, but I would like to have this lady for a couple of turns around the floor." Holding out his hand he helped her up. Ignoring the fact that Hollis was fuming.

"Pike," she murmured, "go very easy. That last set just about finished me."

"I noticed you seemed to be turning pale. The shoulder thing?" In an oddly jovial humor he led her sedately at the slow pace of the dance, singing along, ". . . do not hasten to bid me adieu," in a deep baritone that was oddly pleasurable. "I told the band to singlefoot for the next ten minutes or I'd put 'em in jail. I wanted to talk to you without it looking like business."

Pike was a great dancer, smooth as glass, leading her firmly, but with care for the shoulder. She began to relax. "Any news about our friend, Virgil?"

"Yeah, that's what I need to tell you: his identity was picked up by the FBI, after I told them about the phone number. They have taken an unexpected interest in the business."

"Hoo boy. That's all I need."

"I got to confess," he went on under his breath, "the other day I thought you were laying it on kind of thick. But this sort of bears out your story, that they should send a special agent to investigate."

"A special —"

"When I dance you around again check out the character in the corner booth." He did a graceful half-turn and she could look over his shoulder. No doubt who he meant, the gray man with the pallid face, clean-shaven, bland, in city duds. Sipping iced-tea and trying to make it look like bourbon as he scoped out the dancers. "Ever see him before?"

"I don't think so — those Bureau types are such clones it's hard to tell. So what reason did he give for descending on us in all that neutral camouflage?"

"He says your hit man was wanted by Interpol, on suspicion of a couple of assassinations over in Europe. He's wondering what the goon was doing here. I didn't mention you, of course. That's why I'm sort of putting on an act now, so he won't get any ideas." Webster fox-trotted her away to the far side of the room.

"It's just a matter of time." She tried not to sound bitter.

"I don't know why. The story is that I just saw a suspicious car parked out on the desert, matched the description of a stolen vehicle on the wanted list. I moseyed over, found the body, didn't take a lot of notes about the crime scene. But I did toss his motel room, found that number. No idea what it means. What the heck, I'm just a hick cop."

"Pike Webster, you are an inspired liar."

"Good to have a sideline," he said. "Not that I enjoyed it. But I share your doubts about the ability of the Bureau to keep a secret."

The music had segued into an old favorite, the girl bawling, "Take me home, country roads . . ."

Cass caught a glimpse of Hollis, crouched on the edge of the booth, ready to snatch her as soon as they were near enough. "Take me across the room again, will you?"

"Hollis being a pain, huh? I got a few doubts about that boy myself. We've had a couple of complaints, tourist women who didn't like being hustled." He did a classy little whirl that carried them over toward the bandstand at which point they were tapped on the shoulder and paused to find Guy Magee at hand. His greenish eyes bright beneath the bush of ruddy brows, he was smiling wickedly.

"Pike, old buddy, give the rest of us a chance at the sweetest l'il gal this side of the Pecos."

Cass moved into his arms. Her shrink would have been proud of her, she thought, tolerating the embrace of three men in a row without running out into the night, screaming hysterically. Of course, Guy was of a different dimension, small and undemanding, quick little feet and no sexual overtones. Between the two of them there had never been anything physical, even back in high school. He had been popular with the girls, but hardly a dream-boat. His main attraction was his continental manners — the only kid in Panhandle who had ever been to Paris. He'd spent a year there studying impressionism and could speak fluent French, which made him a Panhandle legend, but no lothario. His image was more that of an historic icon, togged out in white leather from head to well-turned boot.

"You look like an N. C. Wyeth painting in that mountain-man suit," she chuckled.

"Shoot. I was trying for Buffalo Bill. Hope you didn't mind me cutting in that way, but I couldn't imagine you have much in common with old Boxcars."

The nickname made her smile in remembrance of days past. They had bestowed the nickname on Webster back in Algebra class when he kept likening equations to a freight train hauling loads marked "a" "b" and "x", leaving some cars on sidings and picking them up again, she never did get it.

"We were talking postage stamps. My father's collection," she told him, unnecessarily, but it had been a sober conversation, he was obviously curious. Keen eyes studied her face, one skeptical brow cocked.

"Well, I'm glad you're back in the small-town swing. You've got to come out to the Hacienda and see what I've done with it."

"The Hacienda? Did you really acquire it finally?" The oldest building in town, an adobe ranch-house draped in grapevines, the place had always been a source of mystery and spine-tingling delight to the young fry of Panhandle. The dark little man who had owned it was said to be descended from the original Spanish grandee, who held the grant from Mexico more than a century ago. All the kids had fantasized about it, but Guy was the one who really lusted after the place, swore he would own it some day, lock, stock and carriage house. "Not many people ever manage to fulfill a dream," she said. "How did you do it?"

"Long story . . ." and now they were having to shout above the pyrotechnics of Great Balls of Fire. ". . . nice bunch of people . . . some are even talented . . . students, you know . . . round-table discussions with guest speakers . . . never had a ceramist. Maybe you could come and regale us with your marvelous tale about the old Chinese potter and his oxblood vase. Bring some of your own pots if you've had time to make any. How about it? Next Thursday?"

"Uh — sure — sounds like fun." She was growing distracted. By now Hollis was throwing a full-scale snit, rising to his full height and heading across the dance floor, shouldering couples out of the way.

Reaching them, headlong, he snarled at Cass like a feral cat. "Just who did you come here with? You danced with half the other men in town already."

"Andersen, chill out." Guy was a foot shorter, but somehow managed to look down at Hollis. "This isn't the high-school prom. Don't be such an ass."

The last words carried sharply over a sudden lull, the music having stopped, the dancers subsiding, breathless. Nearby Freddie Foreman swung Cluny to a sweaty halt. Her full-skirt print dress was wilted, one of her braids had come unstuck.

"Hoo-boy, I need a beer," she gasped.

Freddie ignored her. "Let's have a square dance," he yelled, stamping the floor with a hard-heeled boot that was definitely not for pretty. Even in clean jeans and flannel shirt he managed to exude of an aura of grease rack.

"Square, square," others took up the cry.

"Turkey in the Straw!"

"Buffalo Gals!"

Meanwhile Hollis was trying to repossess Sandy physically. He smelled of something stronger than beer, must have traded up to rye in the interim. She looked for Izzie and Ilsa, but they had left. And where was Pike?

"Freddie, pu-leeze, gimme a break," Cluny whined. "I need a beer."

"Shut up, you dumb broad." Carelessly, Foreman swept a hand, clouting his wife in the mouth with the accuracy of long practice. She reeled sideways and would have fallen if someone hadn't lunged forward and caught her, a mountainous man, six-six by two-sixty, with shoulders that could have shrugged off the entire Bronco defense. He set Cluny aside to get to Freddie, lifting the mechanic off the floor by his collar.

"Nobody," the giant roared, "y'hear me, *nobody* hits a woman while Ah'm around. We don't hold with that, down Texas, because it's not polite and beside which, it *hurts!* See?" He slapped Freddie hard across the chops. "A real man doesn't do that to a female person. You get the message, you little cowchip?"

Over at the bar, Foreman's friends were knocking back their drinks fast, moving to wade in and make a fight of it. The Texan tossed Freddie at them like so much used Kleenex. By then his own contingent of pals was emerging from a nearby booth.

"Where's Pike?" Cass struggled to remove her arm from Hollis's grasp.

"Who needs him?"

"You will in a minute if you don't let go my elbow."

"Huh?" He dropped the object in question and stepped back, bug-eyed. "Hey, don't look at me like that."

"Then don't drag me around, I don't like it."

Meanwhile the two groups of bully-boys

were wading into each other in the center of the dance floor. It looked like the Texas Star on fast-forward, Cass thought. She saw the Chief now, angled against the far end of the bar with Mae. They seemed to be comparing notes as if in a replay booth.

Guy saw the direction of her look. "Don't worry, that's Boyd Ruger, I doubt if he ever lost a fight. Web will step in if anybody pulls a knife or busts a bottle. We only have three jail cells in our little town, so he doesn't round up people who are simply enjoying themselves. Anyway, Rafe's about to blow the whistle."

Gollager was making signs at the band like a third-base umpire: thumbs up, then a circular motion, and finally a brief salute. They nodded — a-one-and-a-two-and they unfurled the Star Spangled Banner at full decibels.

Oddly enough, it worked. Combatants and cheerleaders broke off the furor as Mae's hard soprano pinned everybody in place.

". . . and the rockets' red glare, the bombs bursting in air . . ."

Alone in his distant booth, the FBI was standing at attention over an empty glass with a twist of lemon. Staring out the window, he seemed to be looking for flags in the enigmatic darkness.

13

There was an old saying of her father's, Cass remembered: Skip church and you'll get "in a back-slid condition." It described her uneasiness as she dressed for services that Sunday morning. Ten years since she had been in a house of worship, and then it had been part of an assignment. A small chapel in the Bavarian Alps with strange icons and chanting, it hadn't moved her. But then religion had always seemed distant from any of her life's black experiences. It was only after the night on the waterfront that she began to regret the lack of any belief to cling to, in much the same way you wish you had learned to play a musical instrument. Too late now. The practices which gave others so much peace of mind were foreign as an ancient language.

She felt like a hypocrite, putting on Sunday apparel — silk stockings and high heels and a hat. Liz had provided a straw boater which looked turn-of-the-century, but was perfectly suited to Cass's thrift-shop cotton dress with the little white collar, the buttoned sleeves. Like a penitent she walked sedately over to join Liz who was waiting behind the wheel of the car next door. Joe, it seemed, was "down with the wheezes." In younger days he had worked the coke ovens up in Ludlow Canyon and, like most old miners, he probably had the black lung, though it was now called emphysema. Words weren't sufficient to describe the miseries of not being able to breathe. She'd seen too many old wrecks gasping their last around town in earlier times.

When they reached the small white frame meeting house a body of people had already congregated, gabbing and hugging, the air vibrating with Sunday harmonics. Even Cass had to admit, there was comfort in that aura of good faith when the old organ struck its opening note and the parishioners sailed into "Abide with Me," as if they really meant it. Most of them were aging, arthritic, resorting to inhalers — the pollen season was affecting the whole community. The minister himself was forced to dab at his beak of a nose as he preached a sermon out of Job, the part where the Lord suggested he quit feeling sorry for himself.

" 'Deck thyself with majesty and excellence, array thyself with glory and beauty, and thine own right hand can save thee.' "

She liked the old man. Craggy and decrepit, he reminded her of Hume Cronyn. With fingers like dried twigs he shook her hand after the service, gave her a mischievous smile as if he knew she was a sinner and didn't hold it against her. "I hope you will come again, my dear." The old boy still welcomed a challenge.

Afterward they drove home down an avenue of crabapples that tossed white petals at them joyfully. Cass could have sworn they weren't in bloom an hour ago. The sun looked especially proud of itself up in that flag-blue Colorado sky.

"How'd you hit it off with Hollis last night?" Liz asked. "Must have been late when you got home."

"Only about eleven," she said. "There was a fracas out at Gollager's, not my favorite kind of date."

"Boy didn't try anything funny afterward?" Liz had never really approved of Hollis.

"Well, he didn't get a chance, actually. When we went out to the parking lot we found somebody had let the air out of two of his tires. Pike Webster just happened by about then, he brought me home." And Cass still had her suspicions. That was too innocent a look on the Sheriff's face.

As they got out of the car the air was alive with spring's sound effects — bee-buzz in the lilacs, finches making out in the locust tree, giggling of children somewhere down the street. Taking leave of Liz, Cass strolled back across the yards to the house, feeling more relaxed than she had an hour earlier.

Only to have her mini-euphoria snuffed. On the step below the back door lay a telltale twig of lilac — she nudged it with the toe of one white pump. Bending to inspect the locks, she found no scratches. Hard to pick a brand new deadlock without leaving a few marks. Biscuit could do it, of course. So maybe this was no small-town thief. She stepped cautiously into the kitchen and stood just inside the door, doing a visual check, wishing she had the stiletto in hand, but you hardly want to wear a knife down the back of your shirt when you go to church.

Whoever had tossed the place had been careful to set everything back the way it was. Just a few grains of sugar scattered over on the sink counter under the shelf where she kept a package of doughnuts. Having lived in backwater areas where there was a whole sub-culture of six-legged varmints, she was usually careful about cleaning up crumbs. And the chair was tight up against the kitchen table. She was almost sure she'd left it ajar.

Cass was still taking inventory of the room when a tap came at the door behind her. Liz stood looking in, troubled.

"Is anything the matter, child? I saw you kind of tippy-toe around when you went inside just now."

"Yeah. Matter of fact, I think somebody was here in my house while we were at church."

"Oh, that can't be." She pushed past and went on to the living room. "They didn't take the TV. Kids always go for that."

"You mean there's crime here in Panhandle?"

"We get our share. Them Foreman kids are real little juvenile delinkers. Come on back with me, we'll ask Joe if he seen anybody."

In her kitchen the old man sat hunched in a tatty old bathrobe while a pan of soup steamed on the stove. The room was full of the aromas of cabbage and ham. "Hon, whiles we was gone, did you notice anybody fooling around Sandy's house. She thinks she was broke-into."

He blinked his bleary eyes and tried to focus on the problem. "What'd they take?"

"I haven't checked yet," Cass said. "What I wondered — is there any possible way they could have swiped my key from your collection?"

Liz shook her head, grizzled woolly curls a little awry where the hat had come off. Reaching onto the top shelf she took down a sugar bowl, pink with roses in underglaze. Shaking the pair of keys into her palm she showed it. "Nobody would dast poke around my kitchen, especially not with Joe home."

He said, "Well, I wasn't out here the whole time. I was in the parlor listening to that preacher on TV. Last week I sent him five bucks to pray for my lungs."

"Did he do it?" Cass asked trying not to sound skeptical.

"Yup. Least, he prayed for all the sick people out there in the TV congregation. It was a strong kind-a prayer. I got my money's worth." The old man looked like death's early warning, his skin a muddy gray from lack of oxygen.

"I'm sorry you're not well," Cass said and she meant it.

He shrugged. "Miner's pension. Been bustin' coal all my life, started on the pickers' table when I was right out of sixth grade.

Down the shaft when I was fifteen, along with Pa."

"He must have been here at the time of the Ludlow strike." She was thinking how her own father would have been interested to know somebody connected to the Massacre.

"Yep, he seen the tents burn, heard 'em scream, the women and kids hiding down in them dugouts." Joe went into a fit of coughing, but came up still telling his story. "Pa was with the men that next night when they went up the canyons. They burnt out them mines, showed the whole country we wasn't going to take it from them rich crooks no more. Blew up every tipple from Trinidad to Walsenburg. Even old Goddamrockefeller off in New York City had to sit up and take notice."

That sent Cass back to her childhood; she'd been ten years old before she learned that Goddamrockefeller wasn't one word. How many people know, she wondered, that terrorism is not some new-fangled Twenty-first Century phenomenon. It must have made an impressive light-show, the explosions tearing up the night sky in the canyons of King Coal. She seemed to remember the President had to send federal troops in to restore order.

"Well, thank the Lord we don't have no more of that kind of thing," Liz said firmly. "It's bad enough we got a world where kids break into houses. If I was you, hon, I would call Pike Webster about it right away."

Cass nodded. "As soon as I get home."

It went against the grain to ask for help, but it was a necessary courtesy and besides, he would find out anyway. Sandy Butterfield would obey the rules. Within twenty minutes he had pulled the cop car into the driveway behind her truck. By then she had a pot of coffee brewed; he accepted a cup with a nod as she told him her suspicions, the lilac twig.

"Just like in a detective story," he snorted.

"Don't knock it. It works. Somebody opened the back door and didn't leave a scratch on the lock."

"Take anything?"

"Not that I can see. I think they may have been looking for something. At least they poked around my shelf of staples." Or maybe they just got hungry for a doughnut.

"That scrap of paper you found? Where is it now?"

"Gone. I memorized the number and flushed it. But if that's what they were hunting you know what it means — there's more of them out there, not just the guy with the rifle." It wrung her inside with a renewed pang of perplexity. *What could bring a whole team down on me? What have I done, or what have I got that they want?* It made her angry, the whirlwind of fear. Didn't need any more danger, wasn't ready for any more risks. Then magically from the ether came the words she'd heard this morning. "Gird up thy loins like a man, for I will demand of thee . . ." To which her inner coward whined, *Aw, cut it out!*

Meantime Pike was prowling the house. Like a primitive tracker stalking game he moved silently through the rooms, sniffing, listening, looking into closets. Back in the kitchen he paused at the door down to the cellar, bent over to stare at a film of dust and dabbed a finger in it. "Flour?"

"Clay. I probably tracked it from my work room. I am test-firing the kiln down there, I put in a few samples of my new throwing batch to see how they would mature." She swiped some up. "Kentucky Ball, Old Mine #4, noted for its plasticity."

"You mean your oven is on down there right now?"

"Yeah, just about ready to fire off. Want to see? It's a great experience, to look bare-eyed at twenty-two hundred degrees."

"Aren't you afraid you'll burn the house down?"

"The kiln is certified to Cone 7, high-fire brick, well engineered and insulated with asbestos. I am only firing to Cone 5 today, I'm not trying to make porcelain, just a decent stoneware." She started down the steps, turning on the light below — and something moved. A subtle shifting . . .

Pike was quicker to identify it. Holding her by the arm, he eased ahead of her. The naked bulb in the center of the cellar threw hard black shadows behind the appliances, the furnace, the hot water heater, the kiln. The buzzing of its elements sounded odd to Cass, raspy, like a whirligig. She'd had one once when she was a kid, it spun in the wind with a rapid *tick-tack-tack.* And then she realized the noise was coming from beneath the metal framework.

She could see the thing now, coiled in the corner inches from where she would have stood to look into the peephole, its tail vibrating at an angry pitch. Mesmerized she froze in place. Pike glanced around, located the sponge mop hanging on the wall near the stairs and reversed the squeeze plate. With a swift move, he lunged and pinned the rattler, then grabbed it in his bare hand right behind the head and held it up, writhing.

"You got a plastic bag?" He looked downright pleased.

Why do men love snakes? She got out a garbage sack and held it open while he dropped the deadly creature in. Made her shudder. She'd seen plenty of diamondbacks out in the arroyos, but here in the house it made her sick. Back in the kitchen Pike found a fork in a drawer and stabbed the sack with it in several places to let air in.

"What are you going to do with it?" Not that she really wanted to know.

"Oh, I'll dump it tomorrow, out on the grassland over-east. Too many prairie dogs over there, we could use a few more good snakes." He tied the bag with a double twist.

"I can't see how it could have got in here."

"Oh, it had help," he said. "Look there." On the stairs, one patch of clay dust bore the unmistakable print of a boot, about size 12. "Your visitor didn't come to steal something, but to leave you a little present."

14

Monday morning, everything looks more possible. The day was beautiful, her night had been dreamless, and the kiln was ready to be opened. At this point the pyrometer came in handy, showing that the temperature had backed off from its pinnacle of 2185° to a mere 500° — time to crack the lid. Never fling it wide, you would create a rush of cool air that might damage the elements. But she could prop it a few inches and peer in with a flashlight.

Late yesterday evening when she had fired off she had watched the cones go down, pushing to see through the fiery brilliance of the heat and glimpse the vase at the moment of vitrification. Trembling with metamorphosis as the components fused, it was in that instant so vulnerable the least flaw could cause it to collapse, cave in or twist or sag. Now she could see that it had come through the fire with integrity, standing straight and a little cocky. Her heart jogged with an unexpected bump of pleasure. Then claustrophobia sank in its claws and she fled the narrow cellar.

Back at the kitchen table, she took long swallows of air to get rid of the panic. It made her angry, this weakness that came over her in closed quarters. She used to try to argue it away, excuse it. But it was part of her make-up, the atavistic fear of a trapped animal. Even Kuzu couldn't shame her out of it.

"Difference is, you are not a lower animal. You have a complicated brain, opposable thumbs and a capacity to believe in your own destiny. You must have faith in something to make it this far. Maybe you believe in God, or Mother Earth or Lady Luck, whatever, it's the glue that will hold you together when you feel like coming apart. So take up Zen or learn to pray, and don't give me any more crap about animal behavior." *Yes, sir.*

But it wasn't something you could argue with. She needed wider spaces than the kitchen offered. Going out onto the back porch, she let her eyes reach out to the remoteness of the distant mountains, the vastness of the plains beyond the back of the lot. It always stretched her vision, that broad blue sky — Colorado was almost as beautiful as its advertisements in the brochures.

In an hour she was ready for another excursion below, by which time the kiln had cooled to a mere 200°. She took the piece out and brought it up to set on the kitchen table, viewing the little vase with critical eye. It stood on the white linen cloth exuding a charm that surprised her. The blue leaves she had swashed on were dotted with white berries of clay, a kind of engobe she'd concocted out of kaolin and water. The cobalt glaze she had used for the interior was purely experimental, it had crawled around the bottom, but no one was going to notice that. In fact she thought the overall aspect was good enough to take the piece along to illustrate her talk to Guy's artists tomorrow night.

Depending on the artists of course. When he had phoned her to confirm his invitation to the Hacienda she had tried to pump him for details of his "students," what level of creativity they were achieving. It had only provoked a sort of nervous humor, so she suspected they were probably a bunch of rich amateurs with more airs than art.

It gave her a few misgivings. If they were expecting a lecture on coloring-book ceramics, how to make cute little ashtrays out of bisque greenware using glazes from small premixed bottles, she was going to disappoint them royally. On the other hand she didn't want to come on as an arrogant know-it-all. If they really wanted to learn some of the basics, she was ready to tell them all she knew. To formulate her approach she really needed to learn more about the group. And as she wondered who around town would know, a small smile formed. Glancing at her watch she wondered if school still let out at 3:30.

Over on the Court House the mellow chimes were striking four when she walked up the steps of the Public Library. They have said that Andrew Carnegie allowed each community to choose its own design for the libraries he financed, so why then did they all look so much alike? Cass wondered. The dark pile of red brick had a front door of good Midwestern oak, a tree that grew a thousand miles from these sagebrush plains. Why couldn't they have built it of adobe with cottonwood beams?

The desk was deserted, but through an open door on the left Cass saw what had to be a ladies' study group in progress. Seated around one of the big library tables a dozen women listened earnestly to another who was reading Emily Dickinson in a no-nonsense tone: " 'I never spoke with God, nor visited in heaven,/Yet certain am I of the spot as if a chart were given.' "

Slipping past unnoticed Cass browsed swiftly through the lower stacks, then climbed steep stairs at the far end, looking for a shelver's cart. It was parked in an upper aisle near a window where Jessie sat, her head bent over a book. Black braids falling forward, her face quiet in concentration, her genes were showing, Native American blood dominating the softer Spanish characteristics of her mother. When she glanced up the day darkened perceptibly.

"Hi," Cass said quickly. With apologies, the faster the better. "Jessie, I came to tell you I am very sorry — I never would have snitched on you if I had known that Pike was your dad. You might have told me."

"It's okay." Distant and cool.

"No, it's not. I just hope he wasn't too sore at you."

"My father doesn't get angry."

"No, that's right. I seem to remember: he gets two feet taller and looks terribly disappointed, as if, by forgetting to do your homework, you have launched on a life of crime."

The tight lips loosened a fraction. "You had him in school?"

"Math. And I am not good in math of any kind. I never could figure out which boxcar got transferred to what siding, or why the whole train didn't just go on to St. Louis."

Jessie couldn't restrain a small smile. "My father is crazy about trains. Upstairs at our house, you should see, one whole room is model railroads."

"I never knew that."

"He doesn't tell many people. He says his private life should be, like, private."

"I understand. In fact I do too, which is why I got a little upset when you knew so much about me. I couldn't imagine how you had found out. Now that I know I don't mind, and I hope you will still invite me to go see those clay deposits. Only right now I need a different kind of help." Second step, after apology, throw yourself on their kindness. "Tonight I am supposed to give a talk on ceramics to that bunch of artists out at Guy Magee's place, and I have no idea what sort of people they are. But I figured you would — some of them must come in the library at times, right?"

"Yeah, a few."

"So what I wondered is: are they for real? Are they serious artists or just a bunch of dilettantes?" Cass used the word like a bribe, third step, show respect.

Jessie accepted it in the spirit it was given. Closing her book — it was Hillerman's "Dancehall of the Dead" — she frowned thoughtfully. "Well, of course, Guy is kind of neat, but some of the people he goes with are snoots."

"Smart snoots or silly rich types who just paint pictures of cactus?"

The childish lips quirked again. "You can't tell what they're supposed to be. I went to an art show at the Hacienda last Christmas, it was really weird. Like there was this big painting called 'Earthenasia.' I call it 'Bugs Smeared on a Windshield.' "

Cass laughed and Jessie made a *shhh* sound, but she was grinning too.

"There was another one about geese, I think."

"As in flocks of?"

"I don't know. Somebody said they had migraines. I didn't know that birds ever got headaches. And then there was one where your soul melts like cheese over a fire."

"I begin to get the picture," Cass said soberly. "In that case I will go artsy-fartsy and give them a lecture on how ceramics embodies the mysteries of the cosmos, I will positively incinerate their cheddar."

Jessie swallowed a snicker. "You want to go riding Saturday?"

"Uh — sure." Cass had got herself into it, trying to suck up. Now she felt she could hardly turn the kid down. Find some other way to dodge the date, get Pike to help. He certainly wouldn't want his child gallivanting around with a human target. But her mission was accomplished. She now dreaded the lecture whole-heartedly.

When she went back downstairs, Cass saw that the librarian had taken the seat behind the desk again. "Oh, Ms. Butterfield . . ."

Me? Yes, I'm Sandy Butterfield. "Uh, hi. How do you do?"

"I'm Charmian Smith." A sturdy middle-aging lady in a home-made wrap-around of bright India-print cloth, she looked like a relic of the hippy era. Skin like cowhide, wind-beaten henna-dyed red hair that swore at the pink hollyhock blossom she wore behind one ear, she affected a floribunda gaiety that would have seemed phony if it weren't for the purity of her eyes, which were clear as violet glass. She was waving a handsome little booklet, on its cover a brilliant photograph of some contemporary pottery, Santa Clara, Acoma, Maricopa. *If I could ever make ware like that . . .*

"I've heard about you," she was saying.

"I'm so glad that we now have a real ceramist in residence, I thought you might enjoy this."

"It's beautiful," Cass assured her. "The only trouble is, these pictures give me a case of mediocrity blues."

The woman's sweet smile lit up the weather-beaten landscape of her face. "I'll bet artistic insecurity isn't a real problem for you." The spark in her eyes was wise and self-assured. How old? Forty? Fifty? Her hair was showing white at the roots. She went on, "I hear you're going to speak to Guy Magee's flock tomorrow night."

"How did you know that?" The suspicion again.

"Oh I'm the town mystic, don't you know?" Charmian laughed like a child. "I am also the clearing house for news of local entertainment. Here" — from a stack of yellow flyers she handed one across the desk — "for your scrap book." It was an announcement of a special symposium at the Hacienda tomorrow, guest speaker Sandra Butterfield, artist and ceramist, public invited, time 8:00 p.m.

"Good grief!" It slipped out before she could stop it.

"You weren't expecting to be a celebrity so soon."

"I wasn't expecting an open house. I'd better go home and work on my lecture. Thank you for this —" As Cass reached out to take the booklet her fingers brushed those of the librarian, who started, as if a spark of static electricity had passed between them.

Charmian muttered, "Oh dear." Flushing darkly she tried to wave it off. "I'm sorry. I shouldn't . . ." Then, abruptly switching direction, "Yes, I believe I must."

"What? Something the matter?"

"Yes. At least — some people are not tolerant of psychic phenomena, but I hope you will keep an open mind."

"I believe there are a lot of mysteries that can't be proved under a microscope."

"Good. I don't usually go around pushing my peculiar gift on people, but this time there is danger involved."

"What kind of danger?" Cass was at full alert in an instant.

"I'm not sure. I got a flash of precognitive insight when our fingers touched. If it wouldn't offend you, give me your hand for a moment, it may come clearer." Her grasp was cool and dry and impersonal. "It's gone. The images don't accept requests, unfortunately." She was staring at the turquoise clasp lying at the throat of Cass's shirt.

As if she could see right through to the stiletto. "What sort of image was it?"

"Nothing specific, just an impression of an odd, menacing force, a threat to you. It seemed to be cylindrical. And red, for whatever good that does. I'm sorry."

"Red like a — fire extinguisher? Or more like a bottle of sherry?"

Charmian smiled faintly. "Neither of those. Well, it was just a swift flash of my silly intuition. I'm probably exaggerating the threat part." Backing off fast, wary, defensive, she had been laughed at too often.

"I never underestimate an omen." Cass had seen too many strange anomalies, especially when she'd been sent to the middle east for a crash course in Islamic terrorism during the hysteria following the events of 9/11. Afghanistan, Turkey, India, she had seen evidence of psychic powers that couldn't be denied by mere skepticism.

In fact she found Charmian Smith absolutely credible, on reflection, as she walked home, escorted by a light spring breeze that was still chilly enough to make her shiver. Or maybe that was the ghost of her team, following at a cautious distance. Trying to warn her to take this seriously. But how? Even good Spanish steel is no match for, say, a shotgun loaded with red, red cylinders of .12-gauge buckshot.

15

The power of suggestion is maddening. Even the word Colorado means "the color red" and pan handles can be cylindrical. As she drove through town in the early dusk Cass shrugged off the sinister connotations angrily. It was said the little burg got its ridiculous name back in the early days when a rancher arrived from the Uncompahgre with a herd of horses branded "U" to which he had quickly added a handle with a running iron, calling his ranch The Panhandle. More probable was the story that the first villagers, who were dirt-poor refugees from the coal mines, had been forced to mooch off nearby towns, hence, panhandlers.

Whatever its shabby provenance, the newly sprung town must have been painful to the old grandee who had held the land grant on the entire area back in the days when the Spanish still owned the territory. His holdings had been reduced, by war and politics, to consist finally of the Hacienda itself and a few acres of the vast vineyard where his ancestors had grown grapes for centuries. The plants were stunted now, too old to bear, but they still writhed in a green barrier around the old adobe mansion to provide an oasis of mystery in the midst of the flat cactus prairies.

Cass was reminded of hot afternoons when a gang of eighth graders would sneak out to the place and peer through the twisted branches to catch a glimpse of the last old Spaniard to hold sway there. They would see the man hacking away, trying to coax a little fruit out of the aging vines. Because he looked so foreign, with his dark skin and tall black hat, his big mustachio and silver-plated belt, he took on the mystique of a Zorro, retired, but still dangerous. Giggle and nudge and when he looks your way, run, run, the kind of mild entertainment you dream up in a dead little town on a summer day.

Now the place was better kept. The iron gate that hung between the two stone posts stood wide, where it had always been closed before. Cass drove through and followed her headlights down the curving driveway to the clearing in back where a great carriage house stood. It was said its handsome mahogany stalls had once housed some of the finest horses in the southwest and a coach that had supposedly borne Lillie Langtry from the Trinidad railroad station to the opera house. No self-respecting town in the west could refrain from appropriating Miss Langtry in absentia.

Now the big building was modernized with newly added windows, the lofty interior hung with fluorescent lights. Beyond the vast open doorway a crowd milled below the display — paintings on every wall. There were even a few pieces of sculpture. This had all the earmarks of a catastrophe, Cass thought with sinking heart. Not just a quiet little talk among fellow artisans, she was going to be served up as the main dish at an amateur art show.

I'll get you for this, Guy Magee!

He looked tickled as he came toward her, those peridot eyes alight with amusement and a small grin secreted in the reddish goatee. "Sandy! Welcome to our sanctuary. We were so pleased you were coming that the students decided to put on a little exhibit for your benefit. It does encourage them, you know, to hang their best efforts, prepare for future gallery showings and so forth. Come on in, take a look around." He seemed genuinely pleased with the stuff.

Cass shuddered slightly as she gazed at welded junk creations, garish canvases titled "Construction No. 7" or "White on White." Beyond the bugs-on-windshield imitation Pollock she found the geese. On a 6' × 8' dead-white piece of plasterboard two thin black lines, ruler-straight, started at the upper corners and converged on the bottom edge in a kind of V-shape. The title was "Migration." The melted cheese turned out to be a ten-foot square of solid purple acrylic interrupted only by a small wedge of orange that seemed to be liquefying at the bottom. "Soul on Fire." Those two were by the same artist, signed simply with a black, swashing "Q".

Up at the podium, as Guy introduced her, Cass tried to judge their mood. She had spoken to groups of artists who were untaught or badly taught, hungering for someone to make sense. A good audience, they had made her feel humble, she had given them everything she had. But these people — ? Looking down at them from the low stage she saw a score of middle-aging Bohemians, sitting their folding chairs as arrogantly as if they'd paid a thousand bucks a seat. And maybe they had. The women wore imported designer slacks, perfect coiffeurs, not a hair out of place.

Their nails were long and shining with polish. Several sported furs that were definitely not *faux.*

And yet, even rich people can be seekers. She framed her presentation in plain language and spoke seriously about the technology of ceramics, leaving the art of design a long way out of it. Halfway through she was aware that the words were washing over their heads. It didn't matter, by then it was a chore to be got over. She was even amused when the question-and-answer part of the session turned to shrug-and-spit.

"But my dear girl, don't you feel that your craft is so *limited* by all those *dreary* technical requirements, I mean with such a *burden* of detail one would never have a chance to *release* the inner spirit, would one?" That gem was from a woman wearing a beaded headband and a leather Indian-maiden outfit that could have been designed for a Park-Avenue costume ball. Cass, in her $200 jumpsuit, was one of the street people.

She said, "The physical discipline of any art form is the prism which gives us the full spectrum of creativity." *You want artistic crap, I can do that.*

"Oh, baloney!" This from a stocky man in the front row. He was dressed in carefully shabby jeans and an elbow-patched suede jacket, obviously trying for the Hemingway look, stubby gray beard and unlit pipe. "Next you'll tell us that old crap about perspiration being more important than inspiration. And I will just flat-out deny it. I'm here to testify that when I saw that flight of geese, the sound of 'em really yanked my chain. I ran out of here, I mean I *ran!* Soon as they were gone, I grabbed that piece of plasterboard and went to work. If I stopped to get all intellectual about it I would never have caught the spirit of migration." He glanced over fondly at his painting.

Cass frowned a fraction. "The trouble with having to name a painting in order for it to be understood is that someone might misread the title. A friend of mine told me to look for the picture of a migraine headache. The thing is, you shouldn't need to explain what a piece of art is about. In my opinion."

"Are you implying that Quentin's work isn't truly communicating? Because you are wrong, young lady!" The woman in the Indian beads exploded with indignation. "We are all greatly moved by the way his inner soul erupts with fire."

Cass glanced at Guy. *You think this is funny?* To the audience she said, "Passion is great, but if you don't express it coherently the viewing public doesn't benefit — I'm talking about the average man, not your personal friends." *And to hell with being diplomatic.* "The serious artist will want to share his vision with whole generations to come, as the Chinese did, the Egyptians, the Anasazi, all still talking to us across thousands of years, without captions. To achieve that you have to master the brush or the chisel or the formula for a glaze. To learn the techniques of your craft is hard work, and those who can't accept that will never rise above mediocrity. Thank you." She sat down. There was no applause.

Guy was trying to keep a straight face. On the far side of him his wife was furious. A plain small-faced woman, dark of eye and brow, her hair bound back into a knot from which a long, coarse ponytail hung in a curve like a Cyrillic symbol she was whispering to him audibly in Russian.

"I told you it was a mistake to invite that woman here."

Smiling blandly he answered in the same language, poorly pronounced but fluent. "The lady only said what I have wished I could, a thousand times."

Meanwhile the room was buzzing — the image of a hornet's nest was probably augmented by the high-vaulted ceiling into which had been let skylights. The place, she thought, must be a marvelous studio by day. Now under the merciless pallor of the fluorescent fixtures the little group looked sullen, throbbing with bruised ego. Hemingway was shoving forward up to the lectern, ruddy eyes like polished agate.

"Young lady, did you come here to insult us?"

"No. That didn't occur to me until after I was patronized." Cass gave him back look-for-look.

It seemed to put a little fluster in his bluster. "We didn't mean to belittle you. But you have to admit that potters are just artisans, after all. And those who cast stones should be ready to duck. When will we see a piece of your work?"

"Hey," she said, "fair's fair. I just set up my kiln the other day, only finished one piece so far. But I brought it along." From her tote she drew the vase, unwrapped it and set it on the lectern. "There you go. Take your best shot."

The burly man glowered at it while the others hovered, watching him for some signal as to what they should think. Guy didn't have to be clued. Picking it up, he turned it in his fingers with a soft, "Wow."

Quentin was moved to follow suit. "Well,

m'dear, you obviously have got a flare. Why don't we all have some espresso and you can tell us more about yourself. I understand you studied in Germany?"

Guy was still smiling at the vase. "This little gem is a complete biography. It isn't oxblood, but you must have jumped in and out of a few fireboxes to be able to pull this out of a lump of clay. Isn't it a honey, Minka?" He handed it to his wife.

She would only have been interested in my obituary. Taking the vase in her long-boned fingers, she scowled as if personally offended. "Primitive," she announced. "If you like primitive."

Cass hardly heard her. She was mesmerized by the woman's bracelet — a tube of scarlet enamel. Very cylindrical, very red.

The long drive home in the dark made her uneasy; the whole evening had left a bad taste. *Never do Guy another favor, damn the boy.* Afterward he at least had the grace to apologize. Escorting her out to the truck, he'd said earnestly, "Sorry, San, I know they're a bunch of klutzes. But they're such *rich* klutzes, and I've got a mortgage to pay off."

Is that why you married the Russian? And even as she thought it, the truth dawned: it was exactly why he had married the lady. She had probably financed his whole operation. It was obvious in her superior demeanor, her contempt for him and his childhood pal. Only the wealthy can afford that kind of ill manners. *But what did Madam get out of the deal?* Cass wondered. Guy was talented, congenial, bright. For some women that would be enough, and Minka was getting a little long in the tooth.

As she drove past McDonald's their lights went off, leaving the town dark except for the antiquated street lamps. In their refurbishing, the town fathers hadn't bothered to update those. They made a furry glow at each corner, but they didn't illuminate much. And the back streets were deeply black, everybody already in bed. Turning at her driveway she cut the engine. *Why didn't I leave the light on over the back porch?* To which came the instant response: *I did.* On full alert, she sat a minute, thinking. *Yes, I did.*

Taking out the penlight she always carried in her bag, she proceeded toward the back stoop, sending the thin beam to finger the light fixture over the door. Of course the bulb could have burned out — if you believe in the tooth fairy. She raked the porch: bucket, broom, the step ladder she had used yesterday to oil the hinges of the door. It stood just to one side and would have come in handy to anyone wanting to unscrew the light bulb. Cautiously she stopped below the steps and aimed the flash at the crack where she had left the scrap of lilac bark — it was still in place. And yet the hair was up on her neck, the sixth sense working hard . . .

Thank God for amateurs!

A pro wouldn't have left the light off, a pro would have replaced the bulb. By plunging the back stoop into pitch-dark, he had alerted her, forced her to use the flashlight, which now picked up the glint of something bright, low on one of the panels. A new thumbtack. He should have found an older one, with a rusted head — that's what Yuri would have used. The twine was right, gray against gray boards, almost invisible leading down into the latticework that hid the crawl space beneath the porch, but a pro would have put the nails back in their holes.

Taking a deep breath Cass eased the skunk screen away, laying it aside. Lucky. She was lucky he hadn't protected his device with a motion sensor. This was your basic bang: a box packed with sawdust cushioning one stick of dynamite, very red, very cylindrical, and a half-dozen blasting caps. On top of them was a vial full of clear liquid holding down the loose end of the twine. The slightest twitch would tip the acid over onto the detonators, setting off an explosion that would take out the back porch and anybody on it. She shook her head grimly. Shades of Harry Orchard.

In training they had studied the old murderer with some amusement. This device was much like the one he had used to blow up the Independence Depot and demolish a trainload of scabs, in the Cripple Creek mine strike at the turn of the century. It had been news to the training class that terrorism had flourished in such an early time. In these days of miniaturized, transistorized, remote-controlled, heat-sensitive devices this was horse-and-buggy stuff, but it could wipe you out as fast as any newfangled gadget. Which was why it had been included in their hazmat course during training — one Friday quiz had consisted of disarming one. At the time Cass and the others had assumed the flask didn't contain real acid, but they never knew for sure. Nobody flunked the test.

For a minute she sat there on her heels considering her options. In a bigger city she would have called out the bomb squad, but there probably wasn't a competent expert for this kind of thing closer than Pueblo. Maybe Denver. The truth was, nobody within a hundred miles was better trained to touch that vial than she was. Or — not to touch it. No telling what the acid was, might even be nitric, wasn't that used in mining operations? She'd read somewhere that they were leaching the ground up around Victor to get the gold out of the old tailings. So treat it with a little respect.

Adrenaline boosting her now, she stood up and went around the house slowly looking for any further hazards. Found none. The front porch seemed clear and the door looked innocent of tampering. Taking off her shoes she walked softly into the front room and back to the kitchen where she found a candy bar in the drawer and ate it down like medicine. And where had she seen some forceps? In her father's tool drawer, he must have used them on his stamps. Going back to the work room, she found them. Delicate, but they were long enough, with neat curved ends. The vial was tall and narrow like a test tube with a flat bottom. How tall? About three inches, probably fit inside a mayo jar. Glass was the only material impervious to the strongest of acids. Back in the kitchen she found several empties under the sink.

At the kitchen table she practiced picking up the salt cellar with the tongs. She was gripping them too tightly — had to get tough with herself. A fleeting thought came and went: Kuzu had never told them how he lost his left hand. Flexing her fingers she held them out — steady. Now for a better light. In the cellar on a shelf she had noticed an electric torch, the kind that stands on its own.

Carrying it and the forceps and the jar, she went back through the house and out onto the front porch. Night chill struck through her coat. Cass almost welcomed it, the heat-pump of adrenaline was making her sweat as she skirted the house again. Settling down to the job, she took a few deep breaths of cold air to force the oxygen. It was time to start singing. Yuri had taught her that — it steadies you to sing or whistle, and she never could whistle. Didn't know any Bach, her own personal favorite was a folk ditty. Muttering under her breath:

"I said the little leather-winged bat,
I'll tell you the reason that,
The reason that I fly by night,
Because I've lost my heart's delight . . ."

Easing under the porch she inched forward, placing the big beam to focus on the bomb, setting the mayo jar as close to the pile of explosives as she dared.

"How-de-dow-de-diddle-oh-day . . ."

Wiping her hands on her coat, she turned them into the fingers of a robot, moving mechanically, slowly.

"How-de-dow-de-diddle-oh-day . . ."

Picked up the forceps, spreading them as wide as they'd go, she reached for the vial. Don't hesitate or dither, just do it smoothly, steadily.

"Howwww-de-dow-de-diddle-oh-day.
Ho-lo-lee-e-e-eee . . ."

Closed around it and lifted it into the mayo jar.

"De-diddly-oh."

It tipped and spilled harmlessly into the glass bottom giving off a faint fume that made her choke. Screwing the lid on fast she wriggled backward out into the night.

Above, the moonless sky was crisp and

transparent as black glass, strewn with handfuls of hundred-carat stars. As she got to her feet, she was breathing fast, you always hold your breath in those last seconds. Now she drank in the cold air and stood looking up at the sky, a little surprised.

Hey, how about that. I'm alive.

16

The law of the pendulum. After a tight squeak with death you go from a false high to a low that is a sublevel of Hell itself. As long as she was with the team they had fought the battle together, after each operation. Bandying bad jokes, gallows humor, Yuri would sing lugubrious Hungarian folk songs, Renee would dance, the only time she ever lost her shyness. They would all end up a little drunk, and gradually climb back out of the hole. This was the first time she'd had to negotiate the murky ladder by herself.

She sat in the darkened kitchen inside a deeper darkness that was completely of the spirit. Danger past, against all rationale, she felt doomed. Worst of all, she didn't even care a whole lot. If she died tomorrow what difference would it make? The psychiatrist in Dresden had explained it matter-of-factly: "Adrenaline leaves dregs in the system that create a chemical imbalance for a while. You need to restore your equilibrium. Try mild stimulants and exercise."

Earlier on in training Kuzu had put things more bluntly: "Get over it and get on with your life. Assess where you're at and where the next danger lies." It stirred an old instinct, a desire to please the teacher.

So assess the three attacks: rifle, snake, dynamite. She saw at once, as the test sheet would put it, which one of these doesn't fit the other two? No-brainer. The sniper had been a pro, the latter two attempts, strictly amateur. The Flea Circus would never send someone tippy-toeing around with a prairie rattler, dumb way to kill somebody. And the dynamite wasn't in their style either; they would have used the latest plastique. Which didn't exactly cheer her up. It meant there were probably two different enemies who wanted her dead. At least two.

With daybreak lightening the windows she got up, moving slowly, and began to fill a packing box with the lethal ingredients laid out on the table. She had cleaned up the mess under the porch, brought the bomb components inside, put the blasting caps in a coffee can. She sealed the mayo jar with duct tape. It would eventually disintegrate from the fumes, especially if the acid was nitric, but it would hold for the present if it didn't tip over. It was on the floor by the back door. The rest would be safe enough in a carton made of heavy-weight corrugated box-board. It had contained a shipment of coloring oxides. Using the Styrofoam popcorn left over, Cass packed the dynamite in it, the can of blasting caps. The jar of acid she put inside another coffee can and added it to the rest and tied the box with some twine.

Glancing toward the house next door, she made sure it was still dark, then went briskly out to the shed and stashed the lethal package. Time now to make some coffee and some decisions.

As she filled the old blue enamel pot Cass glanced up at the chicken clock. Five-thirty-five in the morning, what better moment to decide what color to paint this rotten kitchen that would be okay by Panhandle standards, yet put some pep in the room? Maybe a cheerful salmon pink. Replace the yellow oil-cloth on the table with black-and-white checks, hang some striped black-and-pink curtains to tie it together, and then, thank heaven, buy a new clock. For two cents she'd yank the yellow chicken off the wall right now and take a hammer to it. Her hands actually clenched.

A knock at the back door made her start half out of her skin. Taking a deep breath she went to let Liz in.

"Are you all right, girl? I been some worried. I looked out the window about midnight or so, I seen a light moving around over here."

"Oh — uh, yeah, it was nothing. I thought I heard a skunk under the porch."

"You don't look like you been to bed at all."

Cass glanced down at her clothes, the ones she'd worn to the Hacienda. She'd forgotten them. The jump suit was ruined, earth ground into the knees, stocking feet with holes in the toes. "Rehearsing for Halloween," she gave a stupid laugh that sounded as if someone else had uttered it. "I guess I did stay up all night, I was upset by that bunch out there at Guy's place. They asked me to come talk about ceramics, but they didn't really want to hear it. They wanted to look me over and put me down, and I guess I snapped back, and it got nasty and I didn't feel like sleeping."

"Them," Liz said with pursed lips. "Rich hoity-patoots, think they own the town. You should see 'em come into the Safeway: 'Oh deary-me, you don't carry truffles?' "

Cass laughed in spite of herself. Her voice

sounded more natural now as she said, "What on earth possessed Guy to open a studio for that lot?"

"Well, they said he needed money." Liz was rummaging in the fridge, found a loaf of bread and got out a couple of slices. "Which I reckon is true, and Lord knows those rich folks spend like a bunch of drunken sailors. He's got hisself a little art store right next to The Boutique, sells 'em supplies at high prices, boy's not completely dumb."

"But I always thought the Magees were rich."

"I guess they made some bad investments, when the market crashed a few years ago they lost their shirt and bobby-socks. Father died of a heart attack and mother got Alzheimer's and was put in a sanitarium up in Pueblo. Guy had to do something fast. I always did think that's why he married that woman." Pop, pop, bread into the toaster.

"Yeah, I met her. She hated me on sight. Don't know why. She doesn't know me. But I think he must have talked me up too much, how I got my schooling in Germany, maybe oversold me and she got jealous."

Liz handed her a tall glass of orange juice. "You look like one of these annie-wrecked types. Go on now, drink it up. And don't worry about Guy Magee. You probably know more art than any of 'em. Here, have some toast."

Cass felt a burst of fondness. She had never expected to feel grateful for a little mothering, but it gave her a strange sense of comfort, a cushion against the raw texture of reality that waited to close in as soon as Liz was gone. Something had to be done with those dangerous components out in the shed.

As the old woman picked her way back across the yards, Cass tried to brace up. Took herself down to the bedroom and slipped out of the grungy jumpsuit, went into the shower and gave herself a shock treatment, ice-cold, steaming hot, and back to ice-cold. It didn't create any miracles. She was moving on automatic pilot now, but the fuel gauge was bumping empty. Needed sleep, but it would have to wait a while longer. Dressed in dungarees and sweatshirt, she went back out to the kitchen and picked up the telephone.

"Yeah? Webster here." He sounded grumpy, as if he'd just got out of bed.

"It's me," she said. "I have a little problem. I thought maybe you could stop by on your way to work."

"What kind of problem?" In those few

seconds he had become completely alert.

"Bigger than a rattlesnake."

"I'll be there in ten minutes."

Only eight had passed when she saw the cop-car pulling into her driveway. As he got out his face was set in a *what now?* look.

"Good morning." She tried to sound business like, but he had brought his own miasma of gloom into the kitchen.

"There's the devil to pay about that sniper," he said, getting down a mug and pouring himself a shot of coffee. "The FBI is in my office twice a day trying to get more of the story out of me. They have a sixth sense, that I'm not telling them everything. I was tempted to give them your name and let you field the heat. You're the one who knows what it's all about."

"Do whatever you think best," she said quietly. "In fact you're probably right. They'll be better at handling the bomb." Not exactly tactful, springing it on him like that. It gave her a small stir of satisfaction to rattle his cage.

"What — ?"

In flat, unemotional words she told him the details as he turned visibly paler. "For the love of God, girl, why didn't you call me at once? Crawling around in the dark that way, you could have blown yourself up and half the town too. What were you thinking anyway?"

"I was thinking like a trained operative certified in handling hazardous materials," she informed him coldly. "Have you ever dismantled an explosive device? If you don't get it right the first time, you can't just erase the board and start over, Mr. Webster, sir. I handled the thing myself because I know how, sir. When it comes to bombs, I am a pro. Sir."

"Oh, cut that out." His color came rushing back in a dark tide that flooded his swarthy face. "I know I still sound like a teacher sometimes, it's a habit that's hard to break. But I just can't — I mean, disarming bombs is not exactly suitable work for a woman."

"On the contrary, we have superior manual dexterity, our fingers are small and our feminine natures are good for ticklish jobs — it's all been documented. For the record," she added, "I did not endanger your town. The dynamite was placed back between the footers of the house. They are old-fashioned heavy-aggregate concrete. The force of the explosion would have been channeled upward to take out the porch, probably lift the roof, but not toss it very far. Not enough charge for a really big blast.

I do have a problem, however, what to do with the stuff. I packaged it up safely and put it in the shed out-back. I hoped you might be able to help me dispose of it."

"Oh God." Then, "Yes, sure, I'll figure something out. I don't suppose you have any idea who did this?"

"You'll be the first to know when I get a clue. Unless you want to hand off to the Fibbies."

He shook his head. "I don't like those guys either. I hate having them poke around our town. I swear, they can make you feel guilty just by looking at you. See conspiracies everywhere. As if I can't handle the law around here. Where's the stuff?"

"In the work shed."

He stood up and headed for the back door. "If anybody asks what I'm doing over here so early, tell 'em I came to borrow your dad's belt sander. I'm going to refinish a floor over at the house. Shouldn't be taking Friday off, but —"

Friday? "Uh-oh."

"Now what?" He stopped, worried by her tone.

"Another problem." This time she was genuinely apologetic. "I have a date to go riding with Jessie tomorrow morning. Ran into her at the library and we sort of hit it off. She was going to show me some sedimentary deposits out there on the Rocking R. Of course I'll cancel out, but I really do hate to lie to her. She's a great little kid. Listen, maybe you could forbid her to see me. Tell her I'd be bad for her or something."

"In other words you want me to lie for you?"

"It's not all that untrue. I could be hazardous to her health."

Fuming, he paced the kitchen, thinking it over. "You'd probably be safe enough out on the ranch. There's dozens of dudes around on the weekends, 'cowboys' everywhere, straight from the drugstores of Pueblo, but they take pretty good care of the guests. Ruger himself is one of those know-it-all Texans, comes on strong — well, you saw him out at Gollager's the other night. But he runs a clean operation, I looked into it pretty thoroughly before I let Pony go out there." He was halfway talking to himself.

"Unless he's got his own secret service, he couldn't protect her from a long-range rifle." That seemed so obvious, Cass was puzzled that he'd even consider the thing. She led him out to the shed and helped him carry the boxes to the black-and-white unit.

So I'll have to handle it myself, make up some story that I can't go.

He got in the car and sat a moment. Then abruptly he said, "I don't think there's any risk about taking a ride tomorrow. Go ahead with it. Keep your promise." Then, with a touch of sarcasm he added, "I'm sure a *pro* like you will take all due precautions. Carry your knife and pack your slingshot and so forth."

She watched him drive off, perplexed. Webster was no fool. With a box full of dynamite in the trunk of his car, a rattlesnake in a bag in the back seat and the FBI haunting his doorstep, how could he possibly allow his little girl to have anything to do with good old "Bunny?" But she was too tired to figure it out.

17

Still too wired to go to bed, Cass felt spaced out, running on automatic pilot as she left the house at ten — hardware store would be open by then. It was the only project she felt up to, a physical chore, to paint the kitchen.

The prospect of running into Hollis Anderson put a further sag in her spirits, but she'd just have to handle it. As it happened she caught a break, slipped in on the heels of another customer and ducked away down a deserted aisle where she found a shelf of Yard Alert spotlights with motion sensors, presumably designed to surprise an errant raccoon in the vegetable patch. She took two. She had reached the paint department before she was caught from behind in a hard, rough grip.

"So there you are!" Hollis loomed so close she could feel the heat of his breath, smell the strong aroma of shaving cream, hair oil.

His dark lanky locks were plastered tight to his skull, giving him the look of a mad heron, that beak of a nose thrusting at her. "Where the Devil have you been? I called and called last evening until ten o'clock, finally went over to your house. I thought you might be lying dead on the rug. I even tried to get in a window but you've got them all braced with something. What's wrong with you, girl?"

"Right now, what's wrong is my shoulder which you are jerking around again. Hollis, if you don't get out of the habit of manhandling me, I'm going to fight back, and it won't be pretty! What business is it of yours where I was last night? I have a life, and I suggest you get one." That ought to be plain enough. "All I want from you right now is to mix me some paint."

"Oh, yeah, I got a life. At least I thought I had a chance at one when you came back." He followed her over to the paint aisle. "It was like I found a piece of myself again, like I found the lost chord. I've been out of tune for years."

"I want a nice shade of salmon," She went on briskly. "Not too dark, I am going to paint my kitchen."

"Red's no color for a kitchen. Rose maybe." He plucked a couple of color samples off the chart-board. "You really need somebody to look after you, San. I nearly went out of my mind last night worrying."

"Why on earth? We are both verging on middle age, Hollis. I've traveled all over the world and survived. Here, this will do." Cass handed him back one of the color chits. It was a cheerful peony shade. She was turning away when he seized her, spun her around to face him and planted a wild kiss on her mouth. The crush of his lips, the hardness she could feel beneath his jeans as he forced her close to him brought a wave of revulsion. *God, please don't let me vomit.*

With a short up-thrust of arms, she delivered a blow with the heel of her hand under his chin, followed by a short jab of her boot to his shin which sent him stumbling into a display of garbage cans. As he scrambled to get his balance, she said, coldly, "I wasn't kidding. You are not to touch me again. I don't want to go to Trinidad for every nut and bolt I need, but I will if I have to."

"Aw no!" he groaned. "If that's not just like a woman! They send you signals, get you all het up, and then play hard-to-get."

"Hollis, I don't send signals. I am as direct as a punch in the nose. I am not looking for a boyfriend, I am not attracted to you. Is that plain enough? All I want is to get that paint mixed."

He went away mumbling. ". . . body language . . . dancing the other night . . . tease a guy . . . fun and games . . ." Wrenching off the top of a can he punched into it some dabs of pigment concentrate and set it in the shaker. When he brought it back to the cash register he was still furious. "Twenty-seven dollars and forty-nine cents."

Cass dug out a twenty and a ten from her wallet.

"So we're still on for tomorrow night?" He followed her to the door.

"No, Hollis. We didn't have a date, we don't have a date. We are not going steady, we are not a couple, we're not anything. Got that?"

Still dead-tired Cass could hardly keep from dragging her feet as she went up the back steps to the house. Ought to get busy and install those lights, ought to . . . Reluctantly she acknowledged the warning signs of exhaustion. Dumping the packages on the kitchen table she stumbled on into the bedroom. Kicking off her tennies, she fell across the bed fully clothed.

At least she was too tired to have dreams . . .

■ ■ ■ ■

THE NIGHTMARE

"Your turn." Gnf gnf gnf. His weight and his breath are gone. With terrible clarity her mind categorizes every throb of her torn body. Slick with sweat, she tries again to make the effort to move — just the least flicker of motion, to make some headway against the iron captivity of the chemical.

The hillbilly is whining now, a high thin voice, hard to make out what he's saying, just a whimper. ". . . All this dang rain, I ain't use — to cold weather. This-here is weird," he mutters, with horrifying understatement.

Barely made it to the bathroom. After wretching until her stomach began to cramp, Cass turned on the hot shower and stood there letting it stream off her, scalding. But not hot enough, she needed the inside of the kiln, the firebox itself. A clean way to die, especially if at the same time you create a thing of timeless beauty, there are worse fates.

She wished she could cry, just normally bawl her head off, get rid of the sadness. A thousand times she had prayed for it, but it wouldn't happen. Tired of the unhealing water she turned it off and went back into the bedroom. Digging down under her shorts she found the bottle of pills, shook one out. A sinister little capsule, it lay in her palm like a tiny fragmentation grenade ready to dissolve and hurl its time-release pellets through her body.

Bring it on.

18

She was running, she was late, the bell was ringing for assembly — Cass came awake. Telephone. Barefoot, she stumbled down the hall, wincing at the flood of sunshine that greeted her in the kitchen.

"H'lo."

"Where are you?" A small wounded voice.

"Jessie! Uh — I'm sorry —" The chicken clock showed eighty-thirty. "I — uh — my alarm didn't go off. I'll be there in twenty minutes."

"It's okay." The patience of a child for a flawed adult. "Go on and eat your breakfast. I'll wait."

"Soon as possible." She hung up and collapsed onto a chair, trying to get oriented. After the nightmare . . . she remembered now, she had taken a pill. It must have knocked her out, stolen eighteen hours of her life. As she went back to her room and pulled on some clothes, Cass felt a dull resentment — toward everybody. The doctor and his brain-numbing remedy, the Sheriff for not calling off this morning's ride. Sore at Hollis, for initiating body contact and evoking ugly memories, sore at Guy Magee and his dilettantes, sore at the entire town of Panhandle, Colorado.

Cramming down a Danish and drinking half-heated leftover coffee, Cass laced up her desert boots. They weren't going to help much to protect her shins from the stirrups. She'd ridden enough to know that. Horses, she actually liked, at the right time and place. This wasn't it. Full of a nameless misgiving she hurried on out to the truck, locking the door, forget the scrap of bark this time, *anybody wants to go in and put poison in my toothpaste, be my guest.*

Some sixth sense told her the area was clear of menace right now. Which meant the danger was somewhere else, like out on that open range maybe. All the way to the Rocking R she tried to formulate a good reason to convince Jessie why they shouldn't go riding today. Old war injury acting up, coming down with the flu, expecting an important phone call, *and my great aunt Nellie just died.* You can't fool a smart kid like that one. So accept it, do the best you can to insure her safety, keep a distance away from her, watch the back trail, stick with other people.

The Rocking R was a rambling spread of barns and corrals arranged around a large adobe ranch house. An old-fashioned covered wooden porch spread across the front, while in back two long arms, recently added, must be tourist accommodations. A separate building with a branding-iron insignia was labeled "The Bunkhouse", obviously home to the hired help. The stable yard was hustling with them, husky young men over-dressed in colorful apparel, checkered shirts, chaps and big clean Stetsons, risking hernias to get the over-weight tourist ladies onto the backs of the fatalistic nags, obviously chosen for their sturdiness. Jessie was like a slender sprite in that crowd, helping adjust stirrups, sweet-talking the horses. When she saw Cass she came over in a rush, her grave little face alight with welcome.

"I'm sorry I'm late . . ."

"It's okay. Really. I thought we could get out ahead of these people, but they'll be gone in a minute and anyway they aren't going where we are."

Bad news. "I don't mind riding with others," Cass protested weakly.

"Well, I do. They just plod along the trail out to the picnic area, get some hotdogs and beer and come back again. It's a drag. Anyhow, I'm going to show you where there's some great clay. We're going to Poker Flats." All the time leading the way to a couple of horses parked at a hitching post to one side. "This one's name is Mehitabel — here, you want to give her this." She handed over a carrot, which Cass passed on to the mare, who chomped it cynically.

That horse knows I haven't ridden in years. Sympathetically, she muttered into the hairy ear, "Just remember, things could be worse. I only weigh a hundred and seven pounds. But I can still handle you old girl, and if you try to step on my foot again I will plant my knee in your ribs."

Jessie was cinching a saddle on a lovely little sorrel filly who seemed delighted. Nibbling her elbow, the darned horse was practically grinning. Everyone was watching the two of them. Cass focused on Boyd Ruger, the massive man who had slapped Freddie Foreman in the chops that night at Gollager's. He stood deep in the shadows of the barn, thumbs hooked into his tooled leather belt on either side of a heavy silver buckle — the stance of a man who owns things.

A ranch hand had come to help Cass into the saddle, rangy prototype of a westerner, red kerchief, ten-gallon hat, probably drove a taxi in Denver in the wintertime. As he guided her foot to the stirrup he was parroting his spiel. "Do y'all know how to run one of these thangs? It steers right and left with them leathers in your hand, and it's got two speeds: slow and stop."

"Thank you. I think I can manage that. And I'll be very careful with her — she must be Mr. Ruger's favorite horse, the way he's staring at me. Does he think I'm going to get lost?"

The kid broke into a genuine grin. "Not a chance. Old Mehitabel is like one of them stud-finders with a little magnet, always points where the ranch is. If you do git confused you just let her go and she'll head straight on back here. Besides, Jessie knows these parts like an Injun. Y'all have a good ride." He went to open the gate to the corral.

Cass turned her mount to follow the string of dudes trailing off in a ragged conga line headed east across the open prairie, shepherded by two stalwart riders in full regalia, fringed gauntlets and flourishing mustachios.

"We're going this way." Politely Jessie took charge of her bridle, turned the mare down a different path along an arroyo heading west.

Cass followed obediently, trying not to look worried as she scanned the landscape around for signs of disaster. Leaving the flat land behind, they were almost at once in broken country, little gullies, arroyos, plenty of hiding places for sharp-shooters. She let Jessie get well ahead, leading the way through the maze of dips and dry gulches. Arid land, it was overgrown with brush, manzanita, grease-wood, shoulder-high sage, as wild as it was in the days of the mountain man. Cass reached back to ease the knife in its scabbard, ready for a quick draw at a second's notice. The whole scene felt wrong, her senses were vibrating with premonition.

And yet it was a beautiful day. The sky as pure as white quartz, not a cloud anywhere, the air so clean you could drink it like spring water. The sun scorched her face, she could feel it on her scalp under its short crop of pale hair. *So grow already.* She was tired of the Fuller-brush look.

Now Jessie — there was hair. The dark mass around her shoulders lifted gracefully with every stride of her loping horse, while her small butt held the saddle as if she were born in it. As they crested a ridge, Cass glanced back; the ranch was only a small cluster of packing crates almost lost in the gray prairie. Its very isolation reinforced a question she had wondered over: What on earth had made Boyd Ruger pick Panhandle, Colorado for his dude ranch? It wasn't part of any historical area that would draw the tourist. It wasn't even all that scenic. To the west the Sangre de Cristos lay distant and unreal under the bright fall of sunlight. To the south the headland behind Trinidad was handsome enough and the small town vaguely picturesque. It had once been a stop on the Santa Fe Trail, but only until the traders had found an easier way around Raton Pass. If you knew where to look the old wheel ruts still showed in places, but not as significantly as they did farther south in New Mexico. So what would make a wealthy Texan pick this spot for an investment?

Town fathers probably offered him incentives. She had learned that the town actually did have a Chamber of Commerce and must have hired a publicist, because she'd heard there was a highway sign out on the interstate that touted the advantages of the reinvented cow-town. The Bank must have floated a few loans to the new businesses, the eateries, but why? Why Panhandle when there are dozens of dying villages across the west that the superhighways have by-passed, left to starve and ghost out in the best American tradition.

Maybe the town fathers even subsidized Guy Magee to start his art colony; Cass hated the idea that the seed money came with a marriage license. She thought of them out there lolling around their easels, infatuated with their own egos, talking languidly about the significance of migrating geese. Cass pictured a ribbon of honkers driving down the sky with their powerful wing strokes and thrusting necks, uttering fierce cries of fellowship. To reduce such magnificence to a couple of mechanical lines — that takes utter insensitivity along with a lot of arrogance. *Guy, I could brain you for importing those charlatans into this clean country!*

Ahead, Jessie and horse disappeared down into a deep ravine. When Cass caught up, the girl was dismounted, scanning the rocky bottom. "I thought there might be some clay here," she called. Sounds traveled so clearly in the thin dry air. From the distance came the toot of an air horn, grinding of gears on a semi, somewhere over south. And yet she didn't think they were that near the interstate.

As she rode down to join the kid, she said, "Is that I-25 I hear in the distance?"

"Uh-uh. That's US 50 from Trinidad to LaJunta. It follows the Purgatoire. Is this an agate?"

Cass shook her head. "Feldspar. Actually this isn't a very likely place for clay, either."

"I know." Jessie's grin did marvelous things to her primitive little face. "I just stopped so you could stretch. An hour on Mehitabel sort of bends your legs in a curve. I know, I used to ride her."

Cass swung down, hoping she could get back on again. It did feel good to walk around. "Aren't you afraid your horse will wander off?" The sorrel filly was grazing the buffalo grass, trailing reins.

Jessie shook her head. "Glinda won't go more than a few feet. All Mr. Ruger's horses are trained to stand ground-tied."

"Glinda — that rings a bell."

"Sure, you remember, the beautiful witch in the Wizard of Oz, the one with the red hair?"

"Glinda, the Good. Of course." Billy Burke, with her sweet smile. "Well named. She's a lovely animal."

Alight with pride, Jessie nodded. "I bought her with my own money I earned helping out at the ranch. I worked there every day last summer, giving them oats and rubbing them down. I can shovel manure too."

That scrap of a kid? Cass began to feel good in spite of herself. It was exactly what she would have done at that age. Now, of course — "Mehitabel is another kettle of glue," she said. *Do this diplomatically, even if you have to feign fatigue.* "I don't think we should go too much farther today or I'll really be bent out of shape tomorrow. Anyway, this rock around us isn't decomposing all that fast. For a good alluvial deposit you need an old dry lake bed or a delta below a prehistoric river."

Jessie was nodding. "That's what it's like where we're going. People call it 'Poker Flats,' and it gets slippery when it's wet. It's not too far now, if you think you can make it?"

As Cass clambered back onto the mare she felt a small hand give her a boost in the seat of her jeans at exactly the right moment. "Here, this just dropped off your belt." She handed over the rock hammer.

"Thanks. I bent the clasp the other day — thought I had fixed it, but I guess not. I would hate to lose it, it's my favorite tool." Cass dropped it down the back of her shirt, remembering another beautiful day and a man with a gun.

"That's a good place to carry things, like a knife," Jessie remarked innocently.

"How'd you know about that?"

"Charmian Smith at the library. She saw that thong around your neck, she said that's how everybody carries their knives in Florida. She comes from Miami."

"Ye-e-eah. I do carry my Swiss Army knife back there, it gets too bulky for my pocket with all those attachments." *You're explaining too much. Shut up.* "Of course, the rock hammer is kind of lumpy if you lean back on anything."

"You ought to get one of those fanny-packs with the zipper and wrap it around your . . ."

"Shh!" A sharp sound had cracked the lazy morning air ahead.

"I heard it too," Jessie said. "Some nerd probably shooting at the poor little jackrabbits."

"Too heavy caliber for a bunny-gun." There had been no whispers of air nearby, but there was the scent of disaster on the wind. The echo of remembered words: *Bring your slingshot. . . .*

And it all fell into place. Cass understood his thinking, his plan. In a shudder, she spoke harshly: "Don't move." Then seeing the child's eyes widen she softened her tone.

"The trouble with hunters is, they don't realize that a rifle bullet can carry a couple of miles. So here's what I want you to do: I want you to ride back to the ranch as fast as you can. I'm going to scout ahead, and then I will follow you. If I don't get there within ten minutes after you do, tell Mr. Ruger there's trouble out here, he needs to send a posse. I think he'll know what to do."

"But you might get lost."

"Mehitabel won't. Jessie, that wasn't a request, that was from God's lips to your ears. Now scoot."

"You think it was another sniper like the last time?"

"I don't know. Please do what I say, go back and keep your head down." *While I make sure the shooter concentrates on me, which means I'd better be moving fast.* As she put Mehitabel at the steep slope out of the ravine the old mare balked and Cass lost patience. "Yah!" With the long end of the reins she gave the horse a hard cut across the rump that sent her clawing up the embankment as if the Devil were on her tail. Aware that Jessie was standing, wide-eyed, Cass slammed both heels into the old nag's sides and put her into a lumbering gallop across the rough prairie. One more slice with the reins, but she was getting all the speed the mare had. Cass muttered an obscenity under her breath. She had a growing fear that she wasn't moving fast enough.

Pike, you idiot!, I know just what you thought: That this is your country, that you should be able to scout it, intercept any imported hit man, make the place safe for us to ride. So you went out ahead of us, hoping you could nail him. Looked good on the blackboard, only you didn't think, if it went sour, what happens to us? Damnation!

19

Cursing under her breath, Cass straightened in the saddle. From far off to the south she heard the high rasping whine of a dirt bike, going away. Another mistake the Sheriff had made, figuring a person had to use a horse to get around the range. The truth is, by now the horse is an anachronism.

At that point her personal anachronism pricked its ears and trumpeted a long, welcoming whinny. Up ahead a bald-faced pinto came fidgeting toward them along a tufted crest in the desert. Saddled but riderless, trailing loose reins, it broke into a trot with another panicky whicker, rolling its mismatched eyes, one brown, one blue.

"Chill out," Cass instructed it. "Show us where you left your boss, huh?"

And then she topped the ridge and saw ahead a broad expanse of dry mud that had to be the bed of an ancient lake. Poker Flats. It might even hold some pockets of alluvial deposit, but right now its main offering was a lump out there in the brush, something that looked very much like a human body. With fear cramping her gut, Cass goaded Mehitabel out into the basin at a gallop, the pinto trailing behind.

From a hundred yards away she knew it was Pike. He lay on his back, arms outflung, sturdy legs sprawled, motionless. Sliding down from the saddle, she snarled at the two horses. "You stay put!"

Crouching beside him she found a pulse, thin and thready. There was a bad lump on the side of his head, probably received when he fell off the horse, knocked out of the saddle by a bullet. There was a hole in his leather jacket, not much blood. She opened his clothes and discovered that there was no exit wound, just an ugly swelling where the lead had struck a rib and traveled to his right side. It must have been a very long shot, the nearest rim to the south was a mile away, so the bullet was almost spent when it took him down. The real danger was the head blow. That swelling was a doozy, but better than a soft depression any day. Cass thumbed back his eyelids, no uneven dilation. Right now the problem was shock. Skin was clammy, color poor.

Going to the pinto, which had quieted

next to Mehitabel, she yanked its saddle and brought it over to prop Pike's feet on it. The saddle blanket was heavy wool; unfolded it was wide enough to cover his torso from shoulders to knees. Hunkering beside him, she chafed his wrists, trying not to jitter. A fallen man, all that drive and energy short-circuited — you want to pluck at him, *wake up, wake up!*

To compound her worries Cass heard oncoming hoof-beats and glanced over her shoulder to see a streak of coppery horse, with black-haired rider, tearing across the lake bed at a dead run. *I will never make an authority figure.* As Jessie pulled the filly to a sliding stop, she threw herself out of the saddle and came running with an inarticulate screech of pure anguish.

"No! Don't touch him! I mean it." Cass intercepted her. "I don't know the extent of his injuries. He's been shot, he has a concussion and he's in shock. He may be bleeding internally. We do not move him. *We leave him alone! Jessie, hear me!*"

"But we've got to — I mean why don't you — we can't just stand here!" The girl's face was paper white. "Do something!"

"You're the one who's got to do something. You should have been on your way to the ranch by now. The sooner you start back the better."

Jessie began to shake that wild hair.

"Or," Cass went on coldly, "I could go. I would be slower, of course, I don't know the country. Meanwhile you would have to restrain your father if he started to thrash around. If he stops breathing you'd have to administer CPR. I assume you know how?"

"All right, I get the message." Fists clenched.

"Take Pike's horse, your filly is spent. Leave me your canteen. When you get to the ranch tell Ruger we will need a paramedic unit here before we move him." She could picture the bully-boy Texan sending some ranch hands to lug Pike home over the rump of a horse.

"There's a rescue helicopter at the hospital in Trinidad." Jessie was getting herself under control. Cass's admiration took a leap. Tears were running down the kid's cheeks, but her hands didn't falter as she pulled the saddle off the heaving sorrel and cinched it onto the pinto. "I've got some lunch here." She dug into her saddlebags and brought a packet over, chin quivering. "He isn't going to —"

"Not if I can help it. Now, it's important for you to move fast, but don't take silly chances. You've got to *get* there. In one piece."

"Don't worry. I will." Squaring her small shoulder blades, the girl swung up on the pinto. She made a spindly figure galloping back across the dusty lake bed, but she had the horse under control.

When they had disappeared over the ridge again Cass returned to Webster. His skin was still cool, but the sun was beating straight down, warming the air. She looked at her watch: 12:24. Take an hour for the kid to make it to the ranch, another hour to get the rescue party organized, expect help around three o'clock. At the earliest.

Meanwhile the unseen biker might still be clod-hopping around out there, maybe take a notion to come back and investigate? It occurred to Cass that Pike wouldn't have ridden out without carrying a gun himself. She got up and began to circle. Fifteen feet away in a clump of rabbit bush she found a rifle, 30.06 with a scope, rancher's gun, old-fashioned, but efficient. She sniffed it — unfired. The Sheriff never had a chance to shoot back at his enemy.

When she returned to his side, his eyes were ajar. Crouching again she spoke slowly, firmly. "Lie still, Pike. Don't move. Help is on the way."

As through a fog, he recognized her. "Bunny?"

"It's me." She held up two fingers. "How many?"

". . . y'believe six?" He tried to turn his head, but she laid a restraining hand on his brow.

"Better not do that yet."

"What . . . hell . . . happened?"

"You were shot."

He processed that, began to look panicky. "I can't feel anything."

It sent a new qualm over her. "Try your fingers." Lifting the saddle blanket, she saw them twitch. "Good. Your feet?" The boots gave a small shrug. She breathed again. "I think it's just shock deadening your body. Take my word, you do have a hole in your side. Here, you want some water?" She held the canteen for him to drink.

Abruptly his eyes flared with new awareness. "Pony!"

"She's fine. Gone back to the ranch for help."

"No. Not alone . . ."

"It was a judgment call, whether she would be safer on the move or here at ground zero. Besides, I heard your attacker leaving in the opposite direction. On a motorbike. Stay with me, Pike!" He had closed his eyes. *Concussions, you're supposed to keep the patient awake.* She took his hand and tugged on it.

With an effort he rallied. "Listen . . ."

"I am. I'm keeping a sharp ear out in case the guy comes back. I don't really think he will, but I have your rifle here."

"Listen, I did a dumb thing . . . came out here, thought I would just make sure . . . scope out any suspicious characters as they arrived, y'know . . . didn't figure they'd be ahead of me."

"I know. I'd give plenty to learn how they found out where we were going."

"My fault. I never dreamed I couldn't . . . anyway, you were right, they're big-time and I'm just a small-town cop. I shouldn't have let Pony come along . . ."

"I tried to tell you."

"Hard . . . hard for me to take advice from somebody who couldn't do compound fractions." He slid back into a hazy stupor, blinking, drifting, while Cass paid deadly attention to the sighing of the wind. To small birds fluttering up from a clump of bush over on the bank. To the rattle of pebbles when a small varmint scuttled into its hole. Time seemed to stand still under the brass dome of the sky.

At some point she ate a cheese sandwich

and finished off one canteen of water. Gave Pike a few more sips from the other, but he was hardly aware. All she could do was sit at his side and hold tight to his hand.

Something about that simple contact took her back to another time — the comfort she had always felt when Ian would hold her. During the pitch dark of night his hand would find hers under the blankets, he guessed when she needed that firm grip. She remembered one morning, she had wakened to find his side of the bed empty. He was standing at the window of their garret, five stories high, looking out across the rooftops of Dresden. The newly risen sun was golden on his naked body, beautiful muscles, long limbs, and above, his homely boyish face under its thatch of uncut hair. As if Michelangelo had sculpted him, then got interrupted at the last minute. She put her head down on her knees and finally wept, the hard hot tears of loss, of helpless grief. Once they got started they wouldn't stop.

At one point she thought Pike's fingers tightened on hers, but his eyes were still closed under the shade of the ranger hat which she had propped across his forehead. He seemed to be breathing a fraction more easily — or was that wishful thinking? Wiping her eyes with the back of her hand, she looked at her watch. It was almost four o'clock. And then she heard the ugly whomp of a chopper, coming in fast and low.

The last long arrows of sunlight were shooting the gaps in the distant ramparts of the Sangre de Cristos, sending shadows far across the darkening land, as the two rode back together. Up-hill and down, Jessie ahead of her was etched in gold one minute, the next just a shadowy figure in the dusk. Sagging a little, but there hadn't been a hint of complaint.

Oh Pike, I wish you could see her, the way she copes.

She had come back with the rescue chopper, directing the parameds to the spot where her father lay, then stood by and watched them cart him off, the big red-and-yellow bird tilting away toward Trinidad. After it was gone, she had grimly taken over the chore of getting Cass back to the ranch along a rough short cut across the prairies, all in silence and dread.

They could see the outbuildings ahead. It was time to talk — Cass gave Mehitabel a boot. She moved well now that she could smell the stable. "Jessie, we need to discuss a few things. I hate to lay any more burden on you." *Especially since the truth will make you hate me.* "But you need to know what went on here today."

"Oh, I know. It's like two weeks ago, that man who had the accident out on the prairie, he was trying to shoot you. You were lucky he fell on his head. Dad put it in his log. So now another gunman came back to do it again. Except my father was out there ahead of us to stand guard, and he got shot instead." There was lingering hostility.

Cass said, "You put things together very well. I guess I never should have come home to Panhandle. I had some trouble over in France, I was working under cover to stop some terrorists —"

Jessie shot a swift glance. "Like nine-eleven?"

"Yes."

"I didn't know there were Arabs in France."

"These aren't Arabs. There are cells all over Europe, some of them neo-Nazis, some of them just plain old anarchists who want to bring down the United States because it's a super power. Some of them have it in for me, they found out where I live. I did tell your father I thought we should call this ride off — we were too vulnerable out here in the open. But he figured he could keep us safe. He doesn't know how evil they are, or how clever."

"So that's why he rushed off so early this morning. I had to ride to the stable on my bicycle."

"What's important now is, do you remember telling anybody where we were going? Poker Flats?"

She thought for a minute. "I told Charmian, at the library. And Izzie, I met her in the Post Office and she said she wondered how you were doing, you never call her. I didn't tell too many people, because I wasn't sure you'd really want to go today. Especially when you didn't show up —"

"I had a very bad night and took a sleeping pill and slept through the alarm, and that's the truth," Cass said. "I am very sorry." She could remember being stood-up by adults at that age. "Listen, do you have a friend you can bunk with tonight?"

"I guess." The body language was total gloom. "I wish I could go to Trinidad. I wish I could be there, but —"

So let's do this right. Make up a little for the debacle. "Your father would prefer that you stay safe in Panhandle," she said. "But I understand how you feel and I'm going to Trinidad myself. Not going home first, not going to tell anybody, I just intend to aim straight for the Interstate. There are no guarantees that the sniper won't be waiting out there somewhere. But my truck is pretty fast, I intend to make a run for it. You can come if you want to take the risk." *And just pray that I can deliver you to your father intact and healthy.*

For an instant disbelief rendered Jessie speechless. Then she came fully to life in one deep breath. "I can show you a shortcut, if your truck has four-wheel drive."

"Good. Let's don't mention it around the stable, either." They were riding into the yards now, deep in twilight. Ruger was waiting, looking relieved.

It took some fast talk, but Cass convinced him that she was the best one to take care of the child's welfare — long-time friends, knew that's what the father would want, so forth. The Texan looked unhappy about it, but Jessie seconded the motion. "We'll be okay, Boyd."

Minutes after they had passed beneath the wrought-iron gates of the Rocking R, Jessie had pointed out a dirt road that was little more than a double track through the sagebrush. With the truck's lights on dim and the rifle lying across the back of the seat, Cass felt marginally safe. Better than back in Panhandle. Wherever they were hiding, they would know by now that Webster was out of play. He was all the guardian she'd had. By now they might have a whole wet squad waiting at her house. Still couldn't figure out *why.* But it wasn't going to get solved right now. She paid close attention to the lumpy back road as they crawled the fifteen miles to Trinidad. When she saw the headlights of the interstate ahead it was close to nine o'clock.

Above them, silvered by the moonlight, stood the high thrust of rimrock that was the area's landmark. This stretch of country had seen a lot of history, the Trail, then headquarters for King Coal back at the turn of the century, scene of bloody combat in the union troubles. Now Trinidad slept with uneasy dreams and a fading economy a good mile off the stream of life's traffic.

Stacked streets were ranked along the slope of the headland; the motel had scratched a flat spot out of the sidehill. Behind it was a steep rise of native rock. Cass was satisfied. Nobody above could look into your windows, there was no angle from which a long-distance shot could come and ruin your day. The truck could be parked within a couple of feet of the door, which had an inner latch and chain. The windows were security-barred. As good a place as any to hole up until morning.

She had called from a pay phone on the edge of town and found the hospital closed to visitors for the night. Report on Sheriff Webster was that he was resting comfortably. She doubted that. She left a message for the nurse, to reassure him that his daughter was safe and in good hands.

Liar! She scorned herself as she glanced at Jessie sacked out cold in the bed at the far side of the room. Down deep under those layers of hard sleep she would be refueling her depleted energies. Kids beat back fast. She had tied into a hamburger with good appetite, something Cass envied her. One more chore to do. She picked up the phone and spoke into it softly.

"Sandy?" Liz bellowed happily. "Well I was about to git worried over you. Where are you at?"

"I'm in Pueblo. Brought Jessie Webster along with me."

"Oh that's good. We heard how Web got hisself shot. Couldn't believe it. How bad is he?"

"He'll do. The bullet hit a rib and lodged there, they got it out easily. But he had a concussion after he fell off the horse, so they'll keep him for a day or two."

"I swear, I don't know what the world's

come to . . .”

Cass let her rave. At least now the FBI wouldn’t raise a fuss all over Panhandle, looking for the little girl. Or her.

“. . . missed the fight out at Gollager’s. Ten big busters near broke the place up, Mae had to foam ’em with the fire extinguisher. Good thing you wasn’t around for your date with Hollis.”

“I didn’t have a date with him.”

“Well, he thought you did. Come over and pounded on your door like a loony. I told him to cut it out, if you wasn’t home it was none of his business. Talk about mad, he footed it off down the street like he was looking for somebody to kick. Well, you take care of the child. I’ll call Charmian, she’s been trying to find Jessie. Where can she get a-hold of you?”

“Uh — she can’t. I’m at a payphone. Thanks a heap, talk to you later, Liz.” And she rang off before she had to start spinning really big lies.

Now, finally, Cass sagged onto the bed, but not to sleep. This was no time to let up, with danger coming at you from unexpected directions. She needed to think. Closed her eyes . . . just for a minute . . .

20

A hand was shaking her gently but firmly . . . "Sandy? It's eight o'clock. Can we go see Daddy?"

"Huh?" *Went to sleep, I went to sleep. Never did that before on a stakeout.* "I'm up."

At the hospital they had to battle assorted little tin gods. The rules classified young women of eleven as children. Cass had to explain firmly, even menacingly, why Jessie was to be allowed to see her father. Then had a few misgivings of her own as they went into the room.

Nobody ever radiates health in a hospital gown. Pea-green cotton, rough-dried, tied at the back like a bib — you'd think they could make at least a gesture toward dignity. Pike lay there looking embarrassed and helpless, but better. His color was almost normal. Unshaven, with the tousled hair falling across his forehead, he seemed younger. Or maybe it was the unguarded fondness.

"Come here, Pony." He held out the left hand and she lurched toward him fearfully, going to cover in the shelter of his arm, breaking into sudden harsh gulping sobs. Cass backed out of the room quickly, leaving them alone. *Which is why hospitals don't allow children.* She went on downstairs in search of something to eat.

As she sat in the cafeteria munching a cardboard English muffin, she tried to remember what it was like to be eleven years old. She called up a snapshot of her father taking her down along the bank of the Purgatoire, baiting a hook with a horrible grasshopper. They hadn't caught any fish, but it didn't matter to Tom Butterfield. The serenity of the day would have been enough. A man of peace, he wouldn't be happy to know his daughter had imported danger into his quiet little town.

And she really wouldn't mind moving on. It had been there at the back of her mind since the beginning, even if it meant to change battlegrounds, to fight on unfamiliar territory where she had no friends. That didn't matter if it brought safety for one child and damaged dad. How to do it efficiently, though? Put the house up for sale? Better still, leave the house. Just vanish. Go get the extra passports and book a flight to anywhere, several anywheres, South America, Indonesia, Boston, Massachusetts, confuse the trail. Then sell the truck, take a bus to somewhere else, maybe buy an RV, hide out in the campgrounds of the northwest. Go on clear to Alaska . . .

She was just getting acclimated to a lot of snow when she saw Jessie coming. A bit puffy, but self-sufficient again. "My father wants to talk to you. I'm going to get some breakfast."

"Good idea. Orange juice, some eggs, oatmeal. We didn't eat much yesterday, you'll need all the protein and carbs and electrolytes you can chug down." Trouble is, no amount of nutrition is going to flush away the shakes, not for a day or two.

Back upstairs she paused outside Webster's door, bracing for his hostility, then went in. After Jessie's visit he was noticeably paler, skin looked closer to the bone, as if he had lost weight overnight — which he probably had. Motioning toward the visitor's chair he said, "Sit down, Bunny, we've got some things to discuss."

"Listen, Pike, I'm sorry. About everything. I should have called off the ride and told her exactly why she better not hang around me."

He held up a hand briefly and let it fall. "I'm the one owes you an apology. And a lot of gratitude."

"What on earth for? Almost getting you killed? Putting Jessie in danger? Turning Panhandle into a red zone? Hey, what more could I do?"

His lips twitched amid the dark stubble. Wearily he said, "You tried to warn me and I didn't listen. I didn't think it through. In fact you've done all you could to clarify the situation, almost got yourself knocked off several times, and I still couldn't quite take the thing seriously. I mean, stuff like this doesn't happen in our part of the world. I was sure if there was any danger I could head it off by getting out there first, chase the enemy off, or bust him. Then I go and pull a first-rate asininity."

"I don't follow."

"A thing any student of a gun-safety class knows not to do: I saw movement out there in the bush and I used my rifle's scope to try to locate it. It must have looked to the other guy as if I was aiming my gun at him. He thought he was in my sights and tried to shoot me first. I mean, how dumb could I get?"

"Well, maybe that wasn't too smart, but I'm the one who's responsible for all the trouble in the first place. I'm the catalyst for some sort of evil spell that's come over the town, which is why I intend to split. It ought to draw them away — they seem to have me under close surveillance. I'll try to do it right this time, lead them on and then drop out of sight. I think I can pull it off."

"No!" And then a flush came behind the tan in his face. "I'm sorry, it's not my decision to make, but I wish you wouldn't do it. I think I sort of need you. Like it or not, we're all part of the problem now. And if I act like a bear sometimes, I apologize. I do recognize a trained operative when I see one, you're good at your craft and I am a rank amateur when it comes to this kind of foul play. Of course you might be better off out of here, but I doubt it. They seem to be two steps ahead of the game. That shooter you took down with the slingshot — he'd been holed up in town for weeks before you ever got home. I checked the motel roster with Mae. He evidently told Harry — the realtor at Remax — told him he was interested in that vacant house and wanted to think about it, plan how to remodel it. After that, nobody paid him any attention. But he must have been staking out your place all that time. So somebody was expecting you to come home. Or — what I wonder is —

were they afraid you'd come home? Maybe discover something rotten going on in Panhandle? It dawned on me bit by bit: suppose your Flea Circus, for whatever reason, picked your home-town to set up a base of operations?"

Cass felt the wheels that had been slipping and slithering under her suddenly find traction.

He was going on. "I know, it sounds crazy, but if they did, you'd be a threat to them. You might recognize somebody, or just smell out the truth from past experience. I mean it would explain why the FBI is so interested. What I can't figure out is why on earth a band of German terrorists would suddenly choose Panhandle for a hideout?"

But by now she was getting her balance. A memory flashed across her mind, orienting her. All at once she knew how it had all happened and that there was no running away.

It had begun on a rainy day in Paris — how long ago? Two years or so. She had come to the city for another of those conferences. The strategy meetings had gone on for the best part of a week. She'd been center-front because her team had the highest success ratio of any of the cells. Now they were being given a tough one: find the double agent within the League, the traitor who was leaking information to the other side, the errant flea from the Flea Circus.

"Of course, one hopes it isn't you." That humorous remark had come from her control, the man whose code name was "Jacques." He had invited Cass back to his apartment afterward for some further brainstorming. Since she had come out of camp he had been her mentor, a man of great imagination and experience at the game of undercover work. He had helped her form a team, train them, give them direction. The person on earth she could rely on to help in a pinch, Jacques had saved her butt several times in those early days.

She had no idea of his real name. She had just assumed that, like many of the members of the League, he was a link to some international business group. They were the people most concerned with removing the terrorist threat that was spreading like a disease across the earth. It had become obvious that it couldn't be done by the governments of the various countries, who couldn't agree on the shape of the table at their grandiose "summit" meetings, much less sign onto new policies that would cut across national boundaries and establish over-riding laws to eliminate red tape. And so, in secrecy and common fury, the League was formed, a small band of grimly determined businessmen.

All identities were carefully cloaked. "Jacques" was the French equivalent of "John", a working code name that he had even used for the rental of this apartment in one of the new high rises on the outskirts of Paris. Beyond the wall of double-paned glass the city lay like a diorama out of history, the slate roofs of the old town studded with chimneys, the crooked streets overshadowed by leaning ancient walls and beyond it all, the square mass of the Arc de Triomphe and its companion edifice, the Eiffel Tower. Pretty as a postcard.

In the afternoon twilight the streets below were shining in the steady downpour that signaled springtime. Wind flapped the awnings of the deserted cafés and umbrellas made a bright counterpoint along the sidewalks. Jacques handed her a glass of cognac. He was a striking man, very Gallic features, large nose, dark passionate eyes, and an amplitude of horsy teeth.

"You are about to be of much value to us. Not just your skills but your provenance. It is obvious since the twin towers that the next focus of our enemies will be the United States. You are our most typical American."

His smile was pure French condescension. Couldn't help it, they are born with a certain arrogance. "So let us play a game of 'pretend'. Let's say you are a terrorist, the grand maréchal of fleas, running your insidious circus. Not an Arab menace, they will always follow their own leaders and fight their silly jihads, let the CIA agonize over them. But let's say you are a German. Suppose the neo-Nazis decided to bring down your great Republican government."

"They already have," she said. "Decided, I mean. All their plotting is in that direction." She could speak confidently because she had recently rolled up a cell of anarchists which was focused entirely on America. Their schemes had been in the theoretical stage, but their aims were massive disruption of a powerful country. "They talked about taking out the Golden Gate Bridge or blowing up the Super Bowl."

"Minor moments of chaos, yes."

"The Superbowl is not so minor to the people of my country."

"Of course. I understand. But if you are their Führer, these fleas, you dream of bigger conquests in the style of 'nine-eleven.' Multiple targets, assassinations, and for that you would need a staging ground closer to the scene of action, no? A permanent base of operations. Where would you set up such a thing? In the heart of Manhattan? In the wilds of Idaho?"

His French was soft and melodic. Her own was curt, she spoke it with a German accent, but was fluent enough to hold her own in an abstract discussion. They talked of the drawbacks of the big city, the professionalism of the modern police forces, the territorial imperative of the entrenched underworld toward any strangers. Not to mention the new militancy of the general population since the World Trade disaster, every citizen a do-it-yourself watchdog. Manhattan was especially suspicious, of course. And as for Idaho, it was the FBI's favorite hot spot, with its far-right enclaves and history of small mutinies.

"Perhaps, then, what you call 'Middle America'?" he suggested. "St. Louis, or Kansas City, one of those innocent prairie towns."

She smiled a little at that. "They don't think of themselves as hicks," she advised him. "Those cities have a tightly knit system of political and social interaction and a population that's as alert to anything phony as a bunch of guard dogs that smells a thief. I lived in Minneapolis and I can tell you, if some little bunch of Fascists tried to set up operations there, they would have city inspectors looking over their shoulders, newspaper reporters asking questions, the hidden power brokers from City Hall investigating their credentials. There is nobody more suspicious than a grain-belt politician."

"Oh come, *ma petite,* you make out the United States as too *formidable.* They seem to me a singularly naïve people. The ruses, the 'scams' that have been perpetrated on them show a propensity for blind trusting that should make it easy for the clever elements of the Flea Circus to exploit."

"Not so blind any more, not in the big cities." She was pacing up and down in her socks, wet boots parked near the door so as not to mar the thick gray carpeting. The room was a study in grays and whites, obviously "done" by some decorator. It didn't really look like Jacques, who was flamboyant in a carmine silk dressing gown and rose-colored foulard. She was flattered that he would ask her to brainstorm with him.

"For a permanent base they would choose a venue they could control." She went on. "An example of how it's done is happening right now in parts of the deep South. Places where the far-right fringe doesn't try to disappear behind the scenery — they become an important part of it. They excite a perverted patriotism in the small towns and manipulate it at will. But you'd have to be a genuine southerner to understand their history, especially the Civil War. I don't think outsiders could ever become legitimate."

"It's no wonder" — lolling on the sectional couch Jacques was watching her journey around the room — "that you never put on an ounce of weight. Can't you settle down, *chéri?* Tell me about this 'legitimate.' I know only the parental aspects of the word."

I'll bet you do, Cass thought, *you probably have sired numerous offspring, of both sorts.* "I mean legitimate in terms of respectability. In the U.S. the standards vary. The Old South relies on heritage. But in a small town out west, it would be a matter of money. You pick a community that is nearly bankrupt and throw cash at it, you quickly begin to make friends. Help rejuvenate the place, even open some small business, make all the right noises, you would soon be solid with the town fathers. After a taste of prosperity the natives would forget to ask questions about these newcomers. In fact they would welcome them to their bosom like the prodigal son."

"Do you think so?" Jacques shook his head. "It's a curious concept for me. Heritage I understand. In the Provençal village where I grew up people can trace their ancestors back a thousand years. No parvenu is ever trusted. But to project respectability on the basis of affluence — how very New World."

"There's nothing else to judge by in the American West. Sodbusters and prospectors and cattlemen have come and gone, leaving only ghost towns behind them, a few little county seats that are anemic for lack of any transfusion of capital. They're all outposts of conservatism, they have to be. They have knee-jerk reactions to buzzwords like 'national security' 'patriotism' 'freedom.' A clever front man coming into a little burg like my home town of Panhandle, Colorado, could dress his fleas in white hats and give them little flags to wear on their lapels and with enough capital on hand and a well-written script he could install his gang as pillars of the community and set up shop on Main Street."

Jacques was beginning nod. "First, he would pave Main Street." Then he added dreamily, "That's what my little hometown longs for — paved streets."

"Jobs are more important. Panhandle has always needed more steady work for its younger generation, to make them stick around, get married and have families. If you bolstered some new home-grown enterprises, lured in some of the larger franchises, you would have given them the bread of life. Then if you built them a new elementary school, they'd give you the keys to the courthouse. In a relatively short time you would have established the sort of presence that would remove you from all further suspicion. It would be simple to devise a cover that would permit outsiders to come and go without arousing any questions. You'd need that to bring in your cells of arsonists or bombers while you formulated plans, a staging area from which to send them out to do their ugly work, provide them with shelter afterward with nobody snooping around. There again your small town would be ideal, especially if the local law consists of one lone Sheriff. At least it did when I lived in Panhandle."

"This town, how long since you have been there?"

"Oh, ten years or so. By now it's probably a little closer to dying. It has no economic base."

"Could it be converted into a tourist town? That would be useful in terms of transient visitors."

"Sure. Why not? You could rig up some

attractions, a theme park, or maybe a super-grand hotel, with lots of trimmings, a golf course, and trail rides, maybe an exclusive health spa, I don't know. Have a regional rodeo, a cattle fair, an Indian powwow, anything that would get you listed on the AAA brochures. Shoot off enough fireworks on the Fourth of July and nobody would ever ask a question about all those incendiary bombs you have in your basement, or the jars of nerve gas on your pantry shelf. And after the big devastation, when the country would be red-hot on the trail of the terrorists, nobody on earth would ever think to look in a place like Panhandle, Colorado."

Webster had lain still and pale against the pillows, listening to her ramble on, analyzing, testing her hypothesis. "This fellow, Jacques? Could he be your 'mole'?"

Cass got up and went to the window, feeling sick at heart. "I don't know, I hate to think so. But it's beginning to look like it. Had to be somebody high up in rank. In the months that followed that conference my team and I dug into the heart of the League's membership. We began to find clues, financial anomalies. We had infiltrated some fringe outfits that provided new insight. We may have been getting close to discovering him, which is why he took us out, in a way that would discredit me and turn the focus away from him. It must have been a shock to him when I didn't die. Especially when I decided to return home. Because by then, if my hunch is right, he and his Flea Circus friends had followed my advice literally and become part of the Panhandle scenery. If so, right now they could be making plans for a massive terrorist attack on this country. That's why they would want to eliminate me fast, before I got suspicious."

The Chief stirred restlessly against the pillows. "It all makes sense. Which it didn't before."

"I'm sorry, Pike." Cass heaved the words out in a gulp of guilt. "If I inadvertently brought down this misery —"

"There's no time for second thoughts now." The words came out fiercely and he straightened in the bed. "The thing we have to do is cope with it. Not that I like keeping you here in the danger zone, but you've been trained in the mind-set of these people, and I haven't. I can offer you backup, as soon as I get free of this joint, but you're the one who can ferret these varmints out. If there are terrorists in our midst I intend to exterminate them before they take over my town."

If you're not already too late. But she didn't say it aloud.

21

Silence was a tangible thing. As she steered the old pickup over the bumpy back road, going home to Panhandle the hard way, Webster sat slouched, wincing occasionally as the vehicle hit a pothole, obviously still feeling that cracked rib, the banged up shoulder. Probably a king-sized headache.

Cass said, “Maybe we should have taken the highway.”

“No.” He stared out the window at the fields of prickly pear they were winding through. A lot of the pain in his eyes came from that leave-taking yesterday. But at least his Pony was safely on her way to the Big Rez.

Around noon her grandmother had appeared on the scene, an impassive Navajo woman of age and great dignity. Tall and still graceful in a flowing green velveteen skirt, a black satin blouse, squash-blossom necklace, she had given Pike a silent smile, black eyes proud. Her son, the sheriff. With age-old wisdom she was reconciled to danger, death, all part of the great experience. She had even telegraphed a message of good will toward Cass, a question. *You stand by him?*

The Chief had matched her stoicism, stony-faced and philosophical as she gathered Jessie to her, a mother of the earth and sky, walking in beauty, the Navajo Way. But once they were gone his façade had shown a few cracks.

"She'll be safe down there," he had muttered, to himself, to Cass. "Let's get going." But the doctors wanted to keep him one more night. In fact it had taken most of the next day to run their final tests until he was ready to walk out without their permission. It was afternoon by the time he climbed into the truck silently, not used to be driven by someone else.

He must be sitting there, loathing me. But saying "I'm sorry" can get tiresome. Doesn't help anyway . . .

"The Bank," he spoke abruptly.

"Excuse me?"

"That had to be their first move. I wondered why anybody would acquire a bank in a dying town. About two years ago some corporation bought the old Colorado National and set it up as The People's First Bank, with a whole new look, a drive-through window, an ATM out in front. They began to make loans, to encourage small businesses. I figured we just got lucky. I never thought to ask where the funds were coming from. Stupid. Nobody ever gives out money for nothing."

"I'd say they got some return on their investment. It wasn't a bad idea to try to revitalize a little town. How could you know?"

"I should have been suspicious when they began to finance things that no other bank would have touched. They gave Foreman the dough to expand his filling station, open that greasy-spoon his wife runs. They helped Anderson modernize his hardware store. I'm pretty sure they're a silent partner in Gollager's road house. I know they loaned him money to put in the motel. Organized a Chamber of Commerce that went to work on bringing in outside businesses, McDonald's, the new Payless, the record shop, the pizza place. I think they helped Guy Magee open his art store —"

"Izzie's Boutique?"

"No, she got that money when her father died. But it was the climate of prosperity that made a fashion shop possible."

"What about Guy's art colony? Did the bank help him buy the Hacienda?"

"No, he got that before the bank came in. He's owned the buildings for years. But it took some cash to fix it up. I think he married money. Not to be unkind to his wife, but you have to wonder why else did he pick that rock-hard woman? She was from New York, they ran in the same art crowd, Guy and Izzie and her friend Ilsa. He had a studio there where they all gathered. I think he hired Minka to decorate it and that's how they met. Got married one Christmas, if I recall, my memory's not so hot today." He lay back and closed his eyes, skin the color of uncooked bran bread.

He should have stayed in the hospital another day, Cass thought. Still dizzy now and limping, but his mind was on the move. As he sat there chewing his lip, frustration written in every rugged crease of his face, he looked the epitome of a stone-age warrior.

Cass almost began to take hope. When a man refuses to lie down and give up — "What do you know about Boyd Ruger?"

"Now him I did look into. I just couldn't swallow it, why a rich man would come to this part of the state to set up a dude ranch. When there are scenic vistas and lakes and fishing streams all over the place, to the west, to the north of here, he goes out to the middle of nowhere and buys a defunct cattle spread with falling-down bunkhouses, spends a fortune fixing it all up, advertising in the swankiest magazines. I figured he was up to some kind of con game. So I poked around. Found out he comes from a Texas family, richer than Uncle Sam, and just about as respected down there in the Lone Star State. He owns one of the biggest Ford/Lincoln/Mercury dealerships in the Southwest, plus ten thousand acres of rangeland, an antebellum mansion and a few oil wells. Everything about him checked out, so I finally just asked him: Why Panhandle? He laughed his big laugh and said it was done on a bet. He bet his brother he could come to a jerkwater town, buy a ruin of a place, and within a year create a thriving business out of nothing. Seems it was a sort of family tradition that he had to uphold. And I guess he did it — the dudes flock in, his place is always full. You have to make reservations a month ahead of time to 'bunk down' out there, as he calls it."

"Yeah, he's a little too western to be true. Did you notice the antennas on those outbuildings? Dish satellite and the tall aerial has to be short-wave. What does he need those for?"

"Says he's got business interests all over the globe, has to keep in touch. Communications, that's where it's at, he says. Family is well known, solid Democrats, old conservatives. Down in that country they'd hang a terrorist from the nearest cottonwood tree."

"So he didn't need financing. But everybody else is counting on the bank. What about that, who runs it?"

"Junior Smithson is president. You remember, Jed Smithson's boy, barely passed algebra, but he came back from college with an MBA and now he's in charge of our savings. I guess he's got accountants to help with the books, he just does the gladhanding. He's good at that. Does a lot of P.R. hustling in Pueblo, has a home up there and belongs to the country club. I can't picture him tying in with a bunch of killers, scare the boy out of his skin."

"Maybe not, but they could use him to cover the fact that the money is coming from questionable sources. And I'd bet that our enemy is hiding in plain sight in one of those new success stories that are rejuvenating the town. Only which one? Right now I'd pick Gollager's. Especially since that's where the sniper was staying."

Webster frowned over the idea. "Well, it may be true, but I can tell you that Rafe isn't just a figurehead. He makes good money on the place, I've seen their books. The motel isn't all that full, but they get their share of historical buffs, scouting out the Santa Fe Trail, or spillover weekenders from Denver, come down for the State Fair in Pueblo or the rodeo over in LaJunta. Big billboard out on the highway has a ten-foot tall cowboy playing a guitar. Eastern tourists go for that hokum."

Cass mulled the information. Had to take the Chief's word, he ought to know his town. "So we've got several possibilities where strangers could come and go without arousing suspicion. The dude ranch, the motel —"

"The trailer park next to Foreman's truck stop."

"How about the art colony? Does Guy check the backgrounds on the people who come there to paint?"

"I guess. At least they sign up for three-month 'semesters', live in the Hacienda itself, so you'd expect him to want credentials. He's got a lot of himself invested in that place."

"Plus his wife's money. Where on earth did he meet her?"

"I heard she ran some kind of studio in New York, taught silk-screen painting. Anyway, they couldn't be plotting anything without Guy knowing. Can you picture Magee making bombs?"

"Not really."

The dirt track was ending, there was gravel road ahead. They could see now the distant bawdy sign above Gollager's. "I'd say you're right — that's the place I'd start." Pike gave a prodigious yawn.

"It's just far enough out of town that you wouldn't notice any funny business going on. I mean you could store explosives, build a death machine out in the woodshed, who'd know?"

"Death machine?" He chuckled without humor. "God, what a life you must have led."

Yeah, I'm a barrel of laughs.

"Listen, when we get back to town, what are we going to do to keep you safe?" He seemed to rally to the effort of thinking about it.

"Don't worry. I'll take care of myself. I'm more worried about the rest of the town. The whole known world, for that matter. Who knows what they're planning?"

"Mmm." He sighed and yawned again. "What do you figure their target would be?

Something pretty big, to justify all the trouble they've gone to."

"Could be anything, anywhere. One thing we learned from nine-eleven," she said, "is that these dedicated terrorists are capable of long-range planning and a lot of patience. It took years of preparation to set up the attack on the World Trade Center. Now, I think they'll try something different, something in terms of those weapons of mass destruction. Germ warfare, nerve gas. Or maybe assassination . . . I don't know, what do you think would disrupt the whole country like the disaster on nine-eleven?"

When Pike didn't answer she glanced over. Head tipped back, mouth ajar, he was dead asleep as they rolled into the quiet outskirts of Panhandle.

22

A small frisson of fear, chilly as a draft of air when a window is open a crack somewhere — the feeling was familiar to Cass. She had lived with it for years. When you're stalking prey, you are always wary of making some small but lethal miscalculation. In early days she had actually enjoyed walking a tight rope.

Slightly less fun when you're the hunted. Of course, for the moment, in the broad light of morning with Liz and Joe looking on, she felt reasonably safe. Up on the ladder, she was happy for their presence on more than one count. This was an operation she wanted to be discussed, even broadcast. Let it telegraph to the opposition that she was not going to run. Wielding the screwdriver with authority she bolted the movement sensor to the eave over the back door. She had already mounted one out over the front porch. Their broad beams of light would flood the whole yard the minute anything or anyone set foot in it.

As she spliced the connections to the back porch lamp, Joe said, "I shore do hope you threw the circuit breaker first."

"If I hadn't" — she tightened a screw the last turn — "I would have fried a few fingers by now."

Liz kept frowning, unsatisfied. "I never knew you was so worried about skunks. We always got a few around, don't hurt nothing. Just leave 'em alone and they'll leave you alone."

"I have a kind of phobia, I guess," Cass fabricated as she worked. "Got sprayed once when I was very young and I remember being drenched in tomato juice, and still the odor hung on." No matter how lame the excuse was, let Liz repeat it. The opposition would be expecting some sort of protective measures. *Let them think this is my best effort.* She went to the circuit breaker and threw the switch; the spotlight blazed fiercely.

"Oh my lands!" Liz marveled, "you're gonna light up the whole neighborhood."

"So long as the skunks get the message and leave my trash pit alone."

Cass folded the ladder and they turned to leave. "We got to run to Trinidad," Liz explained. "Go see the doctor. He's got a new gadget that might help Joe, something called a nebulator."

Nebulizer. Cass smiled and waved them off. "I hope it works."

She puttered around, putting away tools, until the Chev rolled off down the street. Then got them out again. Now for the real mission. Glancing up and down the back yards she saw no one. At the circuit box she went to work on the flexible aluminum conduit that her father had installed, running it underground across the back yard to bring light to his work bench in the shed. With a jeweler's saw she sliced carefully through the tube and separated lips of the opening enough to pull a twist of wires out where she could see them. Snipping the red, she made a loop in the end of it and attached a wire of her own. Going back to the shed, she pulled out the switch plate and found the other end of the red, using the old wire to pull the new one through. It only took a few minutes to connect it to the gadget she'd bought at a hobby store in Trinidad, that day when she was waiting for Pike to recoup. It was a miniature signal, intended for an N-scale model train, a crossing guard with twin warning lights. She set it in the window of the shed, clamping it to the frame to keep it from falling over.

Done with that end of the installation, she went back and spliced the line to connect to the hinge on the back door. Finally, one more wire to a toggle switch that she mounted deep in the ivy that grew on the south wall of the bungalow, next to the spot where the truck was parked. Conduit repaired with duct tape, she turned the electricity back on. Going to the switch she flipped it to arm the system. Then carelessly walked up onto the porch, acting out for an unseen audience, and went on in the house. Turning quickly to peer out the rear kitchen window she felt a spurt of achievement. Over in the gloom of the shed two tiny pinpoints of light had appeared. Never see them if you didn't know where to look.

Cass shut off the switch and went back inside to sit at the kitchen table and pop a beer. Try to get inside the head of the enemy — what would he try next? But when you don't know exactly who the enemy is, it's frustrating. A deer at least can recognize the scent of the puma. Still in the grip of the quarry-mode she was vaguely aware of a rap at the front door. Her first impulse was not to answer it. She needed to concentrate harder, something she was missing, there had to be a clue . . . When the knock came again she got up wearily and went to peer out the slits in the front door. She was surprised, oddly glad, immediately self-conscious of her grungy jeans, grass-stained tennis shoes.

Izzie was band-box clean. As she ankled in on those incredible four-inch heels, wearing an A-line outfit of deep magenta with a tiny pink scarf at her throat, she looked ready for the fashion runway. In one gloved hand she dangled a large designer box on a satin ribbon.

"Don't you dare touch this until you've washed your hands."

"If I'd known you were coming I'd have taken a shower."

"I can wait."

Amused, Cass went off to the rear of the house, stripping clothes as she moved toward the bathroom. A quick dowsing sluiced off the surface grime, and it only took a minute to sling on a dressing gown of blue velveteen that she'd bought in New York on arrival, to get rid of the coarse sensation of all that hospital wear. She went back to the kitchen where Izzie was seated elegantly, an elbow on the oilcloth table, glancing around her with distaste.

"I loved your dad, but he must have had an abominable yellow fetish."

"I've already got replacement paint, give me time. Let's see, anybody dressed like a Paris fashion model would hardly stoop to drink beer. How about some tea?"

"Instant?"

"Bite your tongue! Earl Grey."

Izzie grinned, that pixy-crooked smile. "I should have known you would never get Liptonized. Even though your adventures have turned you into a master of disguise, from chimney sweep to" — looking at the gown with its embroidery — "porcelain shepherdess."

"I hate to disillusion you, but I'm really earthenware at heart."

"Stoneware, from what I hear." Izzie cocked her head, the piled-high black hair tilting. "The tales vary from Sandy-as-Curmudgeon Sandy-as–Florence Nightingale. People keep asking me to interpret. I tell them you're actually an undercover agent who is scoping out an international drug ring here in Panhandle. Got our sheriff shot in the process."

Tea . . . too hot . . . burned tongue . . . "The heroine of that event would be Jessie. She's the one who rode her horse back for help, got the chopper, directed them to the scene. All I did was sit valiantly at Pike's side and watch him concuss."

"And now the child has mysteriously disappeared . . ."

"No mystery. She went to spend some time with her grandmother down on the Big Rez. Pike's pretty protective, something like this sniper business spooks him. That's the second shooting in a month."

"And he was in on both. He's got a point, get the kid away from these awful killing grounds." Izzie's homely face twisted in a thoughtful grimace. "Such violence, for our little village. And all the hostilities started since you came home. Is there any significance in that, do you think?"

"I think a lot of people feel they can plug at our jack-rabbits without a license and don't know how far a bullet carries. Doesn't have much to do with me. I mind my own business."

"Speaking of which, how are the ceramics coming?"

"I'm still running tests. I'm trying to develop a good body. Glazes come later."

"And what will you do with it? If you don't mind my asking?"

"I am going to concentrate on throwing. The wheel is a challenge, you never create the same shape twice, which makes it interesting. Would you like to see?" Another way to confirm her legitimacy, Cass thought, as she led the way back to the work room. On a shelf stood four pieces she had thrown last evening when the doldrums threatened. They were diverse shapes, a flat dish, a couple of small bowls and a fairly nice jar. Eighteen inches tall, it was big enough to bring a spot of color to a room once it was glazed. The neck was small, the shoulder extra high, and the foot thin and simple. It knocked Izzie speechless.

"Cassandra, you are good!"

It seemed to create a new ease between them, as if uncertain identities had been overcome and pleasant ghosts of the past were free to return, shades of the two kids who used to belly up to the table and belt the hot cocoa after school.

Returning to the kitchen, Izzie looked around her. "Can't wait to see what you'll do with the décor. Maybe some patches of chartreuse, melon, and cranberry. Don't mind me, I've become a patchwork junkie." She spread her magenta skirts and stuck out one of the fire-engine red shoes. The stockings were black lace. "It started as a mechanism to get people talking about the shop. But now, it's as if I've turned into my own cubist caricature. I have to put on a persona before I'm brave enough to step out the door." Her dark eyes flared, a little startled at her own confession. "People do tend to forgive you if you baffle and amuse them." The words were touched with bitterness.

"I envy your panache," Cass said, "even if I kind of hate you for being so well-groomed at two in the afternoon."

"Oh, there's nothing to get me grungy, sitting around the shop waiting for rich benefactors to darken my door. I don't get quantities of sales, but the quality makes up for it. Three customers a week pay the food bill for a month. You, for instance, were a rib roast with baked potatoes and cherry pie."

"I hope I made good gravy. But — excuse my curiosity — doesn't that prime location on Lamar Street hit you pretty hard for rent?"

"We own the shop." She gave a cocky little bounce. "That's one of the reasons we have been able to survive. We have a very forgiving mortgage that allows us elbow room when we get temporarily short of pocket."

"How generous. For a bank, I mean."

"The People's Pride and Joy, they ought to call it." Izzie nodded happily. "It's been very good for this town. We were dead on our feet a few years ago, the business district was owned by some real estate outfit in

Cincinnati, Ohio. They didn't care who they closed down if the rent was overdue. Then all of a sudden for some reason a group of investors took an interest in our little burg. They bought out the bank, picked up the paper, stopped the foreclosures and even extended second mortgages to keep the town perking. We began to live again, people had jobs — it was like Panhandle had been blessed, for some unknown reason."

"Must be some powerhouse, this bunch that worked the miracles. Who's the President of the Bank now?"

"Oh, he's just a figurehead. Junior Smithson, you remember, he was a class behind us. Nerdy twit with bifocals, couldn't ever remember his irregular verbs in French? Anyway he knows his way around publicity, I guess, because he organized a Chamber of Commerce, got us a billboard out on the highway, talking about putting on our own rodeo next year. That was Boyd Ruger's idea, I think. Anyway, we're a real renaissance village. So what do you think, is it interesting enough to intrigue our Cassandra?"

She took a swallow of tea. "Actually" — no point keeping it a secret any more — "I had my name changed legally. It really is 'Cassandra.' Well-known bon-vivant and world traveler."

"Not all that 'bon,' though," Izzie observed thoughtfully. "Our returned native is trailing a few emotional tatters. What happened? Not just a bit of brain surgery?" Then she flushed. "I'm sorry. I didn't mean to invade your privacy. It's just that you get to be an expert on reading faces when you're in that — 'different' — category. I see in you a very good replica of a well-adjusted woman of the world, but I get the feeling that, like me, you put on a mask every morning. Beneath it you're probably the Phantom of the Opera."

"Just call me Dorry-Ann Gray."

Izzie snorted, snickered, and grew sober. "God, I've missed you. If only you had been here when I was going through the identity crisis. I mean, you always knew who you were. I had to work at it like a tough assignment, a sort of PhD dissertation with appendices on stupidity and embarrassment: 'Oh, so *that's* why I never wanted a man to touch me.' And '*that's* why I always enjoyed movies about women.' And then when it did become clear, all those wasted agonies of trying to keep the thing secret, deny it, forget it. If you had been here you would have hauled me out of the closet and said, 'Shut up and go for it!' "

Cass felt her breath catch somewhere in the region of her heart. Nicest thing anyone had said since she came home. For a person so tightly held to reveal so much — Clearing her throat she said, "But you found your way by yourself. That's better, isn't it?"

"Better? I don't know. I've developed pretty tough calluses. But it's hard on Ilsa. She's more vulnerable than I am. Which is why I am grateful that you've been nice to her. She can be a bit of a pill, poor darling, she's so insecure, and I talked about you too much. But she'll come around. You'll like her once she stops being jealous."

"I already do. As long as she makes you happy —"

"The word doesn't begin to cover it, but then words usually don't. The ones you need are so overworked. Have you ever been, as they say, in love?"

The idea was so alien to Cass it might have been framed in Swahili. "Well, there were a few very compatible interludes, of course."

"Sex. I'm not talking about that, with all its unwritten rules and time-outs and errors. Scoring is so important and the fouls so devastating. But love," she rushed on feverishly, "is simple. It just means that you would donate all your blood to somebody else if they needed it. Without even thinking twice." Abruptly she shoved back from the table. "Enough of that. You have a box to open. I'm always on the lookout for my special customers, anything out of the ordinary." Leading the way back to the living room, she picked up the package and presented it with a flourish. "This just came in and I thought of you at once."

A stole of natural cashmere, it was like holding a handful of ducklings. Cass buried her face in its softness. "It's gorgeous. I'll take it."

"That's what I like about you. You never ask the price. Germany must have been knee-deep in Deutschemarks."

The League had always recompensed its agents well. "I got lucky in the stock market. Back in the early nineties when it was in a bear mood I took a flyer, and when it hit those record highs I sold out, much to my broker's disgust. He wanted me to keep plunging, but I never have been a great risk taker." Cass cringed inwardly as she spoke the lie. "So I have a small fun account in Lichtenstein." *Somewhere around a million bucks.*

"Ah, life in the fast lane."

"I'd settle for the 20-mile speed limit forever."

"Well, you came to the right place." Izzie was out the door and heading for her old, but carefully polished, Karmann Ghia.

"Hey, wait up. I didn't pay you for this yet." Cass cuddled the stole.

Drawing on a scarlet glove, Iz waved as she got in the car. "It's a present. Wear it in good health."

As she drove away, Cass stood there with a sensation so strange to her she couldn't put words to it. An inner warmth that you couldn't buy, not for twice a million dollars.

23

With a precarious sense of encouragement born of the visit from Izzie, Cass went back to the ceramics work room and looked again at the large urn. She set the piece down on the table cautiously, afraid to overrate it. So easy to tell yourself that you're good. Sitting down she picked up a tool and began to work the foot, scooping out the bottom to leave just a rim of clay for it to stand on. To clean up the rest of the piece she smoothed it with a scrap of felt, then put it on the wheel and took off the dust with a damp brush, leaving a faint texture. An hour later she had a finished jar, glazed inside with a dark cobalt in a zinc base, leaving the outer surface natural bisque. Not exactly a demanding statement, it had an understated dignity. Needed some kind of decoration, though.

Mixing a batch of engobe out of Georgia kaolin and water, she painted a few leaves and twined them with a vine of cobalt sulfate. It felt right. *We'll see when it's fired.* Cass straightened and stretched her back muscles. It was good, to lose yourself in the work so completely you forgot to take a break. To be so intent on getting the piece safely to the kiln you hardly minded going down those stairs into the hole.

Shutting the lid, she stuffed the crack with wet ball clay and turned the control knob to "low." It would cure slowly, driving out the water latent in the body, no need to think of it again for four hours. She glanced at her Timex. 3:37 p.m. And for the first time all day she felt a stir of appetite.

Pizza. Wasn't there a shop over on Lamar? Taking a quick shower, she pulled on slacks and a turtleneck sweater. It would make the stiletto harder to draw, but you can't have everything, and she needed the surrounding wool. The evening was chilly, as she walked out through sundown light.

The town was enjoying its own kind of "rush hour." Lamar was alive with people, cars with bumper stickers: **Rock Hunting the Rockies** and **We stayed at Bent's Fort.** The Bank was still open, the old field-stone building bright with fresh gold lettering on the front door, brass handles polished to a high shine. New businesses clustered around it like chickens at a corn toss — a travel agency flaunting posters of Guadalajara, a curio "emporium" with a window display that seemed to be a miniature of the O.K. Corral, complete with toy gunfighters. The sign said "WALK RIGHT IN, PARD."

From Papa's Place the smell of pizza aromatized the whole block. Cass quickened her pace. Just for now, it was good to forget all the implications and pretend that it's a natural phenomenon, to see old Panhandle alive and kicking. The clerk at the counter in front of the open ovens was dispensing take-outs to a bunch of teens who had just piled off a yellow bus parked outside: the high school basketball team newly returned from a winning game with Trinidad, to judge by their raucous gabbling. Dodging their horseplay Cass managed to get to the front of the crowd long enough to order a medium cheese-and-sausage, carrying it back to the row of booths along the rear wall. As she headed for the farthest corner she realized it was occupied by Guy Magee.

Grubby in old dungarees and paint-daubed T-shirt he was hunched over his elbows, his little goat's beard working as he chewed a slab of pepperoni. His eyes were vacant until they focused on Cass. Coming ajar for a minute he looked as if he were face-to-face with an apparition. More than startled, he seemed dismayed. Then getting it together he leaped up, the smile almost feverish with welcome.

"Sandy! You're exactly what I need. Pizza should never be eaten alone, there ought to be a law." Practically dragging her into the seat opposite he went on nervously, "I was actually on my way to see you after the inner man got stoked. Need to apologize for that awful night I got you involved in. When I asked you to speak to those dolts I really never dreamed they would act so rudely. Gave 'em what for the next day. Of course when they're paying you big bucks to attend the workshops, they grow arrogant, but there was no excuse for their behavior."

"Not to worry," she said. The whole thing seemed a long way back in time. As she balanced a slice of pizza she felt him watching her intently as if she were teaching a class in how to eat with your fingers.

"Of course the way you handled yourself," he went on more slowly, "you've been around the block a few times, haven't you?"

"Oh yeah. I've seen rich phonies all over Europe. The art world is pretty much dominated by them."

He nodded wryly. "I remember my days in Paris. When you're only twenty or so you snicker at all these self-important asses. Never thought I'd be catering to them, but it's a living. Better than hustling fertilizer at the hardware store."

Something in his tone made Cass recall: Guy never had liked Hollis Anderson. "So how often does your clientele change? Do you get new ones in every week or so?"

"I offer a three-month program, and they're welcome to sign up for an advanced course if they want. Some of them have been with me almost a year."

"The guy with the migrating geese?"

For some reason the question made him nervous. "Uh — Quentin. Yes, typical, rich and bored, dabbling in art is his way of life. Plus I think he's got a crush on Minka."

"Your wife?"

"Yep, I reckon I need to apologize for her, too. She was in a rotten mood that night. She tends to be temperamental and her work hadn't gone well that day. Silk screen is a difficult craft, if you do it right, and she does."

"You look a little stressed yourself, for that matter. Hard day at the palette?"

He gave a short self-conscious laugh. "How'd you guess? I've been trying to develop a new technique. I fool around when I'm minding the store — you noticed that art supply shop next to Izzie's place? Yeah, that's one of my enterprises. I sell mostly to my own students, of course, but I thought it would look less exploitative if I kept the thing at a separate location. And it provides me with a kind of hideaway. I get homesick for my loft in New York."

"A real loft? In Manhattan?" Every artist's impossible dream.

"Yeah. Next best thing to the Left Bank. Did you ever get to Paris?"

"A few times."

"Love that city. I was going to live there, attend the Sorbonne and so forth. Then Pop lost every penny he had in the stock market. It killed him, literally — he had a massive coronary, left us with a stack of debts. Mother sold the house for peanuts, the town was on the skids by then. I went to work in New York, did some children's book illustrations, a few minor commissions. Never got back to the old country. How long were you over there?"

"Years," she mumbled vaguely, not wanting to think of Paris.

"Any adventures? I always thought you might become a sort of female Indiana Jones. You had that wild stripe down your back." For a second Cass had a flash of panic: *Does the stiletto show?* "And Paris is such a place for ideological factions, *liberté, egalité,* and cheers for Karl Marx. Did you ever get the revolutionary spirit?"

"Actually," she said, "I was in Germany most of the time. The spirit there was Fascist or bust. At least among the students."

"Easy to be a radical when you're young." And he seemed to settle into a premature middle age before her eyes. Beneath the foxy hirsute effects, his face was gray and sad. "I was thinking just the other day of how free we were in art class, high school. I think I never did better work. And you weren't so bad yourself, remember that clown you painted?"

Cass did recall, a fierce slashing of colors onto the canvas, using every tube of paint in her box. It had been a spillage of impatience with herself, with life in a small town, a teacher who didn't know his trade. It was done only days before graduation and the great escape to live with her mother in Minneapolis.

"That picture," Guy was saying, "kind of scared me. It revealed a streak of violence in you that went beyond those silly pranks you and Hollis used to play on us."

"More like frustration," she told him. "I was tired of Panhandle."

"So you got out. And finally ended up in Europe — how did you manage it?"

"Oh, at first I worked for several embassies around the continent, I was a translator."

"Really? *Parlez vous?*"

"Mais, bien entendu."

"Must have been interesting; I've heard those embassies are a hotbed of intrigue."

"I was strictly a supernumerary. Just glad when I got the scholarship to the school in Dresden."

He had finished his pizza and was sitting elbow on table, chin in hand, staring at her troubled. "With so much creativity in you, I can't help wondering why on earth you gave it all up to come back to the muddy shallows of Southern Colorado?"

"I got tired of pressures. Panhandle's a good place to retreat from the rat race. At least you seem happy here."

"Yes, but I've got the Hacienda. That place always was an obsession with me. I used to hang on the fence and look at the old Spaniard pruning his grape vines and picture myself owning the place. I was going to have horses in that stable and a wine press and a staff of servants to do all the yard work." He shook his head.

"So how did you pull it off then?"

He laughed, self-consciously. "Luck. After the old Grandee died he had no heirs, I bought it for back taxes. Didn't have enough cash to fix it up, but then I met Minka. In New York, one of those big bashes we used to have at the loft, everybody on earth there, Izzie, Ilsa, so forth. I was showing around some pictures of the rancho and Minka went wild over it. Said she could see it developed into an art colony, a new Taos. So we hit it off, and after we were married she sold her shop, which gave us the money to fix the place up. It's been very gratifying, so far. I always did love life in Panhandle. I was glad to come home. But I can't imagine you staying here."

"Believe it," she said, finishing the last bite of pizza, aware that she had overstuffed. "I hope I can do some really good work."

Guy stared at her still with that odd perplexity, then in a sudden surge of impatience he said, "You're already too good for Panhandle. That little vase was a stunner. You have a real style of your own — do you know how rare it is to do something unique and handsome without being weird? You could dominate the scene in any sophisticated venue. San Francisco comes to mind, or Martha's Vineyard."

"Hey, you trying to get rid of me?"

He didn't smile. Instead the melancholy in his face deepened as he drank the last of his Coke, making a grimace as if it were flat. Then straightening in his seat, he said, "Far from it. In fact, the other day I fixed up a welcome-home present for you, which is why I was about to come by your place. It's out in my car. If you're done there, come on."

As they walked out into the night air, a stir of breeze made her shiver, she pulled her parka tighter around her while he rummaged in the back of a dusty Jeep Wagoneer to dig out a paper parcel loosely wrapped.

It came open in her hands. "Guy!"

"You remember it?"

"Vividly." The awkward object had once stood on the teacher's desk in high school art class. A wooden sculptor's model, the figurine was about a foot tall with articulated joints and limbs of the correct proportion. It could be moved into any position and used as a guide for setting up an armature or sketching a figure in a painting. On the featureless round face he had painted a bright red spot for a nose, silly goo-goo eyes and a cynical smile. Years of paint spatters and scuffs still adorned the body, but the elastic was new, the joints were tight. "How did you get your hands on this?"

"It was mine all along. I just loaned it to the class. When we graduated I took it back."

"I always coveted the thing madly."

"I remember. That's why I had it restrung and spruced it up a bit. Thought maybe you'd get a kick out of it."

Cass cocked the stick-man in a jaunty pose. It gave her a sardonic leer, and she almost laughed aloud. "It's a great gift, Guy. Thanks a million."

He didn't return the smile. For some reason his sadness was almost painful. "Set it up in your kitchen and think of me once in a while." Then in a rush he said, "Or better yet, stick it away in a bottom drawer and forget the old days!" Turning abruptly, he strode off down the street like a man who is late to his own life.

24

The encounter with Guy had left her with uneasy churnings all through the night. Something strained about it, not like the easy camaraderie of her first days at home. Something was troubling him. A personal dilemma? Or did it have to do with her appearance at the art party the other night? Cass wondered, as she slumped at the kitchen table on a cloudy morning, drinking a cup of left-over coffee that was more therapeutic than enjoyable.

Maybe, she thought, it was her own guilty reckonings that soured the day, the sneaking suspicion that she was going to have to put her own old buddies under a microscope before she ferreted out the dark places that infected this innocent town. It seemed incredible that even Guy Magee and company would be a research project, soon. From the top of the refrigerator the cocky little stick figure made an indecent gesture.

She had set it up there carelessly last night, sheer chance that one hand was raised in challenge. If only the thing had a middle finger.

Shivering, she went to get a sweater. In Panhandle it had always been considered a sign of weakness to turn the furnace on in May. You just grin and bear the chill. Old habits die hard. Besides, she had a hunch part of her discomfort came from a brooding sense of imminent catastrophe. Cass tried to thrust it aside. What had Kuzu told them? *When you think failure, you're halfway to defeat.*

This time, she had an idea she could not afford to make a misstep, not just for her own sake but so many others. If the musings she and Web had made on the way home from Trinidad were right — and she was pretty sure they were — they were tracking a big operation that had been in the planning for years. The takeover of Panhandle, Colorado would have cost the Flea Circus a mint of money. They would go to some lengths to keep it from being undone.

She wished she could brainstorm with Pike, but at his suggestion they had steered clear of each other. The FBI was still a presence in town and their interest might alert the terrorists before the time was ripe — the fleas might just close up shop and hop to some other location. The Bureau had Virgil on their files as an assassin, but they obviously had no clue that he was part of a whole cell of anarchists in their midst.

Also, if they ever investigated her own background they would jump to the wrong conclusions and start making all the wrong moves. So when the Chief passed her on the street in his squad car it was just a nod or friendly salute, for the benefit of the gray sedan crawling along behind a half block away.

It was okay, they had already divided their activities: Webster to investigate the Bank while she scoped out Gollager's and the bunch at the Hacienda. She was glad they could work together within the same frame of purpose, though the concept of teamwork brought up images of comradeship and shared danger that she'd sworn to forego forever. It was a wretched thought, not to trust the warmth of affection. Even from such a safe source as Liz. *I shouldn't get too close to her, for her sake.* But it felt good to have a few friends.

She watched the old woman come across the yards bearing a pan covered with a napkin and had the back door open. "Hey,

Liz, pretty early in the morning to be baking." The aroma of muffins preceded her guest.

"Oh landsake, I've been up for hours. What-all is that, a can of paint? You gonna re-do your kitchen, ain't you?"

"Sure am. I'm tired of yellow. I thought I'd make it a kind of dusty rose."

"That'll be right pretty."

"These look scrumptious. How about a cup of coffee?"

"No thanks, I got to get back over and fix his breakfast. Meant to ask you — you want some zinnia seeds? I kept a sack full of heads from last summer, plenty to go around if you want to pretty up your yard."

"Gosh, I haven't even thought about a garden. I wouldn't know where to begin."

"Oh, there's nothing to it. Zinnias, you just throw 'em down and stomp 'em into the dirt and they grow all by theirself." She was already out on the back porch again, looking up at the spotlight mounted on the eave. "Good thing you wasn't home last evening. That old Hollis come by again, marched up the front steps and them lights come on, bang! Well, he jumped a foot, I near died laughing. Went charging around back, and bang! More lights. Talk about mad. I thought he'd bust a knuckle on your door. What ails that man?"

"You got me. He seems to think I'm his girlfriend, and when I say I'm not he won't listen. Don't know what makes him so sour, he seems to have a good business going."

"Well, I reckon. All these people we got moving in here now. Stores downtown are selling to them dudes that come to the Rocking R, and Gollager's is so busy Rafe's talking about putting in a casino. Not that this county is ever gonna put up with gambling, not since Central City almost went bust. But he's dying to try, you know Rafe. Course if he ever made it happen and we could offer games of chance I suppose it'd bring the tourists in flocks. Which is good for business, but I'd hate to see it. Well, I got to run."

"Thanks for the muffins." Cass had followed her out onto the back porch.

Abruptly Liz turned and enveloped her in a swift hug. "I swear, it's good to have a woman around."

Cass caught her breath — it threatened to swamp her again, this dangerous pleasure of belonging, the glimpse of peace, the temptation to forget the danger and settle in, enjoy life for once. But not with disaster hanging over the town only a detonator away. Cass looked longingly at the paint can and consigned it to a bottom shelf mentally. There was work to be done. So Rafe wanted a casino? Pulling on her windbreaker she went out to the truck.

Nine o'clock by the time she reached Gollager's, the breakfast crowd was gone, the parking lot empty. When she went inside Mae was swabbing off the bar, looking disgruntled, a mood that sat poorly on her cheerful face.

"What's up?" Cass accepted the cup of coffee and put down a bill. "Come on, have some java on me."

"Darned if I won't." Mae reached into the jar and got them a couple of doughnuts, drew herself a cup and came around the counter to take a stool. "This was supposed to be my day off."

"What happened?"

"Rafe knows I need the time. I go to Pueblo and shop and I have lunch at McDonald's, let somebody else do the cooking. I look forward to it. So there he goes this morning, kiting off and won't say why or where. I wish he wouldn't act so mysterious. Reckon he don't want to admit that it comes over him like a craving — the gambling thing, he's got a yen for it. Goes up to Cripple Creek and plays blackjack. He usually wins, so I can't complain, but I wisht he wouldn't do it on my day off."

"Especially when you're the one making this place a success," Cass said. "Sure you do, it's your cooking, you run the motel."

"Well, that's no bonanza. Not with Rafe letting his buddies crash there free of charge, he's such a friendly guy. Oh, I shouldn't complain. He says contacts are important and he's probably right. We never run short of cash. Fact this place is in the black all the way. Just the same — you ever get a spooky feeling that things is too good to be true? There's gotta be some kind of bad luck on the way?"

Know it well. Cass searched for incisive questions that might open up the can of worms, if there was one. But obviously Mae wasn't in the know. Her big honest face was absolutely incapable of hiding any malevolent secrets.

Back in the truck she paused at the exit of the parking lot, looking eastward toward that distant huddle of ranch buildings, but she wasn't really ready for Boyd Ruger. A complicated man, she suspected, not somebody you can idly approach for no good reason. Exactly the kind of bigger-than-life character who might front a secret op. She wished she could poke around the place, talk to some of the "cowboys." What sort of story would he buy? I came out there to check on Jessie's horse? Not likely. Got a friend who wants to spend a week on a dude ranch, I need to look around? That excuse was fine for Mae, but it wouldn't pass muster with Ruger, he'd want details, facts, a name and phone number. Especially if his place really is a hotbed of terrorism. She'd need to talk to Pike before she tackled that one.

Which leaves Foreman's operation, truck stop and trailer park, a possibility. And the Hacienda, with all Guy's cuckoo-birds. She needed a new approach and one occurred to her, something he'd said last evening at the pizza place. With a plan developing, she drove back to town.

Leaving the truck in front of the house, she went in and straight down to the kiln. It was cool enough to open, she raised the lid and felt a little jolt of joy. The urn was as elegant as she had hoped. The firing had brought out the leafy decorations, the proportion was pleasing. Taking it up to the workroom, she got out a piece of fine sandpaper and cleaned off the foot, then found some tissue paper and bundled it into a smart little shopping bag she had saved for just such a purpose.

Back out in the truck, she rehearsed her

lines all the way to the Boutique. Don't come on too strong. Don't rush, be patient. Don't be apologetic, but get your point across, you're on her side. Izzie's side. For Godsake try to be subtle . . .

Ilsa was alone, drifting in the nether regions of the store among the racks of clothes. The woman was all fluttering hands and chiffon draperies. "I'm afraid you've missed her. She's at the Post Office."

"That's okay," Cass said brightly. "I really came to see you, to give you something — if you'll have it." Setting the sack on the soda fountain Cass let her come to it in her own time, the way you offer salt to a wild animal in the forest.

Ilsa approached warily, puzzled, dark eyes ready to be wounded. "What is it?"

"A piece of ceramics that I made. The minute I took it out of the kiln I knew it was meant for you."

As the woman opened the tissue with delicate hands, her rosebud of a mouth came open. "For me? Why?" she asked with childlike wonder. "Because it's so fragile?" She held it carefully, set it on the counter with dawning respect.

"Because it's tough," Cass said. "It has gone through a lot of heat without caving in. It will endure."

The woman's body language told a whole story. Ilsa seemed to uncrimp as she smiled over the pot. "It's lovely, and yet, as you say, sturdy. I'm very flattered." She set it with infinite care on a shelf near the office — off-white against the brown wall, it made a distinctive statement. "Of course I will take it home eventually. There's a little niche — we have one of the old adobe casas over on the South Side, and there's this little space built in for a religious figure. The jar will be perfect there. We worship beauty above all."

Cass smiled. It was a charming thing for her to say. "I'm glad you like it. I don't quite know how to put this, but I've been close to Izzie a long time, even if we haven't corresponded. To come home and find her so happy — well, it's like a miracle. She had such a rotten life, she deserves a little joy."

And suddenly it was a whole new ballgame. Cass had been prepared to storm the walls of a truly insecure person, but Ilsa was more confident than she had realized. More mature, too. There was a network of fine lines around her eyes and mouth, as she broke into a smile that could only be described as "merry."

"How about a cup of tea? Do you have time?"

"I'd love it." Cass followed into a snug little sitting room at the back where a steaming kettle sat on an electric coil.

"We're tea-hounds," Ilsa confessed. "The water is always hot." Her fingers fluttered over a choice of antique cups and settled for a pair of flowered beauties, English bone china with that dazzling white glaze. Good will pervaded the air like the essence of oolong.

Determined not to fracture it with any headlong questions, Cass approached her mission obliquely. "I always knew Izzie was fascinated by fashion, we used to make paper-doll clothes together when we were ten years old. But this shop goes so far beyond any childhood expectations, I am truly impressed. It's part nostalgia, part new-age, and it all works together."

Ilsa sipped her tea happily. "I'm glad that comes across. We try to be eclectic and yet harmonious. The mannequins, the window display and so forth are all Izzie's. The soda fountain idea was mine. And of course we both delight in Guy's murals. He and I go way back to New York, you know."

"No, I didn't know that."

"Yes, I was in the crowd that used to gather at his loft. That's how we met. At the spackling party." Ilsa chuckled, a musical sound so engaging it caught Cass off-guard. "It was a wonderful place to hang out. Down on the lower east side, it was zoned strictly commercial, didn't even have a bathroom, just a toilet and a sink. Guy bought this huge old tub with claw feet and set it near the stove. Which was also forbidden, a potbelly stove to which he rigged a pipe that ran out an improvised vent hole. If the building inspector had ever seen it we were dead. The parties we had — especially weekends when there was nobody around to hear us, the whole district deserted. Anyway one week Izzie came to town to check out the import houses. She was planning to start a gift shop with the money her father left her when he died. Actually it was her grandfather so anyway Guy talked her out of it. 'Forget that,' he said, 'you belong in fashion.' Of course even in those days she was wearing those wild colors, always experimenting. Funny, I never believed in love at first sight. Until then." The tone of wonder was tinged with an old dread, as if there was still an underlying danger that the dream would vanish.

"What's even more incredible," Cass said, "is that it turned out to be mutual. Izzie is one gone girl. When she talks about you her eyes turn on like halogen lamps at sundown."

The cherubic face crinkled with pleasure. "I'm glad she — well it's nice to hear that. You can be so close to a relationship you can't get a perspective."

"I envy you those memories of the good old days. I suppose those people out at Guy's now are left-overs from his New York crowd."

"Oh, heavens no. We were all real artists. Now he has surrounded himself with a bunch of rich egocentric dabblers. They haven't a lick of talent between them, except of course for his wife. Minka is a gifted silk screen artist, but she's such a lip-twitcher."

Even as Cass smiled at the word, she could picture it, the supercilious scorn of the woman toward anyone with a different orientation. "She can't stand minor ceramists, either. In fact, I couldn't help wondering what on earth attracted Guy to the lady."

"Oh, he wasn't —" She broke off, uncertain how far to trust.

Ignoring the break, Cass went on. "I ran into him over at the pizza parlor last evening. Eating alone. He seemed kind of unhappy, not like himself."

"Yes, he goes over there after he closes the art supply shop next door. You saw it? It's one of her enterprises, but he's the one who puts in the time. The truth is, Minka is the business head of The Hacienda. You won't say anything if I tell you a story?"

"Of course not." Cass helped herself to more tea from the pot and freshened Ilsa's cup.

"Well, the whole thing has been a matter of mutual convenience, their marriage, I mean. When Guy met Minka she was only in this country on a temporary visa — I believe she's Ukranian, something. Anyway she offered him a deal: marry her and secure her U.S. citizenship, and she would provide money for him to turn The Hacienda into an artist's mecca. With their combined contacts they could set up an art colony and operate it together. Well, of course, it's something less than he expected, but it's only temporary. The law requires that they live together a few years, I forget, two, three? In due time they'll divorce and she'll move to San Francisco, that's where she wants to live anyway. He'll be left with the Hacienda, which by then will presumably be solvent."

"I suppose it makes sense," Cass agreed slowly, "but what a price to pay, even for a childhood dream."

"Especially since Minka listens only to Tchaikovsky."

"And Guy a Gershwin man!"

"You knew that?" Ilsa clapped her hands. "That brings us back to the spackling party. You should have been there! In the loft he had this huge upright piano, very old, very conservative. We decided it needed a touch of impressionism, so we Van Gogh-ed it with a spackle gun. Guy ended up looking like an Arlesian flower garden."

They were laughing like fools when, out front, the bell dinged and a minute later Izzie stood in the doorway, wearing one red-gloved hand on her black-and-white striped hip, viewing them from under the brim of a black straw hat and trying not to look idiotically happy.

"I see," she said, "that we've acquired a new piece of ceramics. Pickle, you know we can't afford an original Butterfield. People will think this shop has gone high-tone."

As Cass drove home with the pleasant aftertaste of a cucumber sandwich shared at the counter of the old ice cream shop she felt a little sad. So silly, that others savored their prejudices, nursing their hatreds, when it would be so much easier to accept people as harmless as those two. Of course Izzie could be a mouthy confrontational brat, but Ilsa was shy as a doe. The way she had rushed through the door of friendship, she must be starved for a little civility. It was a miracle that Panhandle had let the couple exist here. There were other small towns where they would have been hounded out of the community.

Panhandle — once again she had this temptation to like the little burg. And even as she considered it, she turned in at her own yard, heading around to the back of the house, glancing automatically toward the tool shed. And halted in her tracks. High up on the wall, in the dark cubby-hole where she had installed it, the diminutive railroad signal twinkled, its red lights burning two bright holes in her day.

25

As she passed the switch Cass surreptitiously disarmed it. Then approached the back porch with featherweight care. Proximity bombs can be set off by vibration or even body heat. You have to believe the other side would begin to use more sophisticated devices. Tossing aside her windbreaker, she deliberately steadied her breathing to a regular pitch before crouching slowly to scan the area under the porch. Empty. Circling the house she tested each window. All secure. She had left the curtains open so that anyone inside would have a tough time hiding unless they were in a closet or under the bed. Whoever had come was gone.

Returning to the rear porch she found Liz and Joe waiting for her, looking puzzled. "Sandy, what in tarnation is wrong with you, sneaking around like a cat after a canary." Liz fluffed her apron nervously. "I been watching you twenty minutes now. You act plumb skeered."

"That's how I feel," Cass said, "when I come home to find somebody has been inside my house again."

"Oh no. You think so?"

"Yep. This time I'm sure. I set up a signal, goes on automatically whenever anybody fiddles with the doors."

"Where?" Joe looked past her through the kitchen windows. "I don't see nothing."

"Were you at home all morning? Anybody snooping around?"

"Not a soul." Then Liz added, "Well, I went to the library, but Joe was here all along. Anybody start messing with your door he'd have noticed."

He thought about it, frowning. "Them Foreman brats came through the yards a while ago. Maybe they set off your booby trap."

"Kids couldn't open those locks, not without a key." Cass was muttering to herself. "And yet the door has been opened, it's the only thing that would set off my alarm system." Puzzled, she glanced at Joe — it happened that the sun was full on his leathery face, striking deep into the folds that usually hid his eyes. Hard and sharp as obsidian arrowheads, aiming a look at her that brought a salt taste to her mouth. She looked away quickly, hoping she hadn't revealed the instant of comprehension.

"Oh, heck," she said heartily, "you're right, it probably was kids. Guess I'll have to get a camera installed after all."

"Cameras? For heavensake girl!" Liz's voice rose querulously, "Have you lost your mind?"

"Nah, I just get a kick out of gadgets," Cass tried to make it sound like a joke. "Don't mind me. I guess I get a little nervous living alone." It felt safe enough to walk up the back steps with Joe standing a few feet away. She turned the key in the door, giving them an idiotic grin.

Once inside, she stood and eyed the kitchen cautiously, orienting herself to an entirely new scenario built around one cagey old miner. Now it made a certain amount of sense. He obviously had experience with explosives, knew how to rig a detonator, not to mention being handy with rattlesnakes. Though why — ? But that wasn't hard to figure either. The odor of lifelong poverty hung over the old codger like swamp-fog. Years of hard labor with an annuity of arthritis and rotten lungs, he was probably bitter enough to rationalize practically any minor crime if it would bring him a little folding green. Maybe a taste of revenge on the world for its failure to provide.

Cass watched the two of them mosey back to their home, picking their way across the uneven lawn. What would he have left this time? Poison in the oatmeal? Or maybe a listening device, a bug. And if there was one she needed to alert Pike, so he didn't phone her and begin discussing their countermeasures.

Sitting down at the table she got a notebook from the drawer, tore off the page that reminded her she needed butter and lettuce. In short angry words she set down what she had learned, what she suspected, adding the strong possibility that the kitchen might be bugged. Then, picking up the phone she called the police station.

"I'd like to leave a message for the Chief," she told the mechanical answering service. "This is Bunny. I need that sander back, please. I am going to refinish my kitchen."

Grimly, methodically, she checked every room in the house for a sign of explosives, though she was fairly sure it wouldn't be dynamite again. Nothing apparent came to light. Returning to the kitchen she began to dismantle the cupboards. Into a large plastic bag she emptied every open box or canister of its contents.

A half hour later she was starting on the refrigerator when she heard the sound of boots on the back porch and Webster came in, carrying the sander under one arm.

"What in tarnation are you up to now?" he said irritably.

So he was feeling a little raw, missing his Pony, increasingly sore at the situation if not at her personally. Cass understood that. But the sharpness of his tone made her wince and she realized that she had been hoping for a little support. Sign of weakness.

"I'm getting ready to paint the kitchen," she said, and handed him the piece of paper.

He scanned it fast. Glanced around nervously, then chewed a lip for a minute. He said, "Actually the sander has been acting up, but I think I can fix it. Let's go out to the shed, see if your dad has any wire." Without waiting for an answer he turned around and headed for the back yard.

Cass followed, admiring the quickness with which he adjusted to the situation.

"You really think your place is bugged?" he demanded, once they were inside the shed with the door shut.

"I haven't located any device yet, but I'm just getting started on a sweep. Joe must have had some reason to come over."

"You sure he's the one who planted the bomb?"

"Just seat-of-the-pants intuition, some look on his face."

"Your hunches are good enough for me. It makes sense, plant the snake, rig the dynamite, he'd know how. And it's his style — Joe never had a grain of honesty in him. Used to rip off the tourists, take them down to the Purgatoire and tell them there was gold in the sand, sell them a two-dollar pan for five bucks and go off without teaching them how to use it. I put the word out that it had to stop. Town would get a bad reputation if we swindled the customers, everybody would lose. So he quit that, but there's no limit to what he might do if you offered him enough folding green. Question is, who put him up to it?"

"Have you had any leads?"

He shook his head. "The Bank's got a very tight security wall around its computers, I'm not that good at hacking. You find out anything?"

"Just that Rafe Gollager likes to disappear and comes back with a stack of money, but he's a gambler. That could account for it. I got the whole story on the Hacienda from Ilsa, apparently the Russian lady made a deal with Guy: if he'd marry her and give her citizenship she would finance his art colony. So that accounts for that. I keep coming back to Ruger, he's the type who might be running an international ring of terrorists, and those "dudes" could easily be his contacts. You checked him out, I know, but I was wondering — did you ever see a picture of Boyd Ruger? I mean, is our Boyd really the man? Or could he just be using the name and the credentials?"

Pike thought about it. "An impersonation of somebody that well known down Texas would be a hard thing to pull off. But I'll follow up on it. There's one piece of news I should mention — not good. One of the Bureau operatives was kind enough to share with me the information that they've had some new intelligence warning of a disaster of major proportions due any day now."

"A nine-eleven type catastrophe?"

"Yep. The government has raised its terror alert to red. Of course he shrugged off any idea that a town like Panhandle would be involved."

"Of course," I repeated. "They'd be counting on that."

"This afternoon I'm going to check out Foreman's trailer park, on the grounds that it may not be up to code on the wiring. It seems a little grungy for a crowd like your fleas. But who knows? Maybe that's the look they have chosen for cover. What's your next move?"

"One that you won't like. It's a little radical, but it can't make matters much worse. I thought I should try to get word to my old outfit, the Libra League. See if maybe they would want to send somebody here to lend a hand. They probably still don't trust me, but they won't shrug off a terrorist threat."

Webster hunched his shoulders and winced, the rib was still sore. "You're right. I don't like it." Then he glanced at her and his face eased a fraction, he suddenly put an arm around her shoulders and tightened the grip for an instant. "You're between a rock and a hard place, Bunny. Do what you have to do. I've got to be moving on. The Fibbies are still all over my tail."

She followed him back to the side yard where his unit was parked. He turned and called over his shoulder. "On second thought, maybe your best bet is just to buy a new sander."

Going back into the house she was already beginning to compose a message in the old general communication code that they all had learned. Opened the notebook and began to print:

ALLERGIES FORCE ME TO SELL MUCH LOVED DOGS. POODLE, TERRIER, SHEPHERD, DOBERMAN, ALL AKC
WRITE P.O. BOX 961, PANHANDLE, COLORADO

Translation:
Poodle: I have intelligence
Terrier: about a flea or colony of fleas
Shepherd: The League
Doberman: needs to go on attack
All AKC: extremely urgent

The box number was her own i.d. plus her location.

Rummaging for an envelope, she found one and addressed it to the New York Times, jotted a note that she wanted the ad to run in the Sunday edition, and wrote a check. She was sealing it up, already mentally on her way to the post office when she heard footsteps on the back porch.

Liz stood there, her peasant's face knotted in an expression of unfamiliar resentment. Without coming in, she reached through the doorway and dropped a pair of keys on the sink drain.

"I just come to give them back," she said. "We don't want to keep them for you no more."

"But Liz! I never implied that —"

"Yes, you did. You said your door got opened by a key and these are the only extras. Joe says you don't trust us and probably been saying bad things about us to Pike Webster. So you just keep your keys. I'm not watching out for your place no more, I don't want to be responsible." Then seeing the stripped-down kitchen, the trash bag, her native dismay took over. "What on earth you been doing?"

"I'm afraid somebody left something over here that might be dangerous. And I certainly don't think it was you!"

"Well, sakes alive, whatever are you afraid of? That you might get bombed or something?"

"That's exactly right. Liz" — she had to know, Cass came to the conclusion in a rush — "that night you saw me crawling around under the porch? I found a box of dynamite under there and some detonators. I'm not kidding."

It was too much for the old woman's mind to stretch around. She shook her head. "I heard you got hurt in the brain and I'm sorry, but you better find yourself a head doctor and get rid of these boogy-man ideas. I think you're going plumb crazy and I can't help you." She turned and clumped back down off the stoop with a dignity that precluded any argument.

Helpless and angry, Cass picked up the keys and put them in her purse. Rotten game. She had discovered Joe, but she had lost Liz, and it hurt more than she would ever have imagined.

26

When time drags build a new clock.

They call it the waiting-for-the-other-shoe-to-drop syndrome. With unanswered questions on every side, there was nothing Cass could do about it until the opposition made a move. At least that's what she had decided a few days later as she hunched over her father's work bench, fashioning a box from some scrap wood, pretty good scraps. Her father had always loved walnut and she had found several nice pieces, cut them to length and screwed them together. Drilled a hole. Took the works out of the yellow chicken and installed them in the new housing, with the center rod sticking through the front, to which she reattached the hands. They were the only yellow left in the room — she'd have to paint them. And buy some colored thumbtacks to mark the hours. What color?

Taking the reinvented time piece back into

the house, she mounted it on the newly painted wall. Around her the kitchen beamed rosily. It was oddly disorienting. Almost saccharine. What would take the curse off all this sweetness? she wondered grimly. It needed to be accessorized, the handles on the drawers, the oilcloth on the table now covered by the white cloth. What color would Izzie pick? Not chartreuse. Not black, *don't like black.* How about orange? Grace notes of orange would be just cynical enough to add spice. Curtains? No. Too much. Over the window she thought a drop of louvered blinds would be good, maybe in simulated walnut.

Standing at the sink she looked out across the yards with a fresh twinge of regret. Yesterday the old Chev had come and gone several times, Liz hadn't glanced in her direction. Cass had put the paint can and brushes along with the drop cloth out on the back porch like bait to lure the reluctant trout. No one had come over to admire her efforts or ply her with life-sustaining cookies.

She looked up at the new clock and fidgeted. Orange — she didn't want to go back to the hardware store for more paint, didn't even need a whole can. A tube would do, a tube of cadmium orange oil paint.

With the thought she was in motion.

As she walked out onto the front porch a gust of wind shook the locust trees. Too cool for late May it felt as if it were newly arrived from the heights of the Sangre de Cristos. She turned back and got her parka. It had rained all night last night, the hard torrents that the Indians call "male" rain because it drives the seed deep into the earth. It had washed the sky of dust, leaving it crystalline, and lacing the air with a freshness that should have buoyed anyone's spirit. Heading for town on foot Cass walked briskly, looking forward to a little shopping, a talk with friends.

At the Boutique she was brought up short by a sign on the door:

CLOSED
SPRING BUYING TRIP
GRAND REOPENING
JUNE???

Disappointed, she stood staring until footsteps coming from behind made her glance around.

Head-down, Guy almost barreled into her, then shied away looking bewildered. For a minute he stared at her like a startled forest creature, eyes wide beneath the frowsy brows. "What are you doing here?"

"Hi, Guy," she spoke gently, *take it easy. What's the matter?* "I just came by to see the girls. Where'd they go?"

"Oh. Yes, New York. They left yesterday. Don't usually leave until after Memorial Day, but they were upset. This damned police state we live in . . ." He had moved past her and was unlocking the door to his shop. "Those androids from the FBI are incapable of feeling any decency or kindness. I mean, to pick on a helpless child like Ilsa — ?"

Following him inside, Cass tried to read between his lines. "What on earth are you talking about?"

"Oh, it goes back to our wild-oats days. The last of the hippy era, everybody had a cause, for heavensake. So Ilsa marched in the May Day Parade one year, so what? I guess she took part in some gay-rights demonstrations, well, you know. You must have carried a few signs yourself, or didn't they allow protests over in the old country?"

Cass backed off from that subject. "But what's that got to do with anything now? Surely they don't haunt the trail of everybody who waved a sign."

"Actually, she got tied in with some activists, people associated with the Weathermen.

Remember them?"

That rang all sorts of bells. At the training camp they had studied the history of anarchy in the United States. The hot coals of revolution were said to be still burning in the hearts of aging flower children. She personally had doubted it. Fires tend to ash out after a few decades, don't they? "That was all so long ago."

"Nobody on earth has a longer memory than the Feds. What I can't figure out is why they suddenly descended on our little backwater. What are they looking for? You didn't do anything naughty lately, did you?" He forced a laugh, but it never reached his eyes.

Cass returned it in kind. "All I've been up to is painting my kitchen. Which reminds me, I was going to stop in here after I saw the girls. I need a tube of oil paint, I'm going to spark up my cabinets with a little raw cadmium orange."

Guy looked puzzled, almost skeptical. Leading the way back through the store he grabbed a tube off a display rack and handed it to her. "On the house." Then in a burst he asked, "Sandy, what did you get into across the pond that sent you running home? You're obviously hiding out. They say you put motion sensors all over your house, alarm systems."

"Where'd you hear that?" she demanded.

"Oh, Liz Spinney was gabbing along about it at the Library when I was in there yesterday. Silly old woman, but she was really upset. She thinks you're nuts."

"I know. She's not even speaking to me. But Guy, my house has been broken into twice since I came home."

"Geez, I didn't know that. We never have a lot of crime around here. What were they after?"

"Me," she told him, on impulse. "I have reason to believe that an old enemy from Germany is tracking me, trying to settle a score. They even planted a bomb under my back porch."

"My God! Did you tell Pike Webster?"

"Of course. He got rid of the thing. He may have mentioned it to the FBI, I don't know. And I'm sorry if it caused Ilsa any troubles. But the fact is, I feel kind of snake-bit, so please don't listen to any more lies about me. I need all the friends I can get."

For a few second he stood trying to take it in and process it. He seemed confused. Then with a gesture of impatience he threw up his hands and muttered cryptically, "Oh, to hell with 'em all. Listen, how would you like to come back and see my sanctum?"

Cass sensed that it was an invitation he didn't make easily. "I'd be honored."

The door at the rear of the shop wore a large KEEP OUT sign. Unlocking it, he stood aside to let her into a spacious storeroom that was empty of everything but the easel in the middle, a paint-encrusted work stand and canvases stacked against the walls. Lifting the blinds that hid two large windows, he let in a flood of north light, the kind an artist would kill for, and never mind that the view was of a weedy vacant lot. This was a sanctuary, of twisted tubes and old frowsy brushes and the strong odor of turpentine. *Ian would have loved this!*

The canvas on the easel was draped with a paint-spattered cloth. Guy hovered by it, nervous, reluctant to unveil it. "I don't invite my 'students' here." He invested the word with sarcasm. "Sandy, I hate the lot of them. Just between you and me they haven't got the talent of a sack of hammers. The hokey stuff they think is so innovative, I tried it all out when I was in knee pants. Cubist junk, 'found' materials, once I painted a picture out of mashed bananas and axle grease. Called it 'On the Skids.' We've got a fool out there who paints with blue toothpaste, yellow shoe polish and his own blood. Last week he brought in some slime that he called 'engobe,' smelled bad enough we made him throw it out."

"Hey, wait a minute," she interrupted. "I've been looking for deposits of ceramic materials. Engobe can be used for interesting decoration on a bisque pot. Will you ask him where he found it? I don't mind the smell, believe me."

He eased up enough to chuckle. "Okay, I will learn to be open to new media. I just get impatient with the idiots. It's hard enough learning to handle the traditional. I've been trying for a new style in oils, but it's so illusive. At least nobody 'gets' it but me." Circling the easel, he had the look of glass that has been fractured so finely it hasn't fallen in pieces yet, but could at any minute.

"Guy, will you kindly quit putzing around and unveil the thing?" That had to be why he asked her back here.

"Why don't I make us some coffee . . ." Then he grinned and shrugged. With a kind of reverence he lifted the spattered drop-cloth. For a moment Cass was confused. It was as if the rag and the painting were part of the same project. The canvas was splotched with random colors, Naples yellow predominant. Freezing her facial muscles into a non-committal rigidity Cass studied the mess intently. *Dear God, please let me 'get' it.* She had always found pointillism a bit dizzying, but this whirling daubery made her a little nauseous. Such an intense bombardment of the creamy golden pigment, he must have used a dozen large tubes.

Unable to bear the silence, Guy began to stammer. "It's . . . it's . . ."

She held up a hand to stop him. Squinting until the whole thing was a blur she began to sense the form underlying the helter-skelter surface. Those dabs of umber had to be shadows, arch-shaped, and below them a streak of blue. So — a bridge. Under a torrent of noonday sun, the kind you see in Venice, but Guy never lived in Italy, he was in France the whole time. Southern France. Cautiously, she said, "It's obviously the Midi, the hard sunlight that stuns you. Is it the Pont d'Avignon?" Glancing up she caught the sudden glint of tears in his eyes.

He turned away fast and went over to the coffee maker on the work table. "I guess I haven't totally lost it," he sniffed.

"Lost? You've captured it, you have painted sunlight itself, *mon vieux.* All it needs is a bit of definition. Which you were working on, obviously, it isn't finished. But what a statement."

He turned back with a smile that broke her heart. The happiness. It took years off his face. She wondered what had happened to send him off into such a chaos of style, such a confusion of purpose. *Damn those charlatans out there, I don't care if they do pay a mint, it isn't worth it.*

Guy was gently ushering her toward the door. "Sandy, you have given me a boost you couldn't imagine. Now get out of here so I can go to work."

As she walked slowly back uptown Cass was thinking of the conventional ethics: to be truthful, to be honest with your friends. Especially your friends. But Guy Magee was beyond the reach of wisdom, ready to shatter at the smallest blow. She wondered if he weren't on the verge of a breakdown of some sort, the kind that happens when you sell your soul to the Devil. Also known as Minka Moneybags, a woman who would marry to gain citizenship — a true dominatrix. Only why would she use her wealth to come to a little town like Panhandle? It wasn't her style. Cass could feel red flags beginning to flutter. On impulse she turned down a side street and veered toward a building that bore the sign:

PANHANDLE POLICE DEPARTMENT.

It was just a converted store, one big room with several desks and along the rear wall a row of make-shift cells, empty now. At the dispatcher's telephone a young man lolled in a chair reading a comic book. Glancing up, a look of recognition crossed his face, a simple-minded curiosity, you could almost see the wheels turning: *the crazy lady.*

"Help you, ma'am?"

"I was looking for the Chief."

"He's out of town. You want to report a crime?"

Cass shook her head. "No thanks, my business with him can wait. Where did he go?"

"Texas, ma'am. Be back by the end of the week."

"Thanks." So he had taken her question about Boyd Ruger seriously. And the only way to make sure was to visit the man's home territory. But she felt a bit deserted, as she walked home along Lamar Street where workers were stringing a banner from light pole to light pole.

WELCOME TO PANHANDLE
MEMORIAL DAY PARADE

27

Memorial Day — that was no bona fide reason to jump to a conclusion. Most of the recent acts of terrorism had happened at random, as far as the calendar was concerned. No particular symbolism in a date, September 11th. Or, for that matter, April 19th, Oklahoma City. And yet Cass felt uneasy when she thought about the upcoming holiday with its crowds, vacationers, celebrants, special events. Where had she read that the President was going to speak at the Air Force Academy graduation?

Of course that would be an unlikely place to stage a scenario of mayhem, every other person would be combat trained and its locale was perfectly set up for security. What other events, though, she wondered? Ought to check into it, if she had access to a computer. Not the best time for Pike to be gone. *He might have let me know he was going out of town!*

Dabbing the final stroke of orange paint on the hands of the clock, Cass stepped back to view the effect. Against the rose-colored walls it was like the stamen of an exotic flower. The drawer handles were nice accents too. Still, the pastel shades seemed to swallow the sunlight, the kitchen was darker than it had been when yellow. *And I am wasting time, because I don't want to go out there again.*

The Hacienda. Guy's precarious state of nerves had tripped some wire inside her, probably a false reading brought on by the fact that she didn't like the lady he'd married for whatever reason. It's a stone-hard woman who would use a sensitive artist for her own purposes — at least it seemed to warrant a little more investigation.

With some reluctance she cleaned up, went to change clothes. This could be important, and time was running out, *so get with it, girl . . .* Still, she wished Pike were somewhere available, as she got into the truck. Not that the bunch at the rancho were going to attack with anything but scathing words and sneers — the picture of them wearing tiny guns stuffed down their smocks made her smile. And yet it wouldn't be a bad place to hatch a plot, the ancient estate so far removed from the rest of the world.

As she drove through the gates she could see more of the grounds than she had the other evening. The pasture where the carriage horses had grazed was now planted with a strange collection of objects. On a piece of driftwood the words were burned:

SCULPTURE GARDEN

Cass brought the truck to a stop so she could take it in. At the center of the brushy enclosure was a huge construction made of stacked plywood boxes painted kindergarten colors. It bore a large sign: "Foundations of Faith." O-kay. And that granite boulder showing some feeble hack marks, it would have its own title too, something like "Hope" or "Despair" or "Who knew it would be this hard to carve stone?" To one side a piece of welded junkyard scrap had to be a dead bird, she could make out broken wings and two ugly feet thrust upward. With an inner shudder she drove on to the barn, nosing the truck in between a Beemer and a Jag. These were not your "starving" artists, obviously.

The broad doors were wide open. Cass saw people at work inside, isolated in separate cubicles that offered a modicum of privacy, paint-smeared Bohemians who scowled as she walked past. One man in a pony-tail and gold earring threw a cloth over his creation, glaring at the interloper. At an easel out in the middle of the barn a young woman in a grungy jogging suit with a hundred-dollar raw silk scarf over her hair gave Cass a chilly look and went bravely on with her imitation Kandinski.

On the far side of the big room Quentin was at work, bent over a broad table while Minka seemed to be explaining the use of overlays in silk screen. She had a large frame in hand. Of course color separation is a truly difficult craft, and Cass had to admit that the large dramatic print by the door of the office was magnificent.

In a small space that had once been a tack room a girl sat typing on an old manual machine. The calendar by her desk was comfortingly banal — picture of a puppy chasing a butterfly. The days were scribbled and crossed off. On May 29th a single word had been scrawled: *Denver!*

She looked up with Doris-Day blue eyes and smiled brightly.

"Can I help you? I'm afraid Guy's not here."

"That's okay. Actually I am looking for

one of your artists who works with 'found' materials. Recently, I believe, he discovered a deposit of engobe. I would very much like to know where it's located; it's useful in ceramics."

"That smelly stuff." She giggled. "We all ganged up and made him throw it away. His Lordship was very offended."

"His Lordship?"

"Oh, that's what we call him. His name is Winsor Wright. I'm sorry, but he's gone today, too. I think he went to Pueblo to buy canvas."

"Okay, thanks. I'll try another time." Cass had lingered long enough to be noticed. Both Quentin and Minka had seen her, the latter standing like a pillar of salt, in a stark-white man's work shirt which she wore with the tail out, sandals on bare feet and coarse black hair loose around her shoulders. Now, she beckoned curtly: *Come here and account for yourself.*

Cass wandered over casually, glancing at the finished pieces pinned to the uprights around the barn. From the corner of her eye she saw Quentin move protectively in front of the table where his work lay spread. Still smarting over those remarks about his geese. Brightly, Cass said, "Hi. How are you both?"

"What you vant here?" The ever-tactful Minka.

"Nothing important."

Quentin frowned severely. "Come on now, I don't believe you waste time on things that aren't important, Miss Butterfield. Why don't you tell us what brings you here?"

"Yesz, maybe ve help." Minka looking as if she'd like to help her to an early grave.

Why doesn't she like me? Jealousy, over an old friendship? Professional paranoia? But with that silk screen print, she has nothing to be defensive about.

"Actually," Cass said, "I got some news the other day you might be interested in. Friend of mine back east tells me a group of young artists is trying to put together a traveling exhibit to present at the street fairs around the country this summer. They asked me to suggest names for their mailing list. They intend to put out a color catalog. I thought maybe some of your students would be interested."

Minka stared at her as if she had spoken obscenely. Quentin stiffened, his Hemingway jowls set like hardened acrylic. "Shopping-mall shows are for duffers. Here, we are serious about our art."

"Hey, I wasn't trying to insult you," Cass shrugged. "I've shown my work in street exhibits."

Quentin bestowed a sneer. "You," he said, "are a craftsman, ceramics is a populist art form. Our endeavors, for better or worse, are aimed at higher goals." He stood so squarely between Cass and the drafting table, she got curious.

"I get the message," she told them cheerfully. "Tell Guy I came by — oops. Sorry." She dropped the car keys so that they bounced off her knee and under a nearby cabinet, a tall chest of shallow drawers, suitable for large flat sheets, probably Minka's prints. As Quentin stooped to retrieve the keys she got a glimpse of his newest masterpiece. Totally geometric it could have been done with a T-square, a box-like figure with clusters of arms protruding, a stylized insect. The overlay that Minka had been demonstrating was a complex pattern of red polka dots. *Black Widow Spider with Acne.* Amused at her own fantasy, she thanked him and let him walk her toward the door of the barn.

"Always a pleasure, Ms. Butterfield, but let me clue you on something. Artists are a pretty private lot. You may think we're duffers, but we don't appreciate having our concentration broken by outsiders. Next time, I suggest you phone before you come."

Minka had followed them, muttering in her own language. "Street shows. What did the little (Russian obscenity) really want out here?"

Cass sighed as she climbed in the truck. *That didn't shed any light on anything. Obviously I didn't take the right approach. Sorry Pike, the dog ate my homework.*

As she passed the McDonald's sign she felt a stir of hunger, hadn't had anything but a granola bar since early morning. Now it was after three and the parking lot was almost empty. Where was the after-school rush? Then she remembered it was Saturday of a holiday weekend. The restaurant was blissfully deserted. Cass went to the counter and ordered a small burger and fries, with a large Dr. Pepper. Receiving her tray and the empty cup, she took it to the spigots and filled it with ice and soft drink, stepping aside to make room for the next customer.

"Well, good afternoon." It was Charmian Smith, looking as if she had just walked away from a luau in an olive green muumuu and purple slippers, a peony in her orange hair. "Shall we share a table?" she said smiling, and Cass thought: the warmth of that smile makes up for a curious taste in clothes.

"Let's do." She slid into the nearest booth. "How's the library these days?"

"Well, we miss our little Jessie, of course, but she writes me that she is happy down on the Rez. They've given her a horse to ride. I must say I'm relieved that she isn't in this town right now. I get a very strong presentiment of impending danger."

It occurred to Cass that precognition could be a useful gift in these days. "Do you get any specific emanations from anybody?"

"Oh, there are always good and bad vibes." The librarian attacked her hamburger hungrily. "You try to tune most of them out. If you opened up to every sensation you'd go bonkers. The human spirit is such a supermarket of emotions."

"Some of them perishable," Cass murmured, thinking of Guy. "I can see it might become a burden to have access to so much — uh — unauthorized knowledge."

"I'll let you in on a little secret —" Charmian reached across to lay a hand on her wrist, and the sentence would never be completed. The woman seemed to go into shock. Color ebbing from her face, speechless, she hung there blinking as if something were wrong with her eyes.

"Charmian! Are you okay?"

"I'm — I'm —" Obviously in distress, she was gasping for air. "I never saw anything quite — I can't —"

With deepening dread Cass reached out and took Charmian's fingers in her own. "Does that help?"

It almost sent the librarian into a spasm. She plunged away, out of the booth.

"Come on, you've been my guardian once before. Tell me what you see."

"That's just it, I don't see anything. You're gone. I mean, you're here, of course, but I can hardly see you for the darkness."

The big sunny room was blindingly bright from the late afternoon sun striking in through the large windows. The air was warm, full of grease smell, but Cass could feel a wave of coldness coming at her like fog.

Charmian shook her head. "I can't help you. I'm sorry, I've got to get out of here." She rushed for the door as if her life depended on it.

Cass sat limp. The episode had drawn energy out of her like a sump pump. She could almost feel Charmian's pitch-blackness, that atavistic terror of the dark, the sense of suffocation. It had been her own nemesis for years. Only after intensive trials at the training camp had she gained any power over it, which obviously was a self-deception. The thing could still swamp her. She was filled with nameless terror, with the strong image of a coffin. If that was it, she prayed she was dead before they put her in it.

28

Denial is the body's tourniquet against emotional hemorrhaging. The shrink had said that and tried to get her to face facts, which she usually did anyway. Like now — it was no good telling herself that ESP is an unscientific excursion into realms that have never been charted. In her travels she had seen enough to be a believer. So don't try to ignore it, use the warning and try to prepare for it. For instance: how could that premonition pertain to her evening activities?

The note had been stuffed under her door, big printing in laundry marker: GOLLAGER'S TONIGHT, NINE O'CLOCK, IF YOU'VE GOT THE NERVE. Had to be Hollis. She couldn't imagine his being a real threat, but face it — any man is strong enough if he sets the trap right. Suppose he's in cahoots with somebody else, Rafe Gollager? What if Rafe were a flea? Suppose this was a trap and she ended up locked in a cellar or the trunk of a car. But hell, nobody could kidnap her amid that crowd of Saturday night revelers. Cass tried to think it through, sitting at her kitchen table over the remains of a cheese sandwich. She almost missed the yellow walls, they had distracted her from too much cogitation. The restaurant probably has a big freezer behind the scenes, cold, pitch-black . . .

When the phone rang she almost jumped out of her socks. Clenching it hard, she said, "Yes?"

"Bunny? Is that you? You sound odd."

"Pike! You're back!"

"No, I'm not. I'm calling from — is this phone safe to talk on?"

"No. At least I'm not sure. I never did find the bug, but I think there's one somewhere around here."

"Then I won't go into detail, but what I found will rattle your teeth. I won't go into it over the phone, but I want you to stay put, right there inside your house until I get back."

"You find out about a terrorist attack over this weekend?"

"Nobody's talking, but the way they're pussyfooting around, I could connect the dots. I think your fleas are planning to assassinate the President of the United States. I have a friend who works in Homeland Security. He's flying to Colorado tonight, so draw your own conclusions."

She shivered. "The talk to the Air Force Academy? Why can't he just call it off, the President, I mean?"

"It's an election year, he doesn't want to look like a wimp. But if I can nail down a few things when I get back, maybe I can persuade them I'm not too far off-target. What I found here —" He stopped short. "This isn't good, where can I call you on a safe phone?"

"I'm going out to Gollager's tonight. Try me there about nine-thirty."

"Didn't I just tell you, for Godsake, to stay somewhere safe? Just until I get home, Bunny. I'm flying back tomorrow. When I get there I am going to make somebody listen to me, even if I have to go over their heads direct to FEMA."

"The earthquake people?"

"I've learned they do more than natural disasters. In time of crisis, which includes terrorism, they have almost unlimited power to act. They can suspend the Constitution . . . never mind. I guess you can't get hurt at Gollager's, other than a few broken bones. I will call you out there."

■ ■ ■ ■

The dark brown sweater and black jeans made her look like a stick of hazelnut, whittled to a frizz of sap-wood on top. Cass ran a comb through her cowlick and slung the stiletto. The piece of turquoise at her throat was in startling contrast to the rough clothes. She put on a small stab of lipstick and a quick brush of blusher. Pulling on the red wool jacket she felt a ping in her shoulder; weather must be on the way. *Good Lord, I'm getting old, developing a bone barometer.* Trying to outdistance the thought, she rushed off to the truck.

When she reached the road house the big room was rumbling with gaiety and beer talk. The combo seemed to be on a break, couples were dancing to the juke box. The ancient machine was delivering a worn-out rendition of Johnny Cash's "Ring of Fire." With the booths all full of outlanders, she headed for the bar. At the far end Mae waved a welcome, but it was Rafe who moved in to take her order.

"Draft," she told him. "Miller's if you've got it."

"Sure you don't want to wait on that a little?" He leaned across with a leprecaun leer, speaking in a lowered voice. "You'll find something fancier down in Cabin Six." And moved away, leaving her unserved.

Irritated, she had half a mind to sit there and wait until Mae came to bring her a brew. But another thought was stronger, to get this silly business over with, drub Hollis about the ears, and then come back for a drink.

Six was the last unit on the motel row. Away from the bright lights of the neon sign, the log cabin stood deep in shadow. She could make out a faint glow around the drawn curtains at the front window. Ten feet short of the door she came to a halt. Hollis had always been strong as wire, and after a hitch in the Army the man might have a few new tricks. Especially if he'd been recruited by the Flea Circus — she was sure he was perfectly capable of a little amateur terrorism. And he was no Joe Spinney, he'd be smart about it. Stooping, she found a pebble and shied it at the door.

"Come in," a muffled voice reached her.

Another pebble.

He opened up then, standing there in lanky silhouette against the light. "Well, hell, I said 'Come in.' What you hanging around out there for? Don't you want a drink? I got us some bubbly — Rafe's best stock." He waved the bottle, on which he had obviously already started.

"I don't like champagne and I don't have anything to celebrate."

"Oh brother." He snorted. "No wonder everybody's talking about you being a crackpot."

"You're a fine one to talk. What's got into you, coming around my house, making a racket, cussing and slamming your fist on the door as if I had some obligation to be at home? Hollis, what makes you think I owe you a thing?"

"Well, 'owe' — I don't know." He stood there peering into the darkness, a little unsteady on his feet. "Consarn it, Sandy, I can't yell across at somebody I can hardly see. I asked you down here so we could have some privacy, try to iron some things out."

"I personally don't have any wrinkles, but it's for sure that you do." She advanced a few steps. "We had one date and you thought it gave you stock options on me. You thought wrong, and I want to hear you admit it."

"Aw, shoot. I feel stupid standing out here like this. Come on in, girl. Nobody here but us hardware merchants."

Truth was, Cass felt a twinge of silliness herself. Walking forward slowly, she stepped up onto the porch of the cabin.

"That's more like it." He bowed her inside and closed the door. Then in an instant he had seized her, clamped her to him so tight it knocked the wind out. "Now, let's talk. About women who lead a man on with their eyes and all that playing hard-to-get." Breath strong with Listerine and liquor, lanky hair smelling of pomade, he tried for a kiss and missed, mouthing her neck.

Arms pinned, Cass reviewed her options. His feet were spread, his crotch an open invitation, but it's a mean thing to knee a man in his privates. As he ranted on . . . "knew it, soon as we were together . . . your kitchen that day, could have done it right there on the floor." Cass squirmed enough to lock her hands together in a double fist. With a sharp upward thrust, she knocked his head back, but he still kept his grip on her arms. The shoulder was whining. So it had to be the genitals after all. ". . . way you danced, rubbing up against me . . . ought to be a law against a woman propositioning a man with her body."

"Hollis! Knock it off! There was no way I could have sent you any signals. Six months ago I was raped. Since then, being touched by a man makes me sick. If you don't let me go I will vomit all over you."

But he was past listening. Hard and giving off waves of heat, he fumbled frantically with her sweater, trying to find an opening. Fighting down the rise of bile in her throat she roared, "Let-me-go!" And wriggled into position to give him the knee.

At that point the door burst open explosively and Boyd Ruger loomed over them. The big Texan picked Hollis off her like a worm off a cucumber, gave him a shake and discarded him on the floor in a sprawl. In tones of contempt he said, "Ah thought Ah smelled some shenanigans going on." He wasn't even breathing hard. "You want me to call the law, Miz Butterfield?"

"Not worth the hassle," she said, tucking her shirt in.

"Couldn't agree with you more. Any pore excuse for a man who's got to force himself on a woman ain't worth a spit of tobacco juice. Now you listen up, shorthorn. You ever mess with a lady again Ah will personally burn the Rocking R brand onto your scrawny butt."

Hollis sat up, groaning. "What's it to you?"

"Aside from holding with decency and good manners? Well, buster-boy, let's just say Ah have chosen this town to live in and run a bidness in, and nothing will ruin a place faster than a few bums like you and that Foreman. You got no class. You don't contribute, you just foul the air with your bad talk and disrespect for women. You're like a blight on a wheat field, you spread a kind of rot. So set there and think on it. This is your town too. Only it grew up and you didn't."

Ushering Cass back out into the cold night air, he steadied her with a hand under her elbow, just enough to counter the slight dizziness she felt. Over in the dancehall the combo was back, playing, "Mama, Don't Let Your Babies Grow Up To Be Cowboys."

"You all right, Ma'am?"

"Yeah. Thank you." She heard her voice pitched high with stress and felt a touch of surprise. She hadn't felt all that endangered. But the smell of sweat, the feeling of his hard-on, had brought back memories that were almost paralyzing. "How did you happen to come by just at the right moment?"

"Got to confess, Ah was following you, Ma'am."

"Please, call me Sandy."

"Mah pleasure. Would you let me escort you home? Or would you rather have a drink?"

"I could use a shot of brandy."

"Atta girl." He gave her arm a slight chuck without being offensive.

When they walked back into the bar Rafe gave them a startled look and did a fast fade. Ruger grunted. "Ah'll have words with that l'il gopher too. He he'ped set the thing up. Ah saw 'em plotting back there awhile ago." A booth had become vacant for them as if by magic. Seating Cass, the Texan went to the bar where Mae poured a couple of drinks. She looked puzzled, disturbed.

When he got back the big man settled himself opposite Cass the way a pile of hundred-pound grain bags settles into a wagon bed. "Only thing wrong with a small town, folks begin to mess into each others' bidness, and Ah reckon that includes me. Ah purely don't like that Anderson fellow. He's come on strong to a couple of mah lady guests. Boy's got an off-look in his eye, if he was a hoss Ah'd sell him for dog-food. When Ah come in tonight Ah see him and Gollager bad-laughing around, Ah knew some kind of mischief was going down. Then you headed off for that cabin — couldn't he'p it, Ah had to follow along. Ah got respect for you, Miz Sandy."

Cass was surprised to hear it.

"Out there after the shooting the other day, you were stanch. Stood by the Chief, took care of his kid — Jessie's a right nice little pup. Ah couldn't see you being manhandled by some jerkwater fool."

Cass said, "I thought I could talk some sense into him. We used to kid around back in high school. Now, he's got some strange delusion that we were meant to be a couple." She felt sick, pity is a rotten emotion.

Ruger nodded slowly. "You been through things like this before, you got a kind of sadness about you. A wisdom."

"Not a lot of people would agree with you these days," Cass smiled wryly.

He chuckled. "Small town doesn't need a newspaper, word gets around. But actions speak, and Ah like your moves, lady." He gave her a big honest-Injun grin that set off every bell in her watchtower. On alert now, she decided to try an experiment.

"Trouble is, Hollis was always a hero to the girls in high school. Of course I never was sure whether they liked him or his father's old '62 Mustang convertible. Powder-blue, V-8 engine, we're talking major irresistible."

"Yeah, that was one sweet little car." Ruger didn't want to discuss Hollis any more. There was a slight current of purpose in his idle questions as he went on. "They say you went to some art school over in Europe? Sounds pretty exciting. After all that how on earth could you settle for Panhandle?"

"Easy." She gazed innocently into his eyes. "I wanted to live a quiet life."

At that point, Mae appeared beside the booth. "Sandy, there's a call for you at the bar." And as Cass followed her, she went on, "It's Pike Webster. I don't get it, why would he call you here?"

She picked up the receiver. "Hi, Chief, what's up?"

"You okay?"

"Doing fine, with the help of a friend." *Why did I say that? To needle him? Why should I want to make him jealous? As if I could?*

"What friend!"

"Boyd Ruger. I was having a little wrestling match with Hollis Anderson when he stepped in to help mop up."

An odd sound, like a groan, came from the receiver. "That's exactly what I was afraid of. I had a hunch if you went out to that hootenanny tonight he'd be there. What I couldn't tell you this afternoon, your hunch about the guy was right. Reason I came down to Texas, I decided to check him out in person. When you asked if I was sure this was the real Boyd Ruger I realized I didn't know. So I showed our guy's picture around to all his buddies and they never saw the man before. They said their Boyd Ruger left Texas two years ago for a trip around the world. I did a little checking with a friend in the government, his passport says he is now living in Indonesia. When I think of the kind of money it takes to pull off a switch like that —"

"Flea Circus has unlimited funds."

"But if they've got all that money — ?"

"Why would they want to tear down the government? So they could head up a new one, run the world their own way. It's a power trip, Pike."

"You don't sound too surprised."

"I already found out that our Ruger never ran a Ford agency in his life, he doesn't even know that there was no '62 model Mustang."

"Well, I already figured there was something wrong with the guy. He comes on too big, too Texan, if you know what I mean."

"He's also the kind who would hire a first-class sniper to do his dirty work, but I can't picture him trafficking with Joe Spinney."

"I can," Pike snapped. "Anyway, we've got to figure how you're going to get out of there in one piece."

"He's not going to make any moves with all these people around. Anyway, right now he's having a word with Rafe Gollager. I can wander on out to the truck and be gone by the time he notices."

"I'll be home tomorrow. I fly into Pueblo around ten. Then I intend to get a posse together if I have to and close down operations at the Rocking R. Would you please — please — do me a favor and if you can't bear to stay in the house, at least get out of town just for the day? There may be some ricochet from all this. The Feds have already cancelled most of the President's appointments, over the weekend. But he's still going to talk to the Air Force graduates. And there's some sort of dedication ceremony scheduled to honor the pilots lost in all the wars — it's a big deal, just the kind of thing that would make your fleas hop. So if we start rounding them up, they might be a little angry at you. I don't want to have to worry. Do me a favor, take the day off, go fishing."

"I hear you. Good luck, Pike."

Cradling the phone, she waved at Mae. "Tell Boyd Ruger I had to leave in a hurry," she said. And made it to the door without notice.

Out in the parking lot it was a different matter. A dark figure angled against her car.

"So you finally got rid of the big boy,"

Hollis said, slurring his consonants.

Oh for the love of heaven! Cass went straight at him. As he came to meet her, arms outspread, she slammed her boot into his crotch full force. He went down, strangling, and she walked on.

29

The Nightmare

The air smells like wet wash, but it's good to be out of the warehouse. Even the mingled stenches of the harbor are welcome because they help clear her head. She senses a dwindling of that awful subservience. As they push her along, she could have resisted.

She doesn't. She lets them manhandle her, even though the temptation is strong, to test herself against the drug. Pain helps, it stimulates the adrenaline to dissipate the chemicals. They must not suspect this, they must not guess, if she's to have a chance.

Her will power is as slow to rise as the morning tide that laps the piers, a few inches higher with each wave. The silent undulation of waters is silvered now with the oncoming dawn, though the lights on the yacht still patch the depths with red. The long row of portholes are dark, friends inside, sleeping, unaware. Of course there should be someone on watch. They'd hear the shot — too late.

"Ain't you gonna use the Tootsie Roll?" The rube has an advanced state of jitters by now.

"Nah. Why would you use a silencer? You heard the boss, gnf gnf, he wants 'em to find the body before it sinks."

They had come up to the edge of the dock, nothing below but a welter of slippery shadows in which a few dim objects float, a wine bottle, a rind of melon. "So go on and do it! Let's git! I don't lahk this place."

"You got no sense of ceremony, man." Gnf gnf gnf. "Dying is important. She got to pay her respects to her executioner." There's a glint of metal as a gun is held up to her face. "Kiss it, girl. It's gonna put you outa your misery."

She swallows a wave of revulsion, bends her head and deliberately touches the gleaming steel with her lips. But by choice, she does it by choice!

Snorting with amusement the man moves behind her, the grip on her arm relaxes — time it right — ! With all the strength she can summon she wrenches free and hurls herself downward toward the black slop below. She never remembers going in.

■ ■ ■ ■

As she lay in bed trembling, Cass was halfway back in the moment of that other sunrise. The deceptive beauty of daybreak lying over the harbor, the masts of the boats rocking on the tide. Then reality set in and she bolted upright. Stumbling out of bed, she rushed to the bathroom and turned on the cold jet of the shower. This was no time to relive old terrors.

Today was going to be the end of the chase. There wasn't much sense of triumph. She had felt a kind of liking for Boyd Ruger, in spite of his overblown caricature of a cattleman. It was hard to picture him hiring somebody to kill her. And yet there was a cold calculation in his eyes that never quite got erased by the cowboy grin. A man who craves power, that was obvious. If the country were plunged into anarchy by another massive terrorist attack, one that would take out the President, he'd have his players in place to step in and bring order out of chaos, run the government and look like a hero doing it.

A chilly morning, clouds were moving in from the west, pouring down over the Sangre de Cristos, swallowing the heights in a gray mist. Here on the plains the air smelled of rain to come. The kitchen languished in the dull light. By now Cass had to admit she missed the yellow, even the ridiculous chicken. Her new clock was invisible, wood blending with the background, except for the orange hands that darted out in search of the time. Eight forty-five. When would Pike be back? Noon, he said. How long before they hit the Rocking R?

I ought to be there.

And that was exactly the kind of thought the Chief was afraid of. She had to admit: he was right. Her part in this was over. But it took all the self-discipline she could muster to set the idea aside.

So go make a pot.

In the converted ceramics studio, she took down a jar that she had thrown and put it on the banding wheel to study it, turning it slowly. A large chunky thing, it needed some graceful contrasting decoration, not brush-work, maybe incised — no, too delicate. As she pondered it the phone rang.

Running back to the kitchen she snatched it up, then controlled her voice. "Yes?"

"Hallo. Miz Butterfield? Winsor Wright, here. You probably don't remember me. I'm one of the ah-tists out at the Hacienda, enjoyed your little talk the othah night."

Very languid, almost an English accent. "I believe you were interested in locating some engobe."

"Oh. Yes, I am. I understand that you use it on canvas. Very interesting. How do you keep it from cracking off once it's dry?"

"Mmm, well, it is a bit of a praw-blem. You lay it on rahther thinly and then use a charcoal fixative. The point is, if you'd like to acquire some, I would be happy to direct you to the place I found it. Rahther nice deposit, actually, if you don't mind the smell."

"I don't. I'd be grateful to know the location."

"Well, I was prospecting around in the ravines below the foothills, looking for metallic effects. All sorts of minerals were washed down in that sump water below the coal mines, don't you know? And there it was, I sweah, liquefied clay, slick as if it had been deflocculated."

"You know some ceramics, then."

"Oh, just to dabble in. I took one course when I was at Bahsten College. We used slip to cast our pieces, and that's what this felt like. Interesting color, I call it 'pond-scum' green."

Copper sulfate from the hydraulic pumps? Cass tried to think what she had heard about the mechanisms that were used to unwater the mines. "It sounds interesting."

"I should add that it was only because the ground was wet that I found it. A day much like this — just a light drizzle, but it showed as a slick against the sandy bottom of the gulch. I'd take you out theah but I cahnt leave my easel right now, the latest work is in critical condition, you understand?" He gave a slight titter. "Do you know where that monument-thing is, the awful sculpture they put up to honor some people who once died?"

"Ludlow? Yes, I'm quite familiar with it."

"Well, it's just beyond that, up a perfectly dreadful road, gross-looking slag dumps, so forth. There's a row of humpback kilns . . ."

"Coke ovens, yes."

"At that point you have to leave your vehicle and walk across a cow pasture. I encountered a bunch of wild cattle that had to be driven off. Better weah your boots, if it rains the place will be a quagmire. Anyhow about midway along you'll see a break in the row. You can walk out onto the bank of a ravine. It's at that point exactly wheah I climbed down, rahther steep, watch your footing — oh, the Devil! I really ought to go with you, woman alone in that desolate place."

"No thanks, Mr. Wright. I wouldn't think of taking you away from your work. I know that country pretty well, I can find it. It was good of you to get in touch."

Putting the phone down, Cass headed for her bedroom to change clothes. A hunt for some ceramic raw materials sounded just right to reorient her. After today she was going to have to make a whole new stab at being Sandy Butterfield, small-town ceramist. Better start right now. The prospect didn't seem as grim as it once had.

Pulling on sturdy short boots she filled her knapsack with old mayonnaise jars to collect samples, slung her stiletto, hung the rock hammer at her belt. *Today we are on vacation, have some fun, girl.*

The word wasn't even in her vocabulary, fun. But she did feel a sense of freedom as she drove westward along the secondary. Had to keep reminding herself that Pike was perfectly able to handle things on his own. She wondered at that reference yesterday to FEMA. Have to ask him about that. She kept watching the back road, force of habit, but nothing moved behind her for miles in the distance. When she reached the highway overpass she stopped and waited; no sign of life appeared in her wake. *Will I ever get over this?*

The radio had been on all the way — now she seemed to have come into a better area for reception, it had picked up a news program.

The anchorman was explaining that the new memorial was a statue to honor the fallen pilots of all our wars, to stand in the middle of the main concourse at Denver International Airport. Dedication ceremonies at one p.m. tomorrow, the occasion to be made historic by the presence of the President of the United States. That was such a prospect for disaster, Cass shivered. Thank the Lord it would be forestalled now. *Here's to you, Pike Webster.*

Following the road across the highway and down into the hollow past the Memorial, she got the usual twinge of nostalgia. How her father had loved this place. Empty of life it was hard now to picture this as the scene of terrible violence, but he could make you see it, superimposing the course of the battle upon the land as if he'd overlaid it with one of Minka's transparencies . . . She felt an odd mental click, as of a tumbler dropping in a combination safe. But the door wouldn't open and she didn't want to puzzle over it today.

She steered the truck across the railroad tracks, past a handful of new cottages off to one side, and up a narrow road that once had led to a mighty coal field. She passed the remains of a tipple — across the decades the deafening noise of grinding rock seemed to echo, the thunder of the black gold from the chutes into the cars on the railroad siding. The tracks were gone, but their flat right-of-way still marked the course of the trains, engines hauling empty gondolas up the canyon that rose steep on either side. The road wound past towering mounds of slag, burnt-out now, but once they had smoked with the inevitable stench of smoldering dross. The sour black water pumped from the mines had added to the heavy mix of odors as it ran into the gullies — a sort of Hell on earth, with miners' families housed all up and down the canyon in the midst of it. The crumbling foundations of their huts were everywhere.

And then ahead the bottom of the canyon broadened and Cass saw the double row of coke ovens, forty or fifty of them. She had poked around them many times, primitive kilns used to convert the coal into a more concentrated form of smokeless fuel to feed the blast furnaces at CF&I in Pueblo. The rounded mounds of firebrick looked like beehives, about six feet high, all fire box. The method was to fill them with coal and light it, then brick them up again tight. Fire doesn't burn well with limited oxygen, it just smolders until the gases and impurities are driven off, takes two or three days. Then they were opened, the big clinkers of coke pulled out and loaded onto the trains. Loose bricks still lay everywhere around the gaping black maws where the walls had been torn down in a wedge-shaped opening from the crown of each oven to the bottom.

In the middle of the rank she saw the break, it had to be the one Wright had mentioned. Parking the truck she got out. The rockhammer promptly fell off her belt. Without a thought, she picked it up and dropped it down the back of her shirt where it lodged against her belt line.

At least there weren't any cattle around today, though the deep tracks in the mud showed they had been here recently. Sparse pasture, scraggly cocklebururs, nettles and prickly pear, and silence so deep it was tangible. It was as if she had come onto a planet and discovered the primitive remains of a vanished society. The old cairns felt like prehistoric ruins, the gaping mouths tinged red from oxidation, their interiors black as lava from a thousand burnings. Her footsteps crunched the gravel so loudly she found herself almost tip-toeing. Not even any birds? Was the canyon so full of deadly echoes that it was haunted forever?

Moving on past the row of ovens she came out onto the bank of the cut where the pumped seepage had flowed. Black grit, overgrown with grama grass in places, no sign of any greenish slick. Nor was there a good place to climb down. As she looked around her she was aware of an anomaly — an oven in the second row whose open maw had been partially bricked up again, using the materials scattered about. She went over for a closer look. It was fairly new reconstruction, done by someone competent. The firebricks were wedged in so tight there was only a thin bead of cement that had squeezed out. She scratched at it with her fingernail, it hadn't completely set . . .

Cass turned to run, but by then of course it was too late.

30

"Forget the knife," Quentin instructed, stepping out of the shadowy depths of a coke oven thirty feet away. "I've heard you're good with a stiletto, Cassie, but it won't beat a bullet." A snub-nosed automatic in his fist, crew-cut hair at attention, little beard neatly trimmed, dressed in a safari jacket and khaki pants the burly man looked as smug as if he'd just written "For Whom the Bell Tolls."

This is how the lion feels before he shoots it.

"Coming off to this deserted place alone," he was saying, "I'm surprised, my dear. I'm afraid you've lost your edge."

Amen to that. "How could you be so sure I'd take the bait?"

"If you hadn't we'd have had to acquire you another way and bring you here. We were tracking you — simple bug on your truck, placed there when you paid us that unexpected visit. You surprised us that day, we barely had time to get into our Bohemian personas."

One thing she had to know: "I can't believe Guy would help you set me up."

"Magee, poor fellow. He's been rather confused about you." The man spoke casually, as if they were having a pleasant conversation over drinks. "We managed to convince him that you're a terrorist hiding out, which would explain the FBI's unusual interest in our town. You helped things along with your strange behavior, all those defense mechanisms you installed around your house. I confided to him that I am the heroic anti-terrorist sent to track you down and so forth. Nice twist, eh? It helped allay suspicions he'd begun to have about me. The man wasn't a total fool, and I make an incredibly bad artist. Fortunately the story we spun began to make sense to him — enough that he planted our bug on you."

"The dummy? But I searched that."

"You didn't scrape the paint off the face. Our receiver is imbedded behind the red spot on the nose. State of the art, very small. That charming girl in our office is quite clever with miniature devices. It's a powerful little gadget, enough to pick up both ends of your phone conversation with our good Chief Webster yesterday. For a small-time cop he's remarkably tenacious. He could have ruined our plan, in fact the entire future of our operation, if he were allowed to contact the forces of Homeland Security. Not to mention FEMA. If the feds ever sniffed out the origin of the disaster that's about to happen, two years of careful planning — and considerable investment — would go down the drain."

Stalling for time while she cast about for some line of escape Cass said, "I know he mentioned FEMA, but I thought they just did earthquakes."

"One of the government's best-kept secrets," Quentin nodded. "FEMA does specialize in disasters, but their underlying mission is to protect the government process in case of a potential take-over, and they have awesome authority. With a quick stroke of the pen they can shut down the transportation in this country, impose martial law, even suspend the Bill of Rights. Their mandate is so sweeping they can move to stop impending anarchy without the bother of due process. So a conspiracy to assassinate the President falls in their jurisdiction."

"The dedication of the memorial to the

pilots?" That notation on the calendar: *Denver.*

"Good of them to place it the middle of an international airport — can you think of a more significant target? What better way to send a message to those quaking Europeans that they'd better keep their heads in the ground and hope the real movers and shakers of this world won't take over their pitiful countries?"

So do something. Fake a faint? Distract him long enough to get a handful of dust, gravel, throw it at him . . . She said, "I don't think you have to worry about Pike, he's on the wrong track."

"Yes. When he went to Texas I supposed as much. Imagine getting all hot and bothered about that ridiculous caricature of a cattleman. It gave us time to set up our defenses."

"Why not just let him follow his false lead? He'll never figure out the real villains here." *Wrong! He'll be on you like itchweed, but maybe not in time.*

"I'm afraid he would. You see, whenever he went back to his home he would find a message on his answering machine which would send him running in our direction. A whole new clue to follow, thanks to the late lamented Guy."

"Late?"

"I know why you keep edging toward that oven, my dear. You figure you can duck inside and I'll have to come after you. But I won't. I'll just spray the interior with hot lead and some of the ricochets will take you down. Hate to do that — you might get killed in the process and we have use for you alive."

"What use?"

"You'll see. I'm waiting for a phone call. In the meantime I don't mind the chit-chat, one spy to another, it's rather invigorating. As I was saying, in his final moments Guy threw quite a wrench in our machinery. He had developed certain suspicions about us, and then you went to see him, at his shop in town. You must have said something that energized him. He decided you were not a mad bomber after all, which meant we must be the bad guys. He began to poke around where he didn't belong and found a very damaging clue, Minka's passport, which gives her full name, Maritza Chernovski. He confronted her and she was happy to admit that she's wanted by Interpol for a long career of talented violence. She never intended for him to live, but he saved us the trouble of a lot of bloodshed. Popped some pretty lethal pills."

"Guy's dead?"

"Quite. Poor fellow, he was living in the wrong century you know. But before he took his own life he managed to leave the message for the Chief — oh, eventually we'll gain access and erase it, but those things have to be handled carefully. We can't afford to draw attention to our base of operations, not after all the time and money we spent setting it up. So we'll have to intercept the Chief when he gets off his plane and steer him in another direction. With your help."

"No!" Cass glanced down the steep drop into the ravine. Rocks in the bottom, nowhere to hide.

"Would you rather we put a bullet in the fellow, right there in the airport parking lot?"

"If you kill Pike Webster you'll activate a whole troop of FBI agents, they'll smell you out eventually."

"I quite agree. We only want to buy ourselves some time, my dear. That's why —" His cell phone made a melodic trill. He flipped it open and listened a minute. "Yes, all right. Just meet him as the passengers deplane, tell him not to make a fuss, we have his little 'Bunny' in custody. Keep a close guard over him until I can speak to him. And watch out for the Feds." The Hemingway beard twitched in a smile as he pocketed the phone. "Confounded nuisance having the Bureau invade the town. That's why we took such small steps at eliminating you. Would have been nice if you'd gotten nervous and taken off for other parts."

"Well, you can blame your man, Virgil. He left a phone number in the cabin. When Pike tracked him down, it turned out the man was on the FBI's dirty list."

"Oh, you mean the sniper? He wasn't one of ours. We didn't even know he'd been given the contract on you. Some of our associates in Paris sent him out, payback for the death of our mole, Jacques, who was one of our best operators. Avenging him is fine, but we never would have approved the use of that uncouth man. We called him *le crapaud*."

"You prefer ham-handed old coots like Joe Spinney."

"Local help tends to be unsophisticated, but non-obtrusive. As I say, we try to keep a very low profile. If one of his attempts had proven successful it would have saved us a world of nuisance."

"That last time he sneaked into my house — ?" Cass was considering the odds of making a dash, around the ovens, dodging and jinking. "What was he supposed to be doing?"

"That was an experiment, one of our new chemicals. Very lethal, almost undetectable. He left a few grains mixed in with your coffee. We hoped it might even take the Sheriff out too."

"I emptied every open container in the kitchen."

"Of course you did. You're a well-trained operative. We knew it was a long shot."

"So now you're going to use the old coot to blow up the Denver airport."

Quentin looked offended. "Certainly not. You should know enough about bombs, my dear, to realize that the job of bringing down an edifice of that size is impractical. On the other hand, Serin gas introduced into the ventilation system at numerous spots, set off by remote control, should be interesting. More conducive of terror, which is what it's all about." The cell phone trilled again. "Yes. Good. Let me speak to him. Sheriff? Never mind that, let's don't waste time. She's perfectly fine, I'll let you talk to her." He moved closer, gun never wavering as he thrust it under her chin and held the cell-phone up. "Say hello, Bunny, dear."

"It's the Hacienda, Pike!" she yelled. "Go get 'em, don't worry about me." But by then

Quentin had jerked the instrument away.

"All right, Chief, here's what you need to do, if you want to keep the lady alive. First, you will not contact any federal agency, in fact you will try to get them off your tail. If they ask, you will convince them that a small-town sheriff got the wind up over nothing. Then you will go north from Pueblo, clear to Fort Collins, it should take you four or five hours. I have reserved a room for you at the Holiday Inn there. Stay by the phone and I will let you talk to our girl again. If you're not there, of course there is no reason to keep her alive and she will suffer a rather unpleasant death. Do I make myself clear?"

He held the phone slightly away from his ear, amused. "Is that a 'yes'? Good man. I knew you'd be reasonable." Flipping the phone shut, he opened it again and pushed the buttons with his stubby thumb. "Joe, you can come back now."

If I make a move, if I force him to shoot me, then he won't have any choice but to kill the Chief to keep him quiet. As long as he has a hostage, Pike will stay alive. She tried not to look at the oven with the opening half filled in — the brick-work left off about waist-high. The opening above was big enough to permit a body to be deposited inside. *I must not let them handle me —*

A mud-spattered truck had come around the bend from up-canyon, a white pickup with red lettering on the side:

AAA Rentals
Construction Equipment

In the cargo bed a small cement mixer was churning slowly. Cass had to swallow hard to keep her stomach from heaving.

"It won't work. Using me to hold over Pike's head — he doesn't give a damn about me. To him I am the biggest nuisance since horse flies."

"To us all, my dear lady. But you are wrong about the Chief. He's quite enamored of you. If you weren't so stressed you would have noticed it."

Enamored? "Boy, have you got that wrong."

"You really don't know? That night after night he has parked on the side street where he can watch your house, just sat there in the dark waiting for your light to go off? Fellow's acting like a lovesick schoolboy."

By now she was shivering, no time to think about what he'd said, she needed the antifreeze of anger to drive off the shakes. "So what did they do to old Jacques, the traitor?

You don't seem to mourn him a lot."

"No one loves a double agent. But I suppose we shouldn't be too hard on the fellow. After all he did come up with the suggestion for an ideal set-up in hinterland Colorado. We scouted a few other small towns in Kansas and Nebraska and a couple in Utah, but none was as perfect for our purposes as Panhandle." They watched Joe climb the slight rise, wheezing, carrying a bucket of wet cement.

As he joined them there was tinge of relish in his stolid face. "Caught us a fish, huh?" He set down his load and took out an inhaler.

"Don't approach her from the front. Our Cassandra has a black belt in judo. She's capable of throwing you down into the ravine. Go around and come up behind her, secure her arms."

"Pleasure," grunted the old man, circling her. Iron hands gripped her above the elbow, no point in struggling. She stood still and waited for her chance. *Mosquito spray.* There was a small can of it in the pocket of her parka. With her left hand she drew the garment forward an inch. Joe wrenched her sharply.

"Cut that out!"

"What did I ever do to you, Joe?"

"I knowed you was trouble the minute you hit town. Way the old lady carried on about you, like you was some long-lost orphan. Now you gone and ruined my whole marriage. Crazy old woman, had to go poking around and found them blasting caps I had stashed in the crawl space. She throwed me out, I lost the best meal ticket I ever had. I wisht I could twist your neck right here'n now."

"Sorry," Quentin said. "That would be premature. The Sheriff may take some further convincing if he fails to cooperate. We really do need to keep him as far as possible from Panhandle."

"You'll never get away with this, your cover is blown, your years of work are down the tubes," Cass taunted him to cover the panic that threatened her as he took out a leatherette folder and extracted a hypodermic, which he expertly filled from a small vial.

"Actually, I think our operation will be all right so long as the federal boys don't link the nervous willies of a small-town Sheriff to the event tomorrow. You and the Chief are the only ones who suspect anything right now. I intend to keep it that way. Hold her still." He advanced with the needle.

"No!" An involuntary, agonized burst.

"Hah. Don't like getting' stuck, huh?" Joe breathed in her ear, so close she could smell the medicine of the inhaler. "Listen boss, maybe you don't know but she got a knife slung around her neck. I can see the leather tie."

"Yes, Joe, I know. It doesn't matter, it's tempered steel, too brittle to be of any use in digging through a brick wall. Don't try to take it, you'll just precipitate a struggle and you can't spare a hand for that right now. Hold her still. Don't squirm, my dear, it's only a sedative, to give you a nap while the cement sets. When you wake up, you may have a slight headache, but there's a jug of water in there. You'll do fine, so long as you're not nervous about closed chambers." Cass felt the needle go in.

The numbing effects began almost instantly. *Got to make a move and make it now.* "Let me go, you toad!" Stepping backward, her boot heel crashed into Joe's shin and she stamped hard on his foot, wrenching free of his grasp. Aware of the gun coming up she snarled at Quentin like a trapped animal. "I'll do it. But don't let that man touch me again."

With the world beginning to tilt, she stumbled over to the opening in the side of the coke oven and summoning the last of her strength dove head-first through the narrow hole. Scraping elbows on hard brick, she went down into blackness.

31

Red . . . dark red . . . as she struggled back to consciousness a sea of oxblood was emblazoned across her closed lids. Slivers of silver floated on her inner vision like shreds of thinly sliced cabbage. With a groan Cass opened her eyes. The red stain still vibrated on the middle air, but beyond, all was pitch black. Flinging out a hand, she scuffed her knuckles on corrugations of stone . . . no, slag, the vitrified coating from many old fires. Coke oven! It all came back on a tidal wave of fear. When she sat up a throb of pain pulsed through her skull, clear out to the face bones. Couldn't breathe . . .

Primitive dread held her paralyzed, sucked the oxygen out of her lungs as she crouched like an animal in a trap. Total blackness, she could feel the walls closing in on her like a smothering blanket . . . Fiercely she fought the rising hysteria long enough for a thin trickle of rational thought to break through.

They must have left an opening somewhere for ventilation. Frantically she stared around her, squeezed her eyes tight shut, looked again. And saw it, a faint patch of lighter darkness far down near the bottom. She flung herself at it, lay with her face pressed close to the opening where one brick had been left out. She sucked at the thread of air that barely touched her face. Beyond was dim daylight, she could hear the patter of small rain on the brushy ground outside.

She could have cried with gratitude, to be in touch with the world. She tore at the hole with her hands, but the bricks were solid, holding the whole weight of the upper structure. Desperately she lay on her back and drove both feet at the wall, *come on, new concrete, it can't be set yet.* But it was. How many hours had passed? Even if it wasn't full hard, those bricks were wedged tight against each other in a shape that was one of the strongest in the world, an arch.

I'm never going to get out of here. They only intended to let me live long enough for their purposes . . .

Lying by the hole, sweating and shuddering, she felt as if she were bleeding to death inside, bleeding hope, bleeding confidence. The only link with sanity was the six-inch gap through which she could drink the wet air in small sips. That and a small spur of self-contempt.

You want to give up, die a loser?

It came back, a memory from her final week of tests at the training camp. Trust Kuzu to scope out your weakness. He had sent her into a four-foot square dark box and left her there for twelve hours. It was his business to weed out the ones who would crack under pressure. She had fought down the phobia, tried to devise means of combating it. They had been taught to use pain as a focal point. She had plucked the skin of her thigh until she felt blood wet on her hands. She had used anger, sheer rage to stiffen her quivering gut. *Damn the man for trying to ruin my career at the last minute!* One way or another it had worked and she had crawled out of the box, ten pounds lighter and a hundred times harder inside. Should have thanked her mentor. Instead she thumbed her nose at him. And passed the course.

That last day he had faced them, the nine who remained, out of thirty-one starters. As they stood at attention in the locker room of the old Army barracks he had spoken their valedictory, in that gravel-voiced growl, an old voice for such a young man — Kuzu couldn't have been more than thirty-five, scars to the contrary.

"Here's a final tip: When you find yourself *in extremis* accept the fact instantly. Don't waste time in denial, assess the danger and begin at once to plan how to cope with it. Never give up. Keep struggling with every skill, every ounce of strength and ingenuity, even if it means you just focus on taking one more breath and then the next. If you think you're lost you will be. The only way you can truly be defeated is in your head. If you refuse to give up, you may die, but you won't die a loser. And you might live." Then, with his only remaining hand, he had operated his wheelchair through the door and out of their lives.

Cass drew in a deep breath of air from the vent hole and sat up. A throb of pain pulsed through her skull. *He said they left some water.* Feeling her way across the crusted floor of the furnace pit she made contact with a familiar shape, a plastic jug. Unscrewing the top with shaking hands, she sipped the lukewarm liquid and the agony in her head subsided to half its strength. Tightening the cap carefully she set the bottle aside and looked at her watch, but the good one was gone, left in Albuquerque, and the Timex didn't have enough glow to cut the darkness. She had to guess that it said five thirty. Or maybe six-twenty-five. She'd been lying there unconscious all day. Or longer, all night too? She could only hope that it was still Sunday, that time had not run out. Quentin must have expected her to wake up within hours in case he needed her to speak to the Chief again.

Of course that ploy, of sending him to northern Colorado, was just a means of getting him away from Panhandle before they killed him, so their precious base would go unsuspected after the disaster tomorrow. She just prayed that Pike didn't fall for it. Surely he wouldn't let them blackmail him, he must have figured it out.

Beyond the air-hole rain was still falling, the steady female rain that causes seed to grow. Maybe weaken fresh-set concrete? She felt around tracing the segment that had been recently laid up. The joints were tight, only an eighth of an inch of bead squeezed out as they were forced together. Cement was never a factor in closing up the coke ovens, it was just a means of holding the walls in place until the final brick was placed. They always worked from the bottom up to the crown.

At the school in Germany her class had built a beehive kiln using a wooden template to hold the sides until the last brick was inserted in the top. Then, with the key in place, the framework was removed and they could stand on the thing, dance jigs on it, nothing could give. The dome is one of the most enduring shapes in all architecture.

An inspired holding cell. No, that implies that you're going to get out again. *This is a sarcophagus.* The word means "flesh-eater." The Greeks used to dig their tombs in limestone that would disintegrate the corpse . . . she had to go back for more air. That was clever, too, to place the hole so close to the ground she'd have to lie still beside it to stay alive. *Except I can't afford that, I have to make some sort of effort.*

As she rolled over Cass was aware of a sharp edge and bolted upright. The rock hammer was still in place, inside her shirt under the parka. It came back to her then, the desperate move to get rid of Joe, to keep him from handling her in those last minutes for fear he'd feel the tool. They'd never have let her keep that. Unbuckling her belt she let the thing fall out, then tightened up again and reached behind her. Felt the tungsten blade with a prayer of thanks. If anything could batter through the walls — no, not the walls. It would take too long to chop each fire-hardened brick out one at a time to create an escape hole.

Moving stiffly, Cass stood up, hand following the curve up to the crown. Find the last one set and dig that out, the whole top becomes unlocked, it should come down easily. It meant working overhead, swinging the rock hammer blindly. The blade seemed to bounce off the surface, no way to tell which spot she should concentrate on. *All you can do is try.* She swung again, and again, skinning knuckles, glad to get back a few grains of grit in her face. But it was hard to gauge where each blow was going. Couldn't aim at the same place because you couldn't see. Had to keep at it on faith. Fiercely she whaled away, as the walls closed in tighter. The oven seemed to be shrinking . . .

She was back at the hole again, gasping for air. Darker outside now, deepening into night. Shades of Charmian Smith! She had been right on the mark again. Blackness, what must it be like to see total darkness in the middle of a sunny day?

As she went back to work her muscles were screaming. *This is never going to work.* Then an accompanying thought: *So why fight? Why not just lie down and die — what does it matter?*

And the answer: *it matters to Pike.* He wouldn't go to Fort Collins. He'd come back home, and they would try to trick him away from the scene of their plots. They'll pressure him some more — return here with the phone. *I won't talk, I won't say anything. Because I won't be here!*

With every ounce of will power, Cass scrambled up and felt for the place she had been pounding. Was there a very slight scratch in one spot? She went at it again, but this time with a plan. Ten strokes right-handed, then ten with the left, and don't cater to the shoulder. Holding onto the hammer so hard her fingers ached, she slammed it again and again . . . *nine, ten.* Switched hands and went at it with her left . . . *eight, nine, ten.* And rest, *two, three, four, five . . .* Now, back with the right, do it for Pike. The thought warmed some of the ice that kept trying to form in her belly.

Odd thing Quentin had said. Enamored? Old-fashioned word, but it fit Webster. If he ever fell in love, he would be enamored. *But not with me, God knows. If the Chief kept a surveillance on my house, these nights when he didn't have anything else to do, with his Pony far away and his town under siege, well that's just his way of being a good cop. Quentin doesn't even know what makes a man like that tick . . . nine, ten.* Gagging for air, she left off and went to get her breath again at the hole.

This time when she went back to work she could feel a distinct groove. One, two, three . . . Don't think about the thin air in this death-hole, concentrate on something else. *Once I'm out of here, how will I get Liz back? I'll ask her to help me put some petunia plants in the yard, she loves petunias. I'll bake a terrible cake and take her some — she'll have to offer to come teach me how to do it right. I'll tell her I'm sick, I can't raise my arms — and that may be the God's truth.*

Her shoulders were in agony and her wrists were beginning to give with each blow. On her knees she fumbled around until she found the water jug, took a long draft. No need to conserve, it was do or die. And don't let things get so bad your muscles quit on you. Cass stripped off the parka, the T-shirt and wriggled out of the shoulder truss. With her pocket knife she blindly cut off a length of the elastic material and wrapped it tight around her right wrist, tied it with a split end, using the other hand and her teeth. Not easy in the dark, but when she got done the joint felt strengthened. She started on the left.

Putting the shirt and jacket back on, she took a hit of wet air, then returned to work, eyes closed against the grains that came down. Now when she felt of the brick above her she was sure there was a depression, wide and shallow, maybe an eighth of an inch deep. At that rate how many hours — ?

Forget it. It won't get done at all if you don't keep working. But after a while a dizziness came over her, a trick of the phobia, or lack of oxygen. Cass barely managed to lie down in time, gasping, light-headed. Make it a good break, five minutes, count to three hundred.

Think about the future. Stay in Panhandle? Why not? She'd had enough of big cities, traveled all over creation. *I actually like the town, or I would if I could be myself there, not Sandy. Maybe not Cass either, somebody in between. Good old Bunny, that's me.* The spell of regular breathing steadied her and she went back to work.

She thought she had the hang of it, now, letting the groove guide her blade . . . eight, nine, ten . . . the shoulder almost refused that time. *This is where I ought to pray. God, I wish I knew how . . .*

Seven, eight, nine . . . a small avalanche of rubble came down on her shoulders, face, mouth, chunks of hard grit. One more blow and this time her hammer's blade hooked onto an edge of brick. She swung again, bringing down larger chunks — she felt a wet splat on her nose. Rain. And air was coursing past her into the chamber. Tomb no more.

32

Cass pulled up the hood of the parka, then realized that her hair was already wet as if she'd dipped it in a bucket. Sweat from those final frantic minutes when she had pulled down the crown of the kiln, slamming the bricks, clawing them loose until the hole was wide enough to clamber forth into the night.

Feeling for footing she picked her way down off the embankment and across the sodden cow pasture, boots getting heavy with mud. And then she was on gravel, she had found the road. The truck was gone, of course. She had left the keys in it, no need to lock up in such a deserted spot. *Quentin was right, you're losing your edge.*

Cass peered again at the dim watch face. It was either 10:45 or 9:50. She began to trot, feeling for the edge of the blacktop to keep her on track, stumbling, legs felt heavy. Probably a touch of hypothermia setting in.

Under the parka she was sweating hard, losing a lot of salt, minerals, forgot to take a big drink from the jug before she made her escape. The need to get out of the trap was too great to permit reasonable thought.

She tried to catch some of the rain on her tongue. Still coming down light and steady, it gave a faint shine to something ahead, bars across the road, a cattle guard. She was nearing the foot of the canyon. And weren't there some houses off to the south?

Dimly a lighted window gleamed in the distance — she headed for it. *God, don't let them go to bed yet.* After some wrong guesses that took her through a field of weeds, she found the turnoff where a dirt road led to the little bungalow. In the pale glow from its windows she could make out a van in the yard: HARDY'S PLUMBING painted on the side panel. A dog had begun to bark in the yard behind the house. The porch light came on and a young man stepped out with a bird gun in his hand.

"Who's there?"

"Just a wet female looking for a telephone." A cheery croak, Cass hardly recognized her own voice. "I need —" she choked and tried again. "I need to put in a call to the Sheriff of Panhandle." As she stood dripping a woman came to peer out from behind him, face-cream and a bathrobe and a fierce scowl.

"Don't let her in, Ralph."

He surveyed the bedraggled clothes, the sodden boots, and chivalry won out. "She's alone and she needs help." He ushered me in. "Go get us some coffee, Junie."

"Thank you," Cass quavered. "Actually, she's right to be suspicious. There are some dangerous crooks roaming around out there somewhere. They stole my truck and left me for dead. I've been assisting Sheriff Webster in an investigation."

"You hurt?" Junie came back a few steps.

"I'm not too great," Cass said with an imitation grin, "but I'm not dead yet." Still dripping on the matt inside the door, she shook her head. "I can't go into that nice living room, I'll mess it up. All I need is a few minutes on your phone. I'll make sure you get paid back for any long distance charges."

As she spoke she had begun to thumb through the pages of the county directory that lay by the phone on the table in the front hall. The number for the Panhandle Police Department rang and rang until finally a recording came on inviting her to leave a message. Hanging up, she tried Pike's home, no luck.

Ralph had brought her a cup of coffee and a chair. She sank down gratefully and took the drink in hands that shook so hard she could hardly get it to her lips. A swallow of the hot liquid burned all the way down and sparked new life.

"Why don't you call Trinidad?" Ralph suggested. "They can radio through to his squad car if he's out on patrol. They've helped me a couple of times when somebody had an emergency break in their water line."

"My husband's a plumber," Junie added proudly. "Sooner or later ever'body needs a plumber."

"That's the gospel truth," Cass said through chattering teeth. "Good coffee. I do thank you." Like molten gold in her belly. "Trinidad's a good idea." She was beginning to think how to frame a message.

"Ask for Billy Hunt, he's a pal of mine," Ralph added.

Finding the number on the front page of the phone book, Cass dialed.

"Las Animas County Sheriff's Office."

"Hi. I have an emergency situation, I'm trying to reach Chief Pike Webster of the Panhandle Police. He may be cruising near Trinidad tonight, we have a flight-to-avoid-arrest situation on our hands. My vehicle was stolen, I don't have a c.b. or short wave."

"Yes, sir, I understand. What's the message?"

I must sound like Boris Karloff. She said, "Tell him, please, that the stolen merchandise is stashed in the pit at the Ludlow Memorial. Tell him this message is from Rabbit. That's my code name. And get the word to him as fast as possible, thank you." Draining her cup, Cass stood up.

"Drugs," Ralph nodded ominously to his wife. "They're a curse upon the world. You with the FBI?"

Cass shook her head. "DEA. Thank you for your hospitality."

Junie warmed abruptly. "You oughta stay here and wait for somebody to pick you up. It's really lousy outside."

"Thank you both, but I have to be down at the highway when he comes. Meanwhile, you folks stay in and don't open to anybody who can't show you an official i.d." Before they could ask for hers, Cass had slipped off out the door into the night.

It pained her to leave the warmth of their little world, but she wasn't about to bring Quentin and company down on that innocent couple. She was sure that the Flea Circus would be monitoring the airways, and her subterfuge wasn't going to fool them for a minute. So now it was a question who would get to Ludlow first. If Pike wasn't in a position to reach her he would know how best to activate the Fibbies who had been trailing him all month. God only knew where they were on a dark and stormy night.

You should have borrowed a flashlight, stupid. But she had come this far by touch and go. Cass trudged on downhill until she stumbled over the railroad tracks. Almost the end of the line. Going forward by guess, she came upon the chain-link fence around the memorial grounds, followed it to its gate and let herself in. Beyond, she just about fell over the cast ironwork that enclosed the monument itself. Negotiating that gate, she thought it was one more thing to slow down any pursuers.

If Quentin got here first, it would take him time to scope out the area and discover that she wasn't down in the pit — no way would she ever get into that pit. It was the original dugout in which eighteen people had died, most of them wives and children. They had dug holes to escape the bullets, but when the camp burned, many suffocated down there. Now the pit was covered with a heavy iron hatch to keep tourists from falling in.

This place where the women had made their last stand — Cass felt a kinship with them tonight.

Her enemy was an international criminal, the stakes were higher than anyone in the old days would ever dream, and yet it came down to basic survival after all. If she played it right Cass figured she might get the jump on Quentin. Provided he came alone. By now she figured Joe was long since in bed. In the darkness she would be invisible, the man couldn't stand off at a distance and bang away with his gun, even if he had a night-scope. She would keep hidden behind the sculpture, he'd have to come after her. To make any sort of search he'd have to shine a light, and that would work against him, make him a target. At close quarters she could put the knife in his vitals before he knew what hit him. At least it looked good in theory.

Now all I have to do is keep alive until the play goes down.

33

The rain was slanting slightly from the west. Crouching under the east side of the monument, she huddled beneath the parka to consolidate her body into one knot of warmth, summoning her yoga techniques, trying to keep the chakras open with firm words: *I can bring this off, I can do it, I have to do it for Jessie and Pike and Liz and Izzie and the President of the United States.*

Anger, use anger to get the blood pumping. Picture Denver International Airport tomorrow, crowded with Memorial Day visitors, top city officials attending the ceremonies, and then the insidious spread of lethal gas upon the air, bodies falling, confusion, death on every escalator, in every shuttle train. Thousands of people in the audience and on the overhead walk-ways, not to mention all the passengers heading home after the long weekend. Quentin had been so sure that she would never live, he had allowed himself the freedom to brag about it. Big mistake. At least she wasn't dead yet, by now the adrenaline was flowing with its false high.

Just in time. A glow flared beyond the low rise that separated the monument from the highway, a car had turned onto the road headed her way. Cass got up out of her crouch and forced her tortured arms to work, reached backward and drew the stiletto. Cold steel between her fingers, she held it under her parka, tested her legs with a couple of quick knee bends. Then, easing around behind the monument, she peered at the vehicle which swung into the outer parking lot . . . *No!*

That was no cop car, and FBI agents don't drive station wagons. In the backlash of light from the headlamps she could make out double antennas that still whipped faintly from the abruptness of the brake. Seconds passed, as if the driver might be calculating whether he could ride down that chain-link fencing. Decided not to try it. The door finally opened — no dome light, but he had left his heads on high, flooding the monument. The gentle rain fell through them steadily.

"Cass. Are you there?" From a hundred feet away the voice was too remote to identify, but it had a familiar ring. "I know you're not down that hole. You'd never make the mistake of dead-ending yourself. So you must be behind the sculpture. Come on, talk to me." He was advancing slowly, hands at his sides, no weapon showing. *And no telling who's backing him up with a rifle from inside the car.*

"I can understand your hesitation, but there's not much time left for palaver. I need your help to catch these varmints." The last word gave him away, even as he walked into the headlights — Boyd Ruger, or whoever, minus the drawl. "Look." He opened his raincoat, London Fog, fur-lined. "I'm not carrying. I swear, no tricks." Buttoning up again he let himself through the outer gate, then the inner one. "If I recall, your file states that you can stick a knife in a marshmallow at twenty paces. So I'll just keep back a bit, okay?"

A good forty feet away, too far to risk a throw.

"Okay, try this on," he said. "I'm here to see about buying those dogs you wanted to sell."

Somehow it didn't come as a complete surprise. If he wasn't one of Quentin's fleas he had to be from the Libra League. But that didn't make him safe. Anybody can double. If this man was true, why hadn't he taken out the operation at the Hacienda before now?

"How about this then: Come on out, Charlie Grandma."

That shook her. It was her working name at training camp. There'd been several people with the initials C.G.; they had assigned her an unconventional *nom d'école.* Hadn't thought of it in years.

"You don't remember me," he was going on, "but I was a D.I. at the camp, a different group, but Kuzu and I shared information about the recruits. He said you were one of the toughest we ever graduated. Come on, Cass, isn't that enough credentials? I'd call in the FBI to attest to my good faith, but they are off chasing shadows. Pike Webster and I have been working together all day in this area, trying to find you."

Talk's cheap.

"He finally shared his info with the Bureau and they reassured him about me. They respect the League, they signed off on my Rocking-R gig, a couple of years ago. I've got a pretty good rapport with them by now. As Ruger would say, we're all trying to rope the same critter."

But if you happened to eliminate me, they wouldn't shed any tears. Almost too worn out to think straight, Cass searched her instinct. What to believe, and what not to, with lives in the balance. She called out, her voice sounding thin and stressed even to her.

"If we're both on the same side, why didn't you make contact with me when I came to town."

"Good question. Which side was your side? At the time I didn't know. After you put that coded ad in the paper, we were convinced you were on our team. I was going to invite you back into the fold that night at the roadhouse when you ran out on me. Look, do we have to discuss this out in the rain?" It was dripping off his Stetson, running down his fingers.

Why doesn't he put on some gloves? Because it's easier to draw a derringer with bare hands.

"All right, tell me about my old friend, Jacques, what's he up to these days?"

"Dead. When we took him in for interrogation he was pretty fast with the cyanide pill. You were, essentially, his downfall. He got a little too clever with that plot to discredit you. But I guess he was desperate. You were due for reassignment to the United States. By then on his advice the Flea Circus had set up an operation in

Panhandle. If you went home, he figured you might realize what was happening and blow the whistle."

"I didn't know I was to be reassigned."

"The League was beginning to beef up its forces over here. Terrorism had come to America. Nine-eleven made believers out of everybody. We suspected that the Fleas were gathering somewhere in Colorado, one of our intelligence teams had picked up the scent. We knew you came from a town named Panhandle. We had intended to send you here to scout for signs. That's why Jacques put that business in motion, to take you out of play. It was pretty clever of him, to destroy one of his own teams. We knew there was a mole, but at that point we weren't sure where you fit in, as a co-conspirator, one that the Fleas decided to get rid of maybe? Maybe you were playing both sides of the game, blackmailing somebody? Anyway, Jacques wanted us to think so. He was too urgent in his condemnation. We began to doubt him, to look into his actions and finally ferreted out the truth. Still, you were his operative, you could have been a double and when you turned up in Panhandle we had to wonder if you were part of their plans."

"Why didn't you roll them up if you knew

they were here? What took you so long?"

"They were pretty cagey. The activities around town looked legitimate. But I realized at once there was too much cash flowing this way. That's why they decided to plant me here on that dude ranch, to get to be part of the scenery. It's not that there weren't clues, there were too many. I didn't like what was going on at Foreman's trailer park, I think it's a way-station for coyotes, bringing in Mexican illegals. I had my doubts about Gollager and even the Hacienda, though we'd never dreamed the fleas would plant their best agent on one of the local boys and get him to bring her back here as Mrs. McGee. I felt the answers were out there, but I hadn't any evidence, so I held my horses, to coin a phrase."

"How did you get the real Ruger to agree to the impersonation?"

"Oh shoot, Boyd was one of the original founders of the League. After he got hurt in a rescue operation, he had to retire. It was his idea for us to use him as a front. I know him, I knew I could do the act. But I wasn't picking up any leads until you showed up. I never believed in coincidences."

"It was no coincidence. I gave Jacques the original idea in a brain-storm session. I trusted the piece of scum!"

"So did we until after he turned on you. He should have been defending you. Cass, you sound like you're about to drop. Won't you get in the damned wagon?"

"So now you know that their headquarters is out there in the Hacienda."

"We do, thanks to Webster. As soon as he got off the phone with you, he called me. Earlier — yesterday — he had tried to sic the feds on me and they'd set him straight, that we're all on the same side. So when he realized they had you, he turned to me for help. He was afraid to tell the Fibbies for fear they would barrel in and get you killed. I had to convince him that there were more lives at stake than just yours. We had to move on The Hacienda fast."

"The woman is in charge of their operation along with a man named Quentin. I don't suppose you managed to get them?"

"The lady is now in the lockup in LaJunta, safe and sound. I didn't trust that flimsy little Panhandle jail. Quentin slipped our net, but there are APB's out all over six states, if Webster doesn't kill him first. The Chief nearly tore a piece off me for moving in on the art colony before we had you back safe. I told him you would understand."

"Thanks a lot." But she knew the League had its rules: no concessions to hostage-takers, ever. You get caught, you're on your own.

"Well, you coped with it, as I figured. But we don't want you to come down with pneumonia. Cass, I need your input. I still don't know exactly what mischief the fleas are planning, but I figure there's some kind of mine field ready to blow. The President cancelled the rest of his visit to Colorado, he's back in D.C. by now. But there may be other innocent lives at risk."

"Oh, only about ten thousand or so." Hypothermia was taking over now, everything slowing down. Cass wanted to believe him, but her mind was sluggish. "They're planning to gas the airport, Denver International."

"God almighty. Well, I'd get right on it if I could just solve my present problem. Look —" Hands up, empty, Ruger walked forward with deliberate steps, as he'd approach a wild animal. "You want to take me, it's your move. Kill me or join me. Help me out here. We found stacks of sophisticated destruction hidden away in those fake sculptures out at the Hacienda. Latest type of explosives, electronic detonators, long-range radio transmitters, now you say gas? What kind?"

"Serin. Through the ventilators. In the

concourses."

"So let's get to it, Cass." He was within fifteen feet of her hiding place. She took a good grip on the stiletto and flipped it. End over end it spun and stuck in the wet ground an inch from his hot-shot tooled leather boots. Mumblety-peg. "Consider that my official resignation from your League." She walked past him into the headlights, wondering vaguely if he would kill her now.

Picking up the knife he followed, saying something. "Look, I wish I could wait for you to get a good night's sleep, but there's really not a minute to lose."

Cass still knew that much. Time was going to run out if she didn't stop the clock. And at that point a new flicker showed beyond the rise, another car crested the top and came down the hill at speed, spitting lights, red, white and blue.

34

Webster cut a long shadow in the double set of headlights as he legged it across the parking lot and through the gates. Cass moved to meet him, so tired she couldn't run, but her emotions streamed out to him. He seized her carefully by the shoulders, without wrenching them, staring down at her in fear and disbelief and a fierce sort of joy. Wordlessly he folded her to him, and she went gladly to shelter in those two strong arms as if it had been ordained.

"By God, you are a tough little cookie." He turned to lead her toward his car, brushing Ruger aside like a minor obstacle. "Come on, I'll get you out of here."

"Hold it." The Texan moved along with them. "I need her."

"Later. She's going into shock."

"And the country's about to have its worst catastrophe since nine/eleven." Boyd kept hovering as Pike half carried her over to his squad car. "Webster, she's got the key to it all, and there's no time — Wait a minute, I've got a thermos of hot coffee." He left them to go to his station wagon and Pike put her in the front seat. Coming back with a steaming cup Ruger said, "It's laced with brandy. Will you just for Godsake listen?"

Webster tucked a car robe around her. Hands shaking, she could barely get the drink to her lips, but the jolt of heat steadied her. She even found voice for what she had to say.

"Pike, he's right. There's something I need to tell him."

"Make it fast." Webster had gone around to slide into the driver's seat, turning up the car heater to its highest.

She chugged the rest of coffee. Brandy burned her sore throat, must have breathed in a lot of dust in the coke oven. She finally got her voice working. "Tell your team to look in the barn at the Hacienda, they'll find a big file with skinny drawers, made for silk-screen prints. In one of them is a line drawing, looks like a schematic bug. I'm betting it's the floor plan to DIA, or at least the ventilation system. They intend to set off a number of gas charges simultaneously."

"God, we'll have to evacuate that whole area. Take the hazmat people a week to search out every cubby-hole . . ." he was turning away when she stopped him.

"In that same chest of drawers you'll find a transparency, an overlay with a lot of red dots on it. I think that'll help narrow the search." *And could I have another cup of that coffee?* But the big man was on the move, back to his wagon, speaking into a mike on the dashboard.

"Is that it?" Webster asked, revving the engine of the squad car.

"Yep. That's all," she chattered.

Without further delay, Pike swung the car in a circle and spun gravel as he headed back for the highway. "Got to get you to the hospital."

"No!" The word came out with a good deal of force. "I just want to go home." Crawl in bed and sleep forever.

At the highway overpass he pulled onto the shoulder. Reaching across, he felt her forehead. "Bunny, you're suffering from hypothermia, exposure, and what the devil happened to your hands? Your knuckles look like raw meat."

"They bricked me up in a coke oven, I had to dig my way out."

"Good Lord, no wonder you look as if you lost weight." He opened the parka as if she were a child, took her hands and guided them out of the arms. "This thing's soaking wet on the *inside.*"

"Happens when you sweat." The heat in the car was beginning to take effect now.

"How did they get the jump on you? Never mind, you can tell me all that later." He chucked the parka in the back seat and drew her over, folding her close inside his coat. A good coat, sheepskin, woolly side soft as a nest. But his voice was hard with anger. "This is Ruger's fault. If he's such a great man why wasn't he covering your back? Leaving you out there as live bait, he ought to be shot." In the glow of the dashboard light, his face was tight with rage. "My fault too. Kiting off down to Texas . . ."

"What happened after the phone call this morning?" *Was it only this morning?*

"Oh, that. Well, I turned north as they instructed, I knew they had a car following me. Wanted to get me as far away from Panhandle as possible before they put me down. Oh sure, I had that figured out, dumb cop that I am. But thank God for cell phones. I called Ruger even as I drove. I thought maybe he just might be trained in search and rescue, figured he might pull it off without tossing away your life, like the feds would. Of course they all have this code: you don't deal with kidnappers and so forth. But at least he got me home — told me to pull into Johnson's Corners, pretend to have car trouble, and by the time I got there he had his personal plane waiting to fly me back to the Rocking R. As far as I know the rental car is still up on the rack and one of your fleas is sitting up in the parking lot waiting for me to come out of the diner. Ruger also stationed a man at the motel up in Fort Collins — he's a powerful man, he waves a hand, things get done. We were going to try a few tricks of our own when Quentin called back. We had apprehended the Russian woman by then."

So it really was over. Cass could hardly stay awake, tucked into that warm coat with his arm around her.

"Did you ever catch up with Joe?"

"He's locked up, too."

"He did the brick work on the kiln."

"Ought to kill him with my bare hands." Pike had started the car, they were heading eastward through the darkness.

"Poor Liz," Cass muttered. "She set a lot of store by her man."

"She'll be better off without him."

Pike, you don't know women. Not at all. But then I don't know anything about men. Enamored . . . that's a funny word. Snugged up tight it occurred distantly to Cass that she should be freaking out, all this masculine proximity. But somehow, she wasn't worried. The night on the waterfront seemed remote, driven off to a distance by the horror of those hours in the blackness of the coke oven. She almost smiled in her comfortable limbo. *I've got a whole new nightmare now. I can dream about being buried alive.*

They were moving along the secondary that would take them back to Panhandle. Eyes closed, Cass hardly felt the bumps, held tight by the careful grip of his arm. *Enamored? I am about as lovable as a wet cat, probably smell worse. In a minute I will shape up. Sit straight, tell him, 'Hey, I'm fine, no sweat.' Not that I've got any sweat left in me.* She snickered down in the depths of the sheepskin coat. Got to keep our sense of humor. Got to keep our independence and self reliance and all that important crap. Got to shape up, in a minute . . .

But by then she was asleep with her head on his shoulder.

We hope you have enjoyed this Large Print book. Other Thorndike, Wheeler, and Chivers Press Large Print books are available at your library or directly from the publishers.

For information about current and upcoming titles, please call or write, without obligation, to:

Publisher
Thorndike Press
295 Kennedy Memorial Drive
Waterville, ME 04901
Tel. (800) 223-1244

or visit our Web site at:

http://gale.cengage.com/thorndike

OR

Chivers Large Print
published by BBC Audiobooks Ltd
St James House, The Square
Lower Bristol Road
Bath BA2 3SB
England
Tel. +44(0) 800 136919
email: bbcaudiobooks@bbc.co.uk
www.bbcaudiobooks.co.uk

All our Large Print titles are designed for easy reading, and all our books are made to last.